THE CURSE

Touch of Eternity

THE CURSE

Touch of Eternity

Emily Bold

SKYSCAPE

SKYSCAPE

Text copyright © 2011 Emily Bold
English translation copyright © 2012 Jeannette Heron

The Curse: Touch of Eternity was first published in 2011 by Emily Bold as *The Curse - Vanoras Fluch.* Translated from German by Jeannette Heron. Published in English by AmazonCrossing in 2013.

Amazon Publishing
Attn: Amazon Children's Publishing
P.O. Box 400818
Las Vegas, NV 89140
www.amazon.com/amazonchildrenspublishing

ISBN-13: 978-1-477-80735-4
ISBN-10: 1477807357

For Patrick, Sara, and Emma
who show me every day what love means.

PROLOGUE

Scotland, 1740

The moon bathed the soft hills of the Scottish Highlands in a silvery glow. Cathal Stuart drew the bloody blade out of the lifeless body of his enemy. The fight had been won.

He peered over the edge of the turret to see how the others in the courtyard were doing. Two of his fighters circled, swords drawn. They covered each other's backs—though they were far stronger than their opponents anyway. The rest of his men had penetrated the stone castle's main tower.

He caught sight of the only woman in the fight, his wild sister. She was almost as good with a broadsword as he was. But on the blood-slicked stones of the courtyard, a single wrong move could mean the end. Despite that, he nearly smiled; it looked as if she were actually enjoying herself.

Nathaira had cut her skirts in preparation for the fight and there was now a giant slash in the fabric of her moss-green bodice. Her black hair had come loose. It swung, damp, around her head, but she didn't even seem to notice it. Her opponent, more than a head taller and at least double her weight, was trying his best to avoid her sharp blade.

Although Cathal had no doubt that Nathaira could win on her own, he decided to come to her aid. She let out a gravelly laugh when she saw him, and together they mercilessly attacked the man in front of them with fast, hard hits. Metal clashed, and the fighters heaved under the strain of the heavy swords. Back and forth, Cathal hit, then Nathaira, as the siblings played a deadly game with their opponent.

They kept slashing at their victim. His once-brown shirt was hanging down in bloody rags, and soon he couldn't use his sword arm. Another hit and the sword flew out of his hand, clanging across the stone in what they all knew was a death knell for him. Seconds later, he sank to the ground. His glazed eyes looked down to the bloody wound in his stomach, and then up to the face of the contented woman who had just driven her weapon through his body.

Cathal praised his sister, and she wiped her blade on the dead man's cloak. The deserted courtyard had grown quiet. The night sky seemed to have swallowed up all the sound—the clashing of weapons, the screams of the dying. All that was left was silence—and a courtyard drenched with the blood of every last inhabitant of the castle.

A woman's lifeless body lay near one of the gates. She was wearing a simple night shift, her hair tidily hidden under a white cap. Her head lolled back where someone had slit her throat.

With a whistle, Cathal called his men to gather around him. One of his men brought a squire, who begged for mercy. The boy shook under the leader's steely gaze.

"We are not being merciful today," Cathal growled. "Get rid of him."

The squire lashed out as he was dragged off to a certain death.

Another of Cathal's men, slightly younger than the other fighters, carried a boy of about seventeen in his arms.

Everyone immediately realized he was dead. Cathal ran forward and laid his hand on the boy's bloody chest. "What happened?"

The man shrugged in resignation. "An axe. From the side, into the bend between shoulder and neck. Kenzie died immediately."

"No!" thundered Cathal. His eyes filled with hatred and hot tears. "How could that happen? Where were you when they did this to my brother?"

Cathal took Kenzie's battered body and laid the boy gently down.

"I don't know what you were thinking, Cathal," said the fighter. He motioned toward the piles of dead bodies. "Are you really surprised that these people fought for their lives? You led us all here. This is your fight, not mine. Yet still, I was at Kenzie's side. I'm sorry I could not save him."

He cast a last glance at the raided courtyard and then turned his back on this place of death. Without another word, he mounted his horse and galloped off through the gate. He stopped just outside the castle, where another victim of the night lay motionless. He slid out of the saddle, sank to the grass, and picked up his younger brother. He had only just turned sixteen.

The fighter clutched him as he murmured, "What was it all for?"

The words went unheard. He looked up to the sky, but neither the wind nor the moon nor the passing clouds could answer. Softly, he cradled his brother in his arms and recited a prayer.

~

The sky began to darken. A band of clouds pushed in front of the moon and shoved the world into a black hole. Everything seemed to stop. Suddenly, a glowing flash of lightning tore across the night and connected with the highest tower. Huge rocks popped out of the walls and rained down on the attackers. Flames began to leap out of the roof.

Over the crackling of the fire, a strange, mystical song began to rise. Everyone turned, trying to figure out where the sound was coming from.

A woman stood on a ridge close to the castle. She was lustrous, illuminated by a single ray of moonlight. Her snow-white hair billowed in the wind, and her arms were outstretched toward the sky.

"Vanora," Nathaira whispered in awe.

Nobody dared take their eyes off her. Vanora started to speak in a curious old language, in a cadence no one knew. The wind grew stronger. The warriors shielded their eyes against the dust whirling up, yet they seemed incapable of looking away.

The unusual sound had them all petrified. It grew more and more intense. The hills, the trees, and the castle itself seemed to grow with it, looming larger and darker.

Screaming, Nathaira broke out of her paralysis. "No—you witch!"

Although the two women were far apart, they were positioned exactly opposite each other. Their appearances were opposite, too: one white, from her hair to her naked feet; the other, dark of hair and smeared with blood. Everything seemed to be circling around these two.

4

"Be quiet, or you will be sorry!" Nathaira shouted, raising her fist to the sky.

Vanora ignored her. When she had finished her song, a final, powerful flash of lightning struck. Then the wind quieted down and the clouds vanished. The woman in white stood motionless. Nathaira and Cathal swung onto their horses and raced toward her.

~

Fearlessly, the old woman kept her ground, conscious of her fate but not budging as the riders came closer. In fact, she felt a strange peace, because at the other end of the valley she could see the old nanny holding on tightly to the back of a gray horse. She caught only a quick glimpse of the child with the nanny, the child whose life Vanora had done everything for this day. The horse disappeared as they slipped into the safety of the Highlands.

When Nathaira's black stallion had almost reached Vanora, the girl leapt out of the saddle and attacked, screaming wildly. Pulling a dagger out of its sheath, she rammed it into the old woman's heart.

Vanora did not raise a hand to defend herself, nor did she seem astonished by the pain. She reached out to her killer's hands and looked inquiringly at the dark-haired girl's face. When she had found what she was looking for, she smiled.

"*Sguir, mo nighean. Mo gràdh ort.*"

Her words were hardly more than a whisper. While she pressed a forgiving kiss onto the girl's hands, the white-haired lady's soul left her body, and she was gone.

~

"What did the witch say?" Cathal asked sternly.

His sister got up, shaking. All the color had drained from her face, and she stumbled weakly to her horse.

"Nothing!"

She would never admit what the old woman had said—or how she had looked at her.

"She was nothing more than a crazy old woman."

CHAPTER 1

Delaware, Present Day

I was sitting in Grandma Anna's dusty attic, surrounded by piles of paper. In front of me were two cardboard boxes with faded labels. The naked bulb above me gave just enough light to illuminate the part of the room where I was sitting. Everything else was in the shadows; the countless boxes and covered pieces of furniture farther back merged into weird, bulky shapes. I was a little spooked, but a moving company was coming in two days to clear out Grandma's house and I wanted to see if there was anything important or interesting up here. My parents were downstairs, sorting coffee mugs and wrapping photos. The house would soon be sold; some potential buyers were actually coming later that same day with a real estate agent.

Digging into the box again, I pulled out another stack of papers. Dust rose and danced in the flickering light, making me sneeze. It was strange; I had never realized that dust could have its very own smell. Old and secretive. Feeling a bit like a grave robber, I kept going. I had no idea what I might find between the old receipts, bills, and newspaper clippings. I sighed, wishing Grandma were sitting next to me so she could tell me the story behind each slip of paper.

If I kept going at this speed, I would wind up spending the whole night up here with the cobwebs. So, determined to pick up the pace, I pulled my hair back in a ponytail and plopped the next two bundles into my discard pile, just as mercilessly as I had with countless other papers. There was absolutely nothing worth a second glance in the next box, and I started to wonder whether I should even bother opening any others.

My stomach rumbled loudly. I tried to estimate the time based on how hungry I was. Still, I was slightly curious, so I decided to try one more box. I figured, why not? My fingers were already black from the newspaper ink.

Pulling the box a bit closer, I was surprised to see that it was even dustier than the others. It looked like it hadn't been opened at all in the past fifty years. I imagined finding secret papyrus rolls, a gold chalice, or even writing carved into stone.

I took a deep breath and removed the lid. No sign of rare antiquities. But there was something about this box that made me think it was worth taking a closer look. A splash of red underneath a pile of yellowed papers caught my eye. It was a book with a leather cover—maybe a journal or a diary, I thought—and I carefully took it out. Next, I pulled out a huge pile of crumbling newspapers. I had almost given up hope of finding anything else interesting when my fingers ran into something hard. I groped around to get a good grip and tugged it out.

I held it up directly under the bare lightbulb. In my palm was a fairly unspectacular piece of jewelry: a tarnished silver chain and a round silver pendant. On the front was a circle with a bundle of arrows inside it. A ribbon was wound around the arrows and tied in the middle. Some words were engraved on the pendant—they seemed to be written in a foreign language—but it was so tarnished I couldn't make them out, even though I rubbed it on my jeans to try and get the gunk off. The necklace couldn't exactly be described as a treasure, but it was the most valuable thing I'd unearthed so far. I couldn't remember ever seeing my grandma wear it, but I would definitely keep it.

I was still turning and twisting my find in the light, trying to decipher the writing, when my dad called for me.

"Sam! Can you please come down? We could really use your help putting all these boxes in the car."

I sighed, shoved the necklace into my pocket, and called down the stairs to say that I'd be right there.

Looking over the papers and garbage bags strewn around the attic, I wasn't sure all of my digging around had been of any use. But that little red book, the necklace, and a pile of letters I'd found—they seemed like they at least might be important. I figured I'd take another look at them at home. I stuffed them into my backpack and started to stand up, but my legs were almost numb from sitting cross-legged for such a long time. As I cautiously made my way down the steps, I heard a creaking sound from above and I turned around for a final look. I guessed this would be the last time I'd be in this house.

"Good-bye, Grandma," I murmured. "I'm going to miss you."

It felt wrong to me that we were selling Grandma's house so soon after she had died, but my parents disagreed. I'd been avoiding them all day. Feeling for the necklace in my pocket, I swallowed the lump that had suddenly formed in my throat and put on an artificial smile.

"I'm here. Which boxes first?"

There was a chaotic pile of boxes in the driveway, and it looked like there was no way it was all going to fit into our car. Even if we could stuff everything in, I couldn't see where I was going to sit.

But believe it or not, we managed to wedge everything in, like a giant puzzle, and I actually wasn't too squished on the short trip home.

Our house was on Silver Lake in Milford, Delaware, only fifteen miles away from Grandma's. I thought about how all these boxes with her belongings would now be put into our attic, probably only to be rediscovered when someone went through our stuff after we were gone.

It was already dark by the time we'd carried everything in. While Mom disappeared into the kitchen to make us a quick dinner, I sat down to do my homework. I hadn't even started it when the phone rang.

"Hi, Kim," I said as I picked up the phone without even checking the caller ID.

Kim hadn't said a word, but she didn't need to. Ever since we'd been in elementary school, she'd called every day at the exact same time to talk about important topics— mostly boys.

"Hi, Sam. How was it?"

"Dusty. But we finished everything."

I was surprised she'd remembered to ask me about Grandma's house. She'd been a little self-centered lately.

"Good, I'm glad that's over with." Then as expected, she quickly changed the topic. "You'll never guess who I saw today."

Kim's enthusiasm practically radiated through the phone. I knew her cheeks must be pink with euphoria.

There was only one boy in Milford who could evoke such excitement, but I pretended not to know. "No idea . . . Tell me, who?"

"Ryan Baker!" She shouted so loud I had to pull the phone away from my ear. "I was in line in front of him, so that means he got in line behind me!"

There was a meaningful silence. I shook my head.

Ryan was the coolest guy at our school. He was seventeen, a junior, just like us, and the quarterback of the football team. He had wild wheat-blond hair, luscious full lips, and cornflower-blue eyes. And, oh yeah, those devastating six-pack abs. Pretty much the entire school either wanted Ryan or wanted to be Ryan.

"Wow," I exclaimed, although I didn't think there was that much for her to be excited about, to be honest.

Hardly listening as she gushed on and on, I went back to my geography homework. I was trying to be a good friend, though, so at regular intervals I'd let out an affirmative mumble or an astonished "Really?" followed by a breathless "Unbelievable!"

For Kim, every day was evaluated in terms of being a good day or a bad day on the Ryan Scale. This was definitely a good day for Kim.

As for me, I tended to avoid Ryan entirely. I'd made a fool of myself in front of him—and half the school—two years before at my friend Grace's birthday party. Her parents

11

weren't home, the party was going full speed, and we had decided to play spin the bottle. On Ryan's spin, everyone held their breath as the bottle wobbled around, telepathically trying to get the bottle to stop in front of them. Everyone was laughing and clapping when the bottle slowed and pointed at me. Ryan had an amused look on his face as he crawled over to where I was sitting. My heart almost stopped beating, and I turned bright red. Then Lisa, of course, had to ruin everything.

"I heard that our little Sam has never been kissed," she said tauntingly. "So Ryan, honey—do your best to give her something to dream about for the next twenty years."

Lisa flounced to the side, laughing away in her size-two jeans. I'd always hated that blonde perfectly perfect daughter of a plastic surgeon, and I sure as hell hated her more at that moment.

"So what?" I shouted defiantly.

Ryan pulled me over to give me the first kiss of my life, but I pushed him aside, scrambled up, and ran away. Tears of humiliation ran down my face as I tore through the living room and out the front door. The whole way home, I muttered dark curses to myself, all along the same lines: what a horrible, mean person Lisa was. Naturally, she'd probably kissed hundreds of boys.

Ever since that night, I'd been avoiding Ryan. I'd hide if I saw him in the grocery store, and I'd duck into another classroom if I saw him coming down the hall at school. I certainly wasn't going to talk to him, much less look him in the eye. Frankly, I thought Kim was getting her hopes a little high by crushing on him. Ryan was the kind of guy who preferred to be seen with the popular cheerleaders, not the whip-smart editor of the school paper.

"Kim"—I interrupted our one-sided chat—"my mom just called me to dinner. We can talk tomorrow, OK?"

"Oh, sure. But think about it, because the beach party this weekend is going to be incredible. And I definitely can't go alone. Please, please, please, if you're my friend, come with me!"

"I'm sorry, Kim. I really don't want to hang out with Lisa and her crowd."

"Please . . . Please . . ." She made whiny little puppy noises. It was unbearable.

"OK, OK. I'll think about it. But I'm not promising anything."

"Thank you, thank you, thank you! You're the best!"

"I said I wasn't promising anything."

"I know. But I know you'll come!" I heard her giggle as I hung up the phone.

I sighed and hoped the beach party didn't involve swimsuits. I mean, I'm fine with my body. I've always liked that I'm thin, but I don't have much to offer on top. And being compared with Lisa and company, well, I bet even someone like Jennifer Lawrence would feel intimidated. But, I thought, if we had to wear swimsuits, I could always wrap myself in a brown towel and try to blend into the shoreline.

At school the next day, Mr. Schneider wanted to see my geography homework. And just as I had feared, he wasn't happy with the poorly done map I'd drawn of the subregions of Europe and he gave me a C. Wonderful. There was only one month left in the semester to improve my grade. Frustrated, I banged my locker shut.

I looked up and saw Kim barreling down the hallway. Jeez, she practically shoved a ninth-grader out of her path to get to me.

Kim's black pixie cut and her chunky black-rimmed glasses suited her journalist-wannabe image. Actually, she was well on her way to her dream, with all the reporting and editing she'd been doing for the student paper.

"So," she said conspiratorially, "I'm on my way to the field to interview some of the football players about healthy food. Want to come with me?"

Although it was spring, the football team still had practice. In the off-season, they'd run sprints, lift weights, and basically just act manly. It was kind of gross, if you asked me, even if their year-round dedication had helped make them the state champions for several years in a row.

Kim was pulling me along by my sleeve when I realized which player she wanted to interview.

"Sorry, I don't have time," I told her. "I just got another C and I really need to do some homework."

"Come on. It won't take long. And I'll buy you nachos after, to make up for all our reporting on healthy food."

Bribery.

Before I knew what was happening, I was sitting on the bleachers behind the school, watching Ryan and the other boys show off in front of the cheerleaders. Lisa squealed loudly when Ryan threw her over his shoulder and ran around the track. They laughed as they rejoined the others. Lisa was shamelessly flirting with Ryan, stroking his arm. Yuck. Kim saw this as her cue, and she marched toward the team with her notebook under her arm, determined to prevent any further advances by Lisa.

"Gentlemen!" she called out. "I'm doing a story on healthy snacks for athletes. Can you help me with some quotes?" She elbowed in, right in front of Lisa, and beamed up at the players, and I wondered if I was the only one who noticed that the football team was featured in the paper with astonishing frequency. I had a sneaking suspicion that raging hormones and starry eyes had distorted most other readers' perceptions.

I was annoyed. Screw the nachos, I thought.

I got up and started walking home. Silver Lake was pretty close-by, just a few blocks from school, past the hospital where Mom worked

I was about halfway there when Ryan caught up with me. Sure, he lived in the same neighborhood, but we hardly ever crossed paths. And he was still in his football jersey, so I was confused. Had he come after me? That seemed unlikely. I was wearing my favorite Levi's 501s, which were a bit worn and frayed at the hem, my gray Converse sneakers, and my mom's old Nirvana shirt. Not exactly the most alluring ensemble.

"Hi, Sam."

"Uh . . . hey, Ryan."

Even an exchange this mundane would rate high on Kim's Ryan Scale, but I stared at the sidewalk, hoping that aliens would come down and take me away.

"I saw you at practice," Ryan said.

Man, his voice was sexy.

"Um . . . yeah. I was keeping Kim company."

"That's what she said. She also said that you're both coming to the beach."

"If she said it, then it must be so."

What was with me? Why was I suddenly spouting philosophy? I had no idea what Ryan wanted from me. I truly did not want to spend time with him; I always felt like an idiot around him. I could hardly wait to get to the next corner when I would turn onto my street and Ryan could go along his merry way. We walked silently next to each other until I crossed the street.

"Bye," I mumbled.

"Bye! See you on Saturday," called Ryan. "I'll see you there!"

I almost stumbled. Do not turn around, I told myself. I felt like he was looking at my back as I walked away, but since when was Ryan interested in me?

When I got home, I went into the kitchen and threw my backpack in the corner. My mom was waiting for me.

"I went to help Kim with the school paper," I said, explaining why I was late.

"It's OK. I just wanted to talk to you about something."

Mom took a plate out of the cabinet and loaded it with lasagna. She put it on the table, with a fork and a glass of water. I started to eat, but—ow!—the lasagna was piping hot. There was hot oil hiding underneath the melted cheese. Swearing under my breath, I gulped down almost all of my water.

"What did you want to talk about?" I mumbled as I tried to examine the roof of my mouth with my tongue.

Mom shook her head and made some soft clucking sounds. I burned my mouth all the time. I just wasn't capable of eating slowly. She set a whole bottle of water next to me and started washing the pans in the sink.

"Uncle Eddie called yesterday and asked if Ashley could visit us for a couple of weeks this summer. What do you think of that?"

I swallowed and gave her a strong, hard stare. She shrugged and turned back to the dishes.

"That's what I thought. But your dad thinks it's a great idea. Ashley's going to come right at the beginning of the summer, since Eddie has a tour to finish then. I'm not sure how long she'll stay. It'll probably depend on the weather. She loves the lake, you know."

Oh, I knew. Ashley is my cousin from Illinois. Her father, Eddie, is a truck driver who seems to always be away on long-haul tours across the Yukon. Her mom died in an accident seven years before, so Ashley had been with us a lot since then. Although we were both the same age, we didn't really have much in common, and I wasn't psyched about her coming to visit.

I pushed the plate away and got up, stopping at the window to look out at the lakefront, which stretched right up to our garden. Silver Lake really was beautiful.

When I was still small, my dad and I built a wooden pier so that we could jump off it into the water, and to have a place to tie up our boat. I had happy memories of us sitting there together, letting our feet dangle into the lake. But since last summer, I didn't like the pier as much.

Ashley had spent the month of June with us, and within a week, half the boys in town were in love with her—if love is the right word. Including Ryan. He'd been glued to her side the entire summer. One evening after I'd said good night, they went for a walk alone and then headed for the pier together, where they did God-knows-what. When Ashley came into the room we had to share, I pretended to be asleep. I couldn't say what annoyed me more: that she sucked up so much of the town's attention or that she had ruined my pier.

The thought that that terrible summer might repeat itself was depressing. And I was pissed that my parents had made the decision without me.

"Great. Sounds just great!" I grabbed my bag and stormed up to my room.

I felt quite content with the loud bang that reverberated through the house when I slammed the door. I turned my music way up and dropped onto the bed. I couldn't believe I'd have to welcome Ashley for her magnificent comeback. And just when Ryan seemed to have noticed me for the first time. Oh well, I thought, who cares about them?

As I raked around in my backpack looking for my homework, I came upon Grandma's red book.

I'm usually pretty tidy, but my bag is the exception—it's ruled by anarchy. I thought I'd put the diary, or whatever this leather book was, onto my bookshelf, but apparently I hadn't.

I leafed through it. Each page was filled with beautiful old-fashioned handwriting—tight, perfect, curvy shapes. I figured I'd have plenty of time to read through it on summer evenings, while dodging the Ashley-Ryan lovefest.

Then I remembered my real find. The necklace.

I tried to recall where I'd left it. I rummaged through the hamper in the bathroom until I found the pants I'd been wearing in Grandma's attic. Phew, the necklace was there, in the pocket. I pulled it out and went back into my room. Twisting and turning the pendant under my desk lamp, I could now see that there was something written on the front above the arrows. The elegant writing was so delicate it was hardly visible.

Cbnicb air a daoi oh d ani g tb

Unfortunately, I couldn't read all the letters. I brushed my fingers over the old words, and suddenly the pendant radiated a strong heat—so strong that I almost dropped it. The feeling disappeared as suddenly as it had come. I wondered whether I had only imagined it. But I could have sworn that the metal had almost scorched my hand. No, scorching wasn't the right word; it hadn't hurt. It was more of a very intense, good feeling—warm, like sitting in front of a campfire. I shook my head to sort my thoughts.

I slid my fingers over the letters again, bracing myself, but nothing happened.

Well, of course nothing happened, silly, I told myself. It was a piece of silver on an old chain! Still, I couldn't help feeling disappointed.

My phone rang.

"Sam! Do you know what just happened?"

It was Kim, of course.

"What?"

"You won't believe this. Justin Summers kissed me!"

"Justin?"

"After you left—and way to say good-bye, by the way—Ryan left in a hurry. And then all of a sudden, I was standing there alone with Justin."

"Ryan's best friend?"

"Yes . . . You don't sound like you're happy for me."

It was obvious that Kim was disappointed with my commentary, so I quickly changed my approach.

"No, it's great. Of course I'm happy for you! I just don't quite understand what actually happened. Start at the beginning."

"We were just standing around talking, and suddenly Justin looked really shy. Then he said he thought it was very sad that I was so into Ryan. And I was totally confused. But before I could say anything, he leaned down and kissed me."

"Whoa!"

"I know, unbelievable! But you know what's weird? I always thought he was kind of cute."

Kim was speaking so fast that I had difficulty picking up everything. I hadn't seen her this excited since we visited that candy factory in fifth grade.

"And, oh my God, he was a good kisser!"

"What about Ryan?" I asked.

"Well . . . it turns out Ryan is in love with someone else." Kim could no longer hold back. She almost shrieked as she burst out, "And that someone is you!"

I almost dropped the phone.

"Me?"

"Well, that's what Justin said, and he's Ryan's best friend."

"Oh, Kim. I am so sorry." I felt awful about this development. "I would never try to take him from you. I swear, I'm not interested in him!"

"Nah, it's cool. He'd probably never be into me. Anyway, he had his chance, right? You should totally go for him."

My thoughts were jumping all over the place. I didn't know if I was happy or not.

"Well, anyway, that's so cool about you and Justin," I said. "I'm really happy for you."

"Thanks! I'd better go now. I need to text Justin and make sure he's coming to the beach party."

"Kim, wait—"

But she had already hung up.

I grimaced. Now I wanted to go to the stupid party even less.

~

Music was booming across the beach and a roaring bonfire threw a red glow toward the sky. Tiki torches lined the wide arc of the shore. Kim was grinning like a Cheshire cat. I could barely keep myself from frowning.

"I don't understand why I have to come with you," I groused. "You're going to be meeting up with Justin anyway. Do you think I really want to sit around watching you two make out?"

Kim laughed. "Oh, come on, it looks like a good party. And Ryan will be here."

I made a face and shrugged. I had a plan: I'd drop Kim off, and then I'd leave.

Justin and Ryan walked in together, carrying an enormous cooler between them. Their arms flexed, and I have to admit, even I noticed. Kim jabbed me in the ribs with her elbow.

"They're here! God, I don't believe it—the two cutest guys at our school, and they want to be with us!"

I didn't really think it was so unbelievable—they'd probably been with all the other girls. We were the only ones left.

"Kim!" Justin bounded over to his newest conquest and wrapped his arms around her. She melted in his arms.

"Hey, Sam," Ryan said. "It's cool about those two, huh?"

"Yeah, cool," I said as I tried to wander away.

I didn't know what on earth I should talk to Ryan about, but he didn't seem concerned. He grabbed my hand and pulled me down to sit in the sand.

"I was thinking," he said, "maybe we should leave the two of them alone. Want to go for a walk?"

"Why would anyone go to a party if they'd rather be alone? I'll just stay here, thanks."

My rudeness seemed to annoy Ryan, and he got up and walked back to the rest of the group.

Why was it always so complicated with boys? I liked Ryan, but it just didn't make sense that he would seriously like me. I certainly didn't want to be the one everyone laughed at later on.

I watched as he opened a bottle of beer with his friends. Then Lisa turned up and got a beer, too. Kim and Justin were dancing, and every few seconds they kissed.

I was in a really bad mood. OK, well, what if Ryan really had been serious, I thought. Wouldn't he just leave Lisa and come to me?

"Sam?"

Ryan's voice brought me back to reality. Oh.

"Here, I brought you something to drink."

He handed me a beer and sat down close to me.

"Thanks."

I took a small sip. I hated beer—I wasn't a big fan of alcohol. Still, I was nervous, so I drank half the bottle.

"Are you going to spend the whole night sitting way over here?" His voice was soft, and he put his hand on mine, stroking it with his thumb.

"What do you care?" I didn't know why I was being so rude.

"Why do I care? I like you. It's that simple."

I pulled my hand back. "And when exactly did you decide that? At practice, when you had your arms wrapped around Lisa? Or last summer, when you were sleeping with my cousin?"

Wow, it must have been the beer talking. I was being awful. Ryan got up and brushed the sand off his jeans. "I think the two of us need to talk."

He took my hand and helped me up, pulling me behind him until we were quite a distance past the torches.

"What's your problem?" he said. "I tell you I'm into you, and you start being mean."

"Please excuse me for not reacting appropriately to your passionate confession."

"I know you like me, too. What I don't understand is why you won't admit it."

"You're awfully full of yourself!" I pulled away and stormed back the way we had come. I hadn't gone far when he caught up.

"Come on, Sam. This is going absolutely the wrong way." He brushed through his hair with his hand, softening me with a remorseful look.

"Ryan, listen," I said. "You're the hottest guy in school. But you need to find someone else to tease because I'm done."

I downed the other half of my beer in one gulp and pushed the empty bottle back into his hand.

"Enjoy the party." I started to take off.

Kim was busy anyway, and I couldn't care less about Ryan. I was even a bit proud of myself. I'd blown off the hot guy before he could make a fool of me.

"Hey, Sam," he called after me. "There's just one thing I want to know . . . Don't you still need to be kissed?"

I pretended I hadn't heard him.

"Damn, I don't see why you have to be so cold. Your cousin Ashley sure isn't!"

I stopped and turned.

"Asshole! If you really want to know, it's true, I haven't ever kissed a boy. But I'd rather eat a handful of sand than kiss you! My first kiss will be with someone worth kissing. And another thing—I wouldn't consider Ashley a big score. She's not exactly picky."

I spent the rest of the weekend curled up in my room. I didn't even return Kim's calls or texts. She was in the throes of her first love, and she wouldn't get it anyway. Even I didn't know why I'd acted the way I did. At least I wouldn't have to worry about Ryan anymore.

～

At school, I tried to lie low. That worked fairly well, but still, trouble found me. After history and geography class, Mr. Schneider wanted to talk to me.

"Samantha, I feel like you're having difficulty finding enthusiasm for these topics." He was sitting on the edge of his desk and slowly stretching his legs.

"No, it's not that—"

"I know you're smart, but you need motivation. I'd like to talk to your parents about a great program that I think you'd be a good candidate for."

Oh no, I thought. He wanted to talk to my parents?

"Mr. Schneider, please . . . Please, don't call my parents. I'll improve, I promise!"

"Samantha, calm down. Let me talk to your parents, and then we'll see what happens." He started packing up his bag, dismissing me. I dragged myself home. The whole week had been crap.

~

"Scotland? You want to send me to Scotland for the summer?"

I was stunned.

My mom was talking and my dad was standing behind me. His arms were on the back of my chair, like he thought I was going to bolt.

"Mr. Schneider says he knows you're really smart, but he's convinced that you just aren't working up to your potential. He thinks this exchange program would be a terrific opportunity for you—and we agree."

Apparently, the teacher had brainwashed my mom; otherwise, she wouldn't dream of letting me go so far from home.

"Sam. Think about it before you say no. We told Mr. Schneider that we'd get back to him by Friday. Just think about it for now."

~

Scotland. I was lying in my bed, weighing my options and gently tugging on Grandma's necklace. I'd been wearing it a lot lately. Kim was head over heels for Justin and would probably spend every waking moment with him. Ryan was probably telling everyone I was a prude. My beloved cousin Ashley was going to come and comfort Ryan—with her boobs—and sleep in my room.

This made Mr. Schneider's offer a lot more appealing. He said that a teacher in Scotland—some guy named Roy Leary—had proposed the exchange, swapping a student from Milford with a student from Scotland. By choosing me, Mr. Schneider was hoping to awaken my interest in geography and history. According to him, Scotland had a very moving and interesting history. On top of that, my parents thought it was a good idea. They'd certainly be happier with me if I were at least giving the impression that I was doing something constructive with myself.

~

On Friday I told Mr. Schneider that I'd love to spend my summer in Scotland.

Chapter 2

Iwoke up panicked.

I peeled my face away from the airplane seat and rubbed my cheek where the synthetic leather had left a crease. I raised my seat back and pushed up the window shade. The long transatlantic flight from New York to London was already over; I was on a smaller plane as I made the short hop to Glasgow, where we would land in a few minutes. From there I would take a bus to the Scottish Highlands. I'd been up for almost eighteen hours, and I'd just drifted off to sleep when a terrible nightmare woke me. I could vividly see the awful images as they replayed in my mind.

~

I was running. I was running as fast as I could on stony, wet ground. I could see waves pounding against the cliffs in front of me, the churning gray waters swirling around the rocks below. A menacing curtain of clouds had pushed itself in front of the sun, and I shivered, despite the sweat running down my back. On the mountaintop behind me was an old lady with white hair. It rose up off her like smoke, billowing around her wrinkled face. Only her eyes were young.

And although she was speaking to me in a language I didn't know, I could somehow understand every word she said:

"You must face your destiny! You can't run away!"

Goose bumps spread over my whole body. I looked for a way out. In front of me, there was only the icy water, and behind me the terrifying apparition. But when I turned around again, she had disappeared. Where had she gone? I scanned the rocky, bare landscape. She had vanished. Relieved, I breathed deeply and sank wearily to my knees as a cold blast of air came down from the mountains.

~

That's when I woke up.

The flight crew was preparing the plane for landing, and we all fastened our seat belts. I shook my head, trying to clear the haunting images. I hadn't even set foot in this country full of superstitions and ghost stories, and already my imagination was playing tricks on me. Probably because I was so exhausted.

By the time I got off the bus in Inverness, dusk was falling. The driver lugged my gray suitcase out of the baggage compartment, and with a curt nod he jumped right back on and rumbled off, leaving me in a cloud of exhaust fumes.

It didn't feel like summer here. It was cloudy and cold. It had rained for half the drive, and there were puddles on the road. I smoothed my hair back under my Wilmington City Ruff Rollers cap, put on the warmest jacket I had, and tried to get oriented. On the other side of the road was the tourist welcome center where I was supposed to meet my host family. I grabbed my bag and dragged it behind me.

Whoosh!

The suitcase was torn out of my hand, and I was knocked flat on the pavement. I had no idea what had just happened. I heard tires squealing and the loud roar of a motor, and quickly, I stood up.

The other side of the road was empty. About a block away, a biker stopped his black motorcycle and turned around to look at me. A man? Yes, a man, I thought. It was hard to tell with the helmet on. When the driver saw that I'd survived what had almost been a terrible accident, he turned around and raced off at full speed. All I could do was swear at him, but there's no way he could have heard me.

My knee was really sore. I guess I must have banged it when I fell. My favorite hat was lying in a puddle, and my suitcase was in the middle of the road.

Weren't there any people here, I wondered. Why wasn't anybody helping me? If that biker had killed me, how long would it have taken for someone to notice?

My mood was getting darker by the second: first, the long journey; then that spooky dream; and now this near collision. I picked up my hat, shook off the water, and rolled my suitcase onto the curb.

Just then, a dark-green Land Rover pulled up next to me. "Samantha Watts?"

A nice-looking red-haired man in his late thirties stuck his head out of the car window. He smiled at me, and then looked puzzled when he saw my wet pants. He jumped out and lifted my suitcase onto the backseat. Then he stretched out his hand.

"I'm Roy Leary. Sorry that I was late. I hope you haven't been waiting long?"

"No, sir, I . . . uh . . ."

"Aye, that's all right then. What happened to you, lassie?" Roy pointed at my pants. He opened the passenger door and offered a hand to hoist me onto the high-up seat.

I felt totally disoriented. This is what a kidnapping must feel like, I thought. I was being taken somewhere by a complete stranger, driving along a lonely street in an unfamiliar place a long way from home.

Roy was talking during the forty-minute trip, but I can't remember answering any of his questions. Now and then, he pointed at things through the wet windshield. As I thawed out in the warm car, I started to feel surprisingly good, considering my exhaustion and the sore knee.

"So this mystic landscape of the Highlands has made us a very superstitious people, aye," Roy explained. "The fog, the bare cliffs, the darkness—it's all part of our heritage and legends. They lead the people here to a deep belief in magic. Dwarves, giants, fairies, and *teine biorach*—that's like a will-o'-the-wisp in English. Stories about such things have been part of our lives for such a long time that we do believe in them."

Roy shrugged, almost as if wanting to apologize.

I wasn't sure if he would laugh at me, but the atmosphere in the car was perfect for strange revelations, so I hesitantly told Roy about my dream. When I'd finished, Roy nodded his head slowly and then turned to look at me.

"Many people come to this country without ever understanding it. Others only believe what they can prove." His voice sounded so serious, as if he were reading from an ancient text. "My wish for you is that you learn to understand Scotland, its beliefs, its history, and above all, its people. So don't be afraid of your dreams. Maybe dreams show the people their destiny."

I had to force myself to look outthe window again. It was hardly possible to distinguish anything now. In the darkness, I thought about what he had said. My destiny? No, thanks—I was there on a mission to avoid my life back in the States. I wanted things to be absolutely harmless. No boys. No cousins. No dark nights at the lake. I was not intending to fulfill any destiny!

I rubbed my arms violently to get rid of the goose bumps. Roy smiled at me, turned up the heat, and switched the radio on. I immediately felt better. I leaned back in my seat and closed my eyes.

"So what did happen to your trousers?" Roy asked.

"Oh, nothing. Some guy almost ran me over on his motorcycle, and I fell when I jumped back out of the way."

Ow! I flinched.

My skin felt burned under my grandmother's pendant. I put my hand up to my collar, but when I touched the necklace, it was just nice and warm. Slightly warmed by my body, nothing else. Don't panic, I told myself. A short nap would chase the silly ghost stories away. The necklace had probably just scratched me. I secretly glanced over at Roy. He was driving, quietly humming to himself and not paying any attention to my strange behavior.

At last we made it to Aviemore. Roy's wife, Alison, seemed a little shy, but friendly. She was so short that she only came up to my chin. Her long light-blonde hair was pulled back into a French braid, and her little nose fit perfectly into her tiny face.

Roy unloaded my suitcase and wrapped his strong arms around his wife's dainty shoulders. Roy was a big man; next to him, even a sturdy person would look delicate. Roy saw me comparing the two of them and gave me a wink. "Now you see what I mean when I talk about dwarves and giants."

He laughed, and Alison elbowed him in the side.

"I hope you haven't been going on and on about Scotland's ancient stories," she warned, wiggling out from his embrace. "Samantha, please come inside. And stop listening to that big, stupid man."

She pulled me into their cottage while Roy stood outside grinning.

~

The silence woke me up the next morning. Seriously, it was far too quiet to sleep. I rubbed my hand over my face, feeling like some jagged Cubist painting. I got up and pulled the curtains aside and slid the window open. Although it was still very early, the day was nice and bright. Cold, damp air streamed in, and I shivered. I wrapped myself up in the quilt from the bed, and then went back to the window. Never before had I breathed such clean air. I agreed with Roy; it really was magical here. Aviemore was only a little place, directly behind the bigger town of Fort William. I couldn't hear cars, dogs barking, sirens. I heard nothing. And there was nobody on the street.

I'd been in a dreamy mood since I'd left home. It was the first time in my life that I'd be away for such a long time. I was thousands of miles away from all the people who were important to me, and I'd be here for seven weeks. No wonder my nerves were playing tricks on me. Still, I was looking forward to this adventure.

The night before, Roy and Alison had given me such a warm reception. I'd had hot food and a warm shower, followed by eight hours of sleep in the softest bed in the world. I almost felt back to normal. The rest of the world was waking up; I saw a few blinds slowly being raised in the neighboring houses. I closed my window and crawled back into bed. It felt like the mattress was trying to swallow me, and I sank into it deeply, giving in to the cozy feeling. Cold, fresh, clear air and a comfy, warm bed—this summer program was starting off perfectly.

～

I didn't wake up again for a whole hour, until Alison knocked on the door. At the breakfast table, I found coffee, tea, eggs, and sausages. Roy's seat was empty, but a used plate was in the sink.

Alison had arranged a surprise for me. She worked part-time at the tourist information center, and had used some of her contacts to book a weeklong series of day trips. She said they thought it was important for me to get to know Scotland as a country. I was a little shocked. I would have preferred to settle in a little more before I started sightseeing, but Alison looked so pleased. I did my best to put on a happy face.

"Thanks, Alison, but you really shouldn't have. I'm sure this is all very expensive."

"No, I have a good connection at the tour company and I told her you were an exchange student. She gave us a really good deal. Don't worry about it at all."

Shortly afterward, Alison dropped me off at the tourist information center in Fort William, which looked exactly like the one in Inverness. That was where our tour group would rendezvous.

"Have fun!" she called out.

"I will," I called back. "Thanks! See you tonight."

As I got on a bus with a few other visitors, a small, bald man introduced himself as our guide.

CHAPTER 3

Scotland

The biker cruised through the countryside, guiding his Ducati Monster motorcycle past a landscape he didn't even bother to register anymore. There was nothing he hadn't seen already. There was nothing left in this world for him, a world that was only gray and damned.

He slowed as he passed through Inverness, knowing he could pick up speed again after the next stop sign.

Suddenly, he was blinded by a flash. He couldn't see anything. Adrenaline rushed through his body. His leg brushed against something hard, but he couldn't immediately react. It was a few seconds before he could get his bike to come to a full stop.

What the hell, he thought. He was in great pain, and yet he knew that was absolutely impossible. He would have welcomed pain. Any feeling would have been better than his unbearable numbness.

There was no question, though—he could feel his heart pounding double-time to pump the blood through his veins. He slowly looked up as the bike underneath him purred, ready to flee at his command.

The street was almost empty. A suitcase was in the middle of the road. But Payton McLean wasn't looking at that. His eyes were looking for her.

There was another flash of light, and a new wave of pain washed over him, almost overwhelming him.

Damn, he said to himself, what was that?

He quickly turned away. The bike's motor screeched full of energy as he sped off in a panic. His heart was racing faster than his Ducati, even after he had left the girl far behind.

Many miles later, in the safety of the dusk, Payton's mind began to clear. He stopped at the side of the deserted road, got off his bike, and eased the helmet off his head. Breathing heavily, he looked around. The loneliness of the Highlands stretched out in front of him. The mountains were mere shadows in the darkening night.

He let an anguished howl escape from his throat. He was desperate to experience feeling again. Pain—how incredible it had felt. After all the emptiness. Nothing. Years of nothing.

He kicked a stone with his boot, hard, and it rocketed away into the darkness. Still, he felt nothing.

Please . . . Please . . . God, redeem me, he silently prayed.

Payton squinted into the night, waiting.

And just as the countless times before, his plea wasn't heard by anyone.

CHAPTER 4

The final stop on the bus tour was a visit to Urquhart Castle, which sits on the edge of the legendary Loch Ness. I was feeling restless—our group was moving slowly—and I broke off from the pack to enjoy the view on my own. As the day had passed, I'd started to enjoy the tour, but I didn't need to hear every single fragment of history to appreciate the beauty of the sights.

A man who looked a bit like Arnold Schwarzenegger was trying to take a picture of himself and his female companion. He set his camera into a small nook in the castle wall, pushed the auto button, ran quickly back to his darling, and put his arm around her hips. They briefly stayed in that unnatural pose, and then Arnold went to check whether the photo had was any good. I shook my head—at this rate, they weren't going to get a decent shot at all—and I decided to pitch in.

"Can I maybe help you?"

"Oh, yes. Thank you," the woman answered, laughing. "Our heads are always cut off!"

Happily, they smiled as I took a few shots, framing them carefully with the Grant Tower behind them. In return, they took a picture of me in front of Loch Ness.

It was hard to imagine that people had actually lived their lives in this castle, that it had once been something more than a ruin. I envisioned rough invaders swinging their swords as they raided the place. People from another world entirely, seven hundred years before. I climbed up the tower and took in the breathtaking view. I could easily see why this lake was the source of so many mysteries: the water looked almost black, and its surface was restless and opaque. Bare branches drifted in the current, standing out like bony arms from the secret depths below.

The wind blew my hair into my eyes, and I went back into the tower. My flimsy jacket wasn't heavy enough for the Scottish climate. I wandered along behind a smoochy couple until I noticed that there was no trace of my tour group anywhere. I quickly scanned the ruin. Crap, I said to myself. Where had they all gone?

I pulled my jacket tightly around me and headed back to the bus. The path led over a small bridge, up a slope, and through the open doors of the souvenir shop. Dozens of people were pushing through the narrow aisles, clutching postcards and stuffed Nessies.

Looking for the shortest way past the crowd to the exit, I scooted along the back wall and tried to squeeze by a metal jewelry rack featuring coats of arms and clan tartans. I stopped dead in my tracks. A necklace on the rack looked just like the one I'd found in the attic.

Reaching into my shirt, I pulled out my grandma's necklace. Wow—I was right! It did match.

I took the souvenir necklace off the display. It was slightly larger than mine and had a label that read "Cameron Coat of Arms, 12 pounds."

I wondered why my grandma would have a necklace with the Cameron coat of arms on it. And why was it so warm again? It wasn't burning hot like last time, but it was much warmer than the necklace from the shop.

When I took a closer look, I saw that the two pieces of jewelry were remarkably similar. Each showed a bundle of arrows bound together in the middle along with some words. The writing was clear on the souvenir: *Cuimhnich air na daoine o'n d' thanig thu.* I held up my pendant to compare:

Cuimhnich air na daoine o'n d' thanig thu

The legible letters were identical. My necklace was much more delicate and expertly crafted than the one I'd snagged off the souvenir stand, but I was convinced the words were the same. Still, I had no idea what they meant.

The shop had largely emptied out, and I looked for a salesperson. A young woman with flaming-red hair was standing at the cashier's desk, looking bored while leafing through a magazine. I assumed she was resting after the siege of tourists she had just survived. Patiently, I waited for her to look up from the magazine, but she ignored me.

"Excuse me," I said.

She glanced at me briefly before looking back down at her magazine.

"Yeah, what?" she barely managed to utter.

"This coat of arms—"

"Twelve pounds." She turned to the next page. The cover of the magazine read "Brangelina wedding, at last?," and I could imagine that for the clerk, answering a thousand questions a day from annoying tourists was not nearly as intriguing as reading about the love lives of movie stars.

Still, I didn't give up. I put my hand holding the souvenir necklace smack in the middle of her magazine, right on top of the photo of the radiant Hollywood couple.

"You don't understand," I said. "I don't want to buy it. I want to know what this writing means."

"Oh yes, I do understand," Ms. Flamehair said snootily. She yanked the magazine away and put it under the counter. "But unfortunately, I'm not a linguist, I'm a sales assistant. If you want to translate that Gaelic writing, then I recommend you get one of those dictionaries." She motioned toward a table behind me, where several dictionaries, tour guides, and maps were laid out. "Or have a look at the books on the history of the clans."

With that, I was dismissed, and Cathy—her name was on the name tag pinned to her shirt—began to sort out the cash-register drawer.

"By the way, we're closing in five minutes," she cheerfully called out.

There was no way I'd be able to find what I was looking for in five minutes. I leafed through the Gaelic dictionaries as fast as I could, but apart from learning how to ask for a bed-and-breakfast, I didn't find a thing.

Cathy cleared her throat behind me. I ignored her for another minute, but then I gave up. Discontentedly, I paid the twelve pounds for the souvenir Cameron necklace and stepped out into the fresh air.

The parking lot was deserted. Cathy came out a minute later and locked the door. She glared at me, opened her car door, and drove off without a second look. It was starting to sink in: I was completely alone at the ruins of Urquhart Castle. Where the hell was my tour group, I wondered. Where was Baldy the Tour Guide? And where was the damn bus? Shit! The wind got stronger and a cold blast invaded my jacket. All right then, I decided. I'd have to call Roy and Alison and ask one of them to pick me up.

I rummaged around in my backpack for my cell phone. Then I remembered that I'd mindlessly tossed my phone into my suitcase after typing in all the important numbers for Scotland. Great. No cell phone. And I didn't see a pay phone anywhere.

I was starting to feel a little panicky. I paced back and forth and considered my options: I could stay where I was, hoping the bus would turn around when someone in my tour group realized I was missing. I could wait for Alison and Roy; surely they'd find me eventually.

There was a roll of thunder. Night was beginning to fall and a mighty black wall of clouds had pushed itself across the sky. The castle was illuminated with spooky greenish lights, which only added to the ominous atmosphere. A bright stroke of lightning flashed across the water.

I added it up. I was alone, at night, in a storm, on the shores of Loch Ness, next to a ruin and all its ghosts, waiting for help when no one knew I needed it. That was too much for me, and I wasn't just going to stand there. I grabbed my backpack and pulled the hood of my jacket down over my face as far as it would go. I walked briskly along the street in the direction of the last town I remembered passing. I figured there was bound to be a phone booth somewhere along the way.

But soon I started to second-guess myself: How far had it been to the town? Was I going the right way? Should I—or shouldn't I—hitchhike?

More than ten minutes later, not a single car had passed. I was freezing. I mumbled swear words to keep myself company.

Suddenly, a car appeared. I thought about standing in the middle of the road to force it to stop, but decided that would probably amount to suicide. I jumped up and down, yelling and waving. "Hello! Hello! Please stop!"

The car raced passed me at full speed.

"Wait!"

I screamed and screamed as the taillights faded away.

I was about to burst into tears. It felt like I'd been walking for an eternity, and I still didn't know how far I was from town. I wasn't about to go back to the castle. Anyone looking for me there would have to pass me on the road anyway.

When it started to rain, I decided to run. My shoes were soaking, and my hood wasn't making a bit of difference. Water was dripping into my eyes and down my neckline, running together with my tears. I desperately shouted, "Fuck it! Where is everybody?"

Then I heard a motor behind me. I turned around and saw a single headlight, coming toward me fast. A motorcycle was going far too quickly on the wet, dark street, spraying plumes of water to the side. I jumped out of the way, to avoid getting drenched.

I was about to yell after it when the bike's rear brake light lit up. The bike had actually stopped! The driver turned, and I ran forward, waving gratefully.

Brushing my wet hair off my forehead and gasping for breath, I looked at my savior. It was hard to tell, because the biker's face was hidden by a black helmet with a shaded visor, but it seemed to be a tall man, with a black leather outfit on.

I was exhausted, completely out of breath, and shaking all over. "I'm sorry to bother you, but can you give me a ride?"

There was a brief silence. Then a voice answered, muffled inside the helmet and a bit breathless and hesitant. "Sure. Where are you trying to go?"

"I need to get to Aviemore, but if you're not going that far, that's OK. I really just need to get to a phone."

Another long pause.

"I can take you to Aviemore. It's on my way. Hop on."

He reached out to me, and when I took his hand, he twitched, as if he'd been zapped by a shock. I raised my eyebrows and paused, expecting him to explain, but all he said, impatiently, was, "Come on, get on the bike!"

Relieved to be on my way to Alison and Roy's cozy little cottage, I swung my leg over the bike, settled onto the seat, and grabbed hold of the unknown driver. He revved the motor, which was so powerful that we almost started to fly. Oh, great, I thought, this guy's insane. I wasn't even wearing a helmet, and he was racing along the dark, wet road at an unbelievable speed.

After the first few minutes, though, I seemed to have used up all my adrenaline and somehow managed to get over my fear of death. I held on to his wet leather jacket with all my might. We sped through the night, along Loch Ness's shimmery coast, with my hair blowing in the wind and the rain whipping me in the face.

The ride didn't take as long as I'd expected, but I was stiff when I got off the bike.

"Thanks. I don't know how . . ."

My knees buckled, and I almost lost my balance. I groped for something to hold on to, and when I grabbed my mysterious driver, he again twitched at my touch. Then he pulled his arm away and rocketed down the road.

Irritated that I hadn't gotten to properly thank him, I stood in the dark, thinking that they were certainly strange people, these Scots.

$\sim$

The warm shower I took that night was amazing. I threw my cold, wet clothes in a heap on the floor and turned up the temperature as hot as I could stand. I closed my eyes and tilted my head back to let the water spray over my entire body.

I couldn't stop thinking about the biker's weird behavior. Why had he bothered to help me when it obviously made him so uncomfortable?

I soaped my hair with a honey-scented shampoo and, at long last, felt I'd rinsed the cold from my bones. Then I wrapped myself up in a big, soft towel, sat down on the bed, and started to sip the cup of hot tea Alison had set on my bedside table. The tea made me feel warm inside, too. I dried my hair, put on my pajamas, and slid into bed.

"Ow!"

My hand went to my chest. That burning feeling under the pendant again.

I went to the mirror and pulled back my pajama top. My skin was bright red, but the pendant itself was cold. Was I developing an allergy to the metal? I hated to think so. Just in case, I took off the necklace and put it on the table. I turned out the light and let myself sink into the mattress.

The clouds and rain had passed, and the night had turned cold and clear. Moonlight shone through the window and danced on the silver pendant. I stared at it for a few minutes, then drifted into my pillow, giving in to sleep.

In the middle of the night I woke, feeling as if something important were missing. Was I homesick? A single moonbeam stole its way through the curtains and shone on my pendant. Dipped in the silvery light, it looked almost magical. Automatically, my hand reached out to it. It felt warm, and a feeling of safety swept through my body. I put it back around my neck, where it belonged, and snuggled back into bed.

～

The black-clad driver turned to look one last time toward the little cottage before he got back on his bike. He had stood for a long time, hidden by the trees, observing the place. He hadn't come for any rational reason; he'd felt drawn here, as if pulled by an invisible rope, the need so great it was impossible to ignore. No one had seen him standing in front of the dark windows, and he wanted to stay. But eventually, he could no longer bear the pain, and he had to go.

As he got farther away from Aviemore, the pain faded, the burning feeling died down, and Payton could finally breathe normally again. However, a dull emptiness remained, and it didn't disappear even when he turned off the main road two hours later and reached his home.

Both his brothers, Blair and Sean, were still awake, playing a game of chess in the living room. The chessboard was set up on a table of ebony and ivory, appropriate for the "game of kings," and his brothers sat opposite each other in chairs that were just as elegant as thrones.

Blair wasn't known in the family as a big intellect, but it was hard for anyone to beat him at chess. In fact, some of the games the brothers played took several days; this match had already been going for hours. Thankfully, it was their nature not to need much sleep.

"What's wrong with you?" Sean said to Payton while playing his bishop. Sean didn't even need to look at him to know something was off.

"Nothing. Everything's fine," Payton replied. The last thing he wanted to do was start a discussion with the clan.

Sean arched an eyebrow and opened his mouth as if about to pose another question, but Payton raised his hand in warning. "I said, it's nothing. Just leave me alone!"

For a few seconds, the two of them stared at each other. Then Sean shrugged and went back to his game.

At twenty-five, Sean was six years older than Payton, and Payton was closer with him than anyone else in his family, including the head of the family, twenty-seven-year-old Blair. Sean seemed younger than he was, due to his thin, sinewy build. He was smart, he was in constant motion, and he seldom missed a thing. Just a few minutes before, for example,

Payton could tell Sean knew immediately that Payton was hiding something big from them. But he wasn't the type to push, either, and Payton was grateful for that. He didn't want to lie to his favorite brother, but he didn't want to talk to anyone about his latest experiences until he knew more about them himself.

Payton crossed the wide-open hall and went up a tightly wound staircase. The old castle was unfeeling and cold, just like the brothers who lived there.

He closed the heavy door to his room and let out a deep exhale. What was wrong with him, he asked himself. What was happening?

He stood in front of the full mirror and scrutinized his reflection. Dark-brown eyes glared back at him. His full mouth was tight; it hadn't been used for a smile in a very long time. The old crescent-shaped scar on his chin made him look dangerous. His light-brown hair stood out rakishly. He subconsciously stroked his hair with his fingers, smoothing it a bit. He was a fairly tall, well-built young man, just as always. He couldn't see anything that had changed. But why then, he wondered, did everything feel different than before?

Chapter 5

My first days in Scotland had flown by. My daily sightseeing tours were on hold for the weekend, so I was spending a lot of time with Alison and Roy. Alison was funny and laughed a lot. While she did her housework, she'd tell me stories—amusing episodes from her life, or small squabbles she'd had with Roy. And although she was the tiny one in this odd couple, she easily won every fight.

I felt really at home with them. The cozy warmth in the cottage, the rosy glow coming in through the pink blinds, and the arch overgrown with roses over the front door—all of it seemed to have brushed off onto me, and I was feeling much sunnier than I had been at home. But I couldn't say everything was perfect.

The whole weekend I'd felt a little on edge. I couldn't put my finger on it precisely, but it was almost as if I were being followed. Whenever I stopped and looked around, I didn't see anything unusual. But it always felt as if someone were looking at me behind my back, and that made the hair stand up on the back of my neck. I felt a little silly about it, actually. It was probably just what Roy had told me when I arrived: Scotland turned people into superstitious scaredycats.

~

On Monday morning I had the house to myself. Since Roy was a teacher, he left the house pretty early in the morning. Alison had already apologized the night before for not being able to make breakfast for me. She was working extra hours at the tourist information office for a few days, filling in for a coworker who had to get her appendix out.

"It's no problem," I said. I was actually kind of relieved to get a little alone time. "I can get breakfast for myself, and then I'll go on the tour."

Alison's expression told me she was worried I might run into trouble again. She'd felt terrible when I'd come home in the dark, soaking wet, after losing my tour group.

I tried to reassure her. "I promise I won't miss the bus again. And I'll always stay close to my group. Please don't worry."

"OK, but do be sure to take your phone with you this time, just in case."

As Alison said good night, it was clear to me that she wanted to believe I'd be fine on my own in the morning, but she wasn't entirely sure.

~

I opened my eyes. Just as I had after my first night there, I unlatched the window as soon as I got out of bed. I could tell it was going to be a nice day. The sun was already successfully warming the air, and I stood at the window in my pajamas, just enjoying the quiet. The delicious smell of coffee and biscuits wafted up from the kitchen. Not surprisingly, Alison had decided to take care of breakfast after all. I wandered downstairs and got myself a cup of coffee with milk. I carried it, and a plate of biscuits, up to my room and had breakfast in bed. I felt at ease. The disconcerting fears of the past days had disappeared, and, for a change, I couldn't wait to see more of Scotland.

My good mood stayed with me the whole day, even during the sightseeing tour. Like lemmings, we followed our guide to the Glenfinnan Monument. We lemmings didn't fall into the sea, but we could be counted on to follow each other into each souvenir shop. This particular little shop could hardly withstand our attack, and I almost had a bout of claustrophobia. Gasping for breath, I dashed out the back door and sucked in some fresh air.

In front of me stretched the wilderness of the Highlands. A gravel path led across the heather and up to the monument, so I headed toward it.

The Glenfinnan Monument is a round, simple tower on the coast of Loch Shiel. The closer I got to it, the larger it loomed. It was built in 1815, our guide had told us, to mark the spot where Prince Charles Edward Stuart, also known as Bonnie Prince Charlie, began the Jacobean uprising. The Scottish clans gathered around him here in 1745 as he led them to battle in the fight for the crown of England and Scotland. They must have really trusted him.

The tower is topped by a statue of a nameless Highlander in a kilt, but since he couldn't say much, a real human Scot in full tartan was on hand. His job was to let only two or three visitors at a time through the arched doorway into the tower. It was very dark and frighteningly narrow inside the old building. I climbed a steep, winding staircase and pushed myself through a tight opening to reach a narrow platform at the top. Another visitor poked his head through right after me.

I stepped up to the stone balustrade to make room for him. And when I saw his face, my breath caught, and I quickly turned away.

I hoped he didn't notice his effect on me. I couldn't say exactly what it was, but the sight of him made me woozy, and I had to lean against the wall. When I stole another look, he was standing as far away from me as possible. Maybe he was trying not to invade my personal space, I thought.

My heart was beating so loudly that I was afraid he could hear it. Every fiber of my body felt electrified. I had only looked at him briefly, and yet his image had burned itself into my memory. He seemed a little older than me, and he was quite a bit taller. His short hair was ruffled, as if he'd just woken up from a dream. His hair was brown, but single strands were lighter, and they stood out like golden sparks. He was wearing black cargo pants and a dark-gray button-down shirt over a white T-shirt.

Despite the distance between us, he kept looking at me. Even when I turned, I felt his gaze drilling into my back. Unable to stop myself, I looked at him again, trying not to be too obvious. There was something strange about the way he was staring at me. His brown eyes seemed slightly glazed, and he had pulled back away from me even more.

I tried to swallow, but felt like I couldn't. The wind blew my hair into my face and a whiff of his scent swept toward me. Indescribable feelings flooded me. His face was scowling, his whole posture unwelcoming, yet I somehow felt inexplicably attracted to him.

The silence at the top of the tower stretched out. C'mon, Sam, I said to myself. Regain your composure! I had to take a deep breath, and then another, before I could even think about starting a conversation.

I turned slightly toward him and pointed at Loch Shiel in front of us. The sky and the even surface of the water melded seamlessly, and the surrounding hills seemed to be watchmen.

"Beautiful, isn't it?" I asked with a weak voice.

He looked past me, took a deep breath, and answered with an equally pressed voice. "Yes, beautiful."

His intense, unfathomable look held me tight in its grasp, and his voice almost physically touched me. I wanted to ask whether he meant the view was beautiful—or something else.

He spoke again and seemed to be waiting for an answer, but I was still so dazed by his first words that I didn't hear what he said.

"What? Sorry . . . I . . . I didn't hear you."

"Payton, I said. I'm Payton. And you?"

"Sam. I mean . . . actually, Samantha . . . but everyone calls me Sam." I seemed to be squeaking rather than speaking. My knees had turned to chocolate pudding, and my voice was giving up on me. God, I wondered, what would Lisa back home say about such pitiful behavior?

The embarrassment got even worse. While I was musing about chocolate pudding and squeaking, I'd missed the next thing that he said. Sure, he had a Scottish accent, but that hadn't given me trouble before. He probably thought I was a complete idiot. There I was, standing in the tight quarters of a famous tower with a boy who was obviously getting to me, and although we were speaking the same language, I couldn't understand a word. Thankfully, I thought, this would soon be over. I seriously doubted he was interested in me.

His tortured expression as he leaned over the balustrade to check out the view made me think he'd rather throw himself over the wall than lean even a millimeter in my direction. It was too much, and I started to laugh—snort, really. I held my hands in front of my mouth to try and stop, but the laughs just popped out of me, giggles gone crazy. I was laughing so hard I was almost crying. My eyes started to water, and I relaxed my body, letting my back drop down the wall to rest myself on the floor.

It took a moment, but then Payton's face changed. It wasn't a smile, but maybe amusement. Yes, I'd say he was at least slightly amused. He studied me, and then sat down opposite me. He didn't say a word. I suddenly noticed that my pendant was doing that burning thing, making my skin feel red-hot, but I was far too caught up in the here and now to give it much attention.

I struggled to regain my composure. Then I gathered all my courage and looked up. Payton was sitting with his legs crossed, leaning against the wall in a way that was meant to look relaxed—and clearly wasn't. His hands were resting loosely on his thighs, but he was obviously tense. The muscles in his arms looked tight, and his face showed not a bit of levity. To be fair, I was probably more capable of climbing Mount Everest than of appearing cool and relaxed myself.

But, slowly, the first shock of hearing him speak was ebbing away.

All of a sudden I felt scared—if I let the moment pass, he'd get up and go away. The thought was awful. Although I still couldn't say what made me so drawn to him, I knew something special was happening. Payton was attractive, despite a prominent scar on his chin, but I didn't think his looks were all there was to it. After all, I had avoided Ryan Baker's hotness for years. Plus, Ryan had a ready smile and an open personality. Oh, and he flirted with every girl. Payton, on the other hand, showed little expression, and he definitely wasn't hitting on me. I decided I'd have to take the first step, because it didn't seem as if Payton were going to make a move.

I looked directly into his eyes, and I felt like I could see pain and desperation in the depths of his being. Then he blinked, and it seemed as if a dense Scottish fog came rolling in, smoothly covering up the feelings he'd revealed there just seconds before.

"Are you all right?" Payton asked, carefully.

"Yes. Thanks. I'm fine now."

I searched my addled brain for a good excuse for my laughing fit.

"I haven't had anything to eat in hours, and I was feeling a bit dizzy. I slid into the wall and, for some reason, that seemed hilarious. I'm sorry if I seem crazy . . ."

He nodded briefly, but didn't ask anything else.

"I could tell you something about the monument," he finally said, timidly, "if you would rather stay seated for a moment?"

"That would be great. I was going to read the history display at the back of the souvenir shop, but I couldn't stand the crowd in there."

"I hate these tourists. They are like vultures, circling around everything of interest and ruining it for those of us who live here."

"Hey now. I'm one of those vultures, you know!" I pretended to be upset.

"Mmm, I noticed that, but you seem to have fallen out of the nest somehow, little vulture fledgling."

I laughed, a little more natural with him now. I had at least reached base camp on the Mount Everest of total calm. "I thought you were going to tell me something about the tower? If you're just going to rant about us obnoxious tourists, I'll have to go back to the visitor center and listen to all the historical information there. And I'll listen to it in four different languages simultaneously!"

"I would be very surprised if you could understand four languages," he countered, "since you weren't even able to answer my questions in one language."

I blushed and threw him a mock angry look. "Very funny!"

"To be honest, I haven't had this much fun in ages."

"Then you must really lead a boring life!"

His expression darkened, and he looked past me, staring into the sky. He riffled his fingers through his hair and took a breath. Then in a neutral voice, he started to tell me about the place.

"The Glenfinnan Monument was built in 1815 to mark the place where Prince Charles Stuart's standard was raised—that's kind of like a large flag."

"The Jacobite Rising, right?"

"Yes, exactly."

My sincere interest in the topic seemed to chase away some of his bad mood, and he kept going with much more enthusiasm. "That was in 1745. Charles came from France and landed on the Western Isles. From there, he rowed to the coast, slightly to the west of here."

Payton's way of speaking seemed a little old-fashioned—almost from another time—but I figured it must be a Scottish dialect I wasn't familiar with yet.

He got up and gestured in the direction of the slowly setting sun. I got off the floor, too, and stood beside him. He immediately stepped back and motioned past me.

"Look there!"

A fawn down on the banks of the lake seemed to be looking directly at us. Its pointed ears swiveled, listening in all directions, before it lowered its head and drank the clear water. The soft movement of its muzzle spread wide ripples across the surface, breaking the golden lake into a million tiny lights. I was enchanted. The last warmth of the day started to creep through my thin chambray shirt, wild spots of light danced in front of my eyes, and a gentle breeze danced softly over my skin.

Payton gasped.

Startled, I turned toward him. His face was white, and he was clutching the balustrade.

"What's wrong?"

"Nothing. Come on, we should go back down now."

Payton seemed to be doing better, so I tried to put it out of my mind. I saw why he thought it was time to leave. A crowd of people was streaming along the narrow path toward the tower. Payton pointed at the tight opening to the staircase, motioning for me to go ahead. But the idea of squeezing myself down onto steep steps that I couldn't see made me nervous.

I reached out for Payton to steady myself. Our fingertips had hardly touched when he yanked his hand back, took a deep breath, and let out some strange sounds.

"Ifrinn! Daingead!"

A moment of déjà vu passed over me, but I couldn't grab the memory.

Then Payton took my hand again. Before I could give it a second thought, I stepped into the narrow opening and carefully felt around with my feet to get a safe grip on the old, rough steps. Payton held me until I felt secure enough to loosen my grip and climb down on my own. A thick rope seemed to be the only safety measure against falling, and I made my way down hand after hand, warily.

No sooner had I stepped through the arched door than Payton was standing behind me. I had no idea how he had managed to get down so fast. The thought of him squeezing through with his broad back and strong arms was absurd, and I would have thought it was impossible if I hadn't seen him come up.

Payton kept his distance, and as a few of the other tourists shoved their way through to the dark mouth of the monument, he moved even farther away. I was just glad to be back on solid ground. I wandered a few steps toward the polished wooden benches set up in a semicircle around the tower. Then I sat down and looked over my shoulder. Payton had followed, but he didn't sit next to me. Instead, he sat on the grass.

His eyes had such an immense intensity, and I wondered what it was about him that made me want to take in every little detail. I was getting used to his company, but inside I was still vibrating, as if I were standing next to a Tesla coil, with its energy conducting through me.

"So have you had enough of the history lesson," Payton asked, "or do you want me to tell you more?"

What I really wanted to know more about was his history, but I told him to go on, that I still had time.

"How much time?" He seemed to have an idea.

I checked my cell phone. I still had an hour before the bus was scheduled to go back to Aviemore. "Actually, I have far too much time."

I didn't know what I could possibly do there for another hour, so I hoped Payton would stick around. If he were to say good-bye now, I'd probably die of boredom and they'd have to erect a monument in my honor. "Here died a bored teenage tourist," the plaque would read.

Mostly, though, I didn't want him to leave. I tried to think if I should throw my hair back lasciviously—or maybe lick my lips. That seemed to work in the movies. But I was saved from having to try any awkward girly maneuvers, because a bemused expression crossed Payton's beautiful, mysterious face.

"What do you think about going for a walk with me, and I'll act as your personal tour guide? I know a path that leads to the foot of the viaduct."

A bit behind the souvenir shop, a gigantic viaduct spanned the valley, all the way from hill to hill. I knew the bridge: it was in the Harry Potter movies. You could buy posters in the shop showing the Hogwarts Express train, which took Harry and his friends over this bridge. But even without the view, Payton's offer would have been enticing.

"Sounds great."

I got up immediately, and he stood up quickly, too, before I could reach out a hand to help him off the grass.

"You should eat something beforehand, though," he said.

"Eat?"

"Weren't you feeling kind of woozy up on the tower?"

"Right . . . I was dizzy. Something to eat sounds good."

We wandered back to the shop next to each other, and I got a bag of chips and a bottle of lemonade. As we sat at one of the small bistro tables, a woman from my group threw a glance our way before turning around to whisper something to her friend. Oh, I thought, the gossip this would cause on the bus! Oh well.

I wiped my hands on a napkin. "So, shall we?"

Payton had also noticed the woman's look. "And I thought the days when pretty girls had to have a chaperone were long over."

Oh my God, I thought. Had he just called me pretty? My heart sped up by about a hundred beats per minute. I felt like I was in a deep, warm whirlpool, swirling around wildly with no protection. I just hoped Payton didn't notice I was having a panic attack at the sound of his voice.

"So," he said, "what brings you to Scotland?"

"Student exchange. I'm trying to improve my grades in geography and history. This trip was my teacher's suggestion. He thought I needed . . . well . . . inspiration."

Payton held me with a long look, as if he were searching my soul to see if I was telling the truth. It made me a little uneasy.

"And you? Do you live here? You seem to know your way around."

"Near here."

His kept his answers so short, which didn't exactly encourage me to ask more questions.

"But why come to a tourist spot then? What with all the vultures stampeding around with their cameras and eating chips."

"Hmm . . . I don't know. Let's say I was drawn here magically. And I am very glad about that, about following my impulse."

If Ryan said something like that to a girl, he would have looked down at the end of the sentence, playing it for all it was worth. Payton, on the other hand, seemed matter-of-fact. He looked almost as if he were challenging me, but the hardness in his eyes didn't match the softness of his voice.

Something about him sucked the truth right out of me, and I couldn't help blurting out, "I'm glad you followed your impulse to come here, too."

We started walking. Ow, I thought. That stupid pendant was burning against my skin. That was it, I decided then and there. I just couldn't wear it anymore.

The brisk Scottish wind kept blowing across the hills and down to us, but I didn't feel cold; being near Payton seemed to warm me from the inside. He told me about the bitter fight for the crown of England and Scotland. Charles's rebellion, which had started where we stood, had been smashed only six months later at Culloden. When the battle had been lost, Charles fled from the English troops and hid near the place where it all had started, back when his journey had held such promise.

When Payton was talking about history, he didn't seem as tense. He spoke with great passion, as if he could see the events of the past taking place directly in front of him— almost as if he himself had taken part. It seemed the past and the present weren't separate for Scots, the way we saw things in America.

The street and parking lot were way behind us as we wandered along the path under the impressive viaduct spanning the valley. A stony riverbed ran parallel to the path, and the quiet gurgling and swishing of the crystal clear water was like music. Butterflies fluttered in colorful clouds around the yellow blooming plants on the riverbank.

"So," I said. "This is the bridge Harry Potter crosses when he goes to Hogwarts?"

"Yes, Scotland offers many magnificent backgrounds for Hollywood blockbusters."

"It's unbelievably beautiful here. I think I could stay here forever."

"Forever? You don't know how long that is!"

A dark shadow crossed Payton's face, and he left me standing alone on the path. It seemed I was always saying the wrong thing.

Payton took two steps toward the water and sat down on a large rock, where he took off his socks and army boots. Barefoot, he waded into the middle of the shallow stream. After a short moment of hesitation, I set my shoes next to his and dipped my toes in. And whoa—was it icy!

"Oh my God," I called out. "This is awful! How are you not freezing?"

Payton smiled, and I must have gone crazy, because I gritted my teeth and waded toward him. It was hard to get a grip on the slimy stones under my feet, and I could just see myself slipping. Fortunately, Payton had stopped on one of the rocks jutting out of the middle of the stream, and he waited there until I reached him. I sat down and rolled up my clammy, wet jeans. The material felt icy on my calves, and goose bumps spread over my entire body.

The afternoon glow of the sun was hitting the viaduct at an angle and making it appear to glow against the sapphire-blue sky. On the riverbank, a row of purple and pink rhododendrons seemed determined to outdo each other with their colorful displays. Payton and I sat next to each other silently and enjoyed the view as crickets chirped and the stream tinkled around our shining little silver island.

After a few minutes, he slid slightly closer to me. His body radiated a comforting warmth. I wondered if he was thinking of putting his arm around me. But I knew I had to go. I'd already missed one bus, and I didn't want to miss another.

"Payton?" I whispered, so as not to destroy the magic of the moment too abruptly.

"Yes?"

His voice was very close to my ear, and his warm breath caressed my neck.

"I'm afraid I have to go back to the bus."

"I'm afraid I knew that you were going to say that."

But neither of us got up.

"You're going back by bus?"

"That's how I came."

Payton raised an eyebrow. "Really? With those gossipy ladies? I can give you a ride, instead, if you want."

My common sense was practically yelling into my ear, Are you crazy? You don't know him at all! He could be a lunatic serial killer!

"That's awfully nice of you, but I don't think I should."

But there was also another voice in my head, and this one was saying, Have you ever met a guy like this before? He's amazing! Take a risk!

I decided it would be all right if I got Alison's permission. I was sure she'd be fine with it. But when I called, no one picked up. I just heard Roy's voice asking me to leave a message.

"Hi, it's Sam. I just wanted to tell you that I won't be coming home on the bus. I'm going to get a ride home with a friend. I just wanted to let you know so that you won't worry. See you soon!"

When I hung up, my heart felt like it was beating in my throat. I had made a decision. I needed to find out more about this spark between me and Payton. My whole body was reacting to him, and I'd never felt anything like this before.

When I looked up at him, a small smile made its way onto his face. "Then we are no longer in a hurry, are we?"

"No, but I should probably tell the bus driver I'm not coming, so he doesn't send out a missing persons report."

He stood up and reached out his hand, and we made our way back to the riverbank. My teeth started to chatter, so we started to run. Once I almost slipped, but Payton's strong grip kept me from falling. Still shaking, we put our shoes on and started back down the path.

"Do you do this often?" I asked quietly.

"What?"

"This."

"Take a walk?"

"No! Pick up girls in towers and take them wading in freezing-cold riverbeds." I felt myself flushing, my cheeks turning as bright as the pink rhododendrons.

"I never do this kind of thing! And you? Do you often go off with guys you've met in towers, following them into rivers?"

I shook my head, embarrassed. "I'm ridiculously sensible, usually."

Payton had stopped walking and looked at me. "Do you think it is sensible to be here with me?" His words were quiet, almost whispered.

"It's the most irrational thing I've ever done." I looked for his eyes, but he had turned his face away.

"But I don't think I'm in danger," I joked, trying to lighten the mood. "You don't look like you've killed that many people recently."

His laugh was hard and forced. "No, you are right. Not recently."

CHAPTER 6

Payton ducked under the stream of hot water in the shower. He shut his eyes and let the water pound against his eyelids. What a day he'd had. In the morning, he'd felt like some remote-controlled robot, drawn mindlessly toward the girl. He hadn't fully considered what might happen. He'd been following her for days, though, so he realized that in some way, he was deliberately asking for pain.

The entire time, he'd thought she could sense she was being followed. She'd look around, puzzled, then go back to what she was doing. But he hadn't let her see him. Hadn't given her a chance. Then the feeling started growing more intense. The pain, the fire, that devoured him every time he got close to her, was rising higher and higher. It had been so long since he had felt something, anything, that the pain he was experiencing—so strong it could take his breath away—felt like a powerful drug. He didn't know where the pain was coming from, but he was determined to find out.

He had watched her get on the tour bus. Then he got in his car—he'd decided not to take his motorcycle—and followed her. He thought about how it might all play out. Clearly, something big had happened to him. He wasn't hollow anymore. But while he was glad to feel sensations, the pain when he was near her was barely tolerable. It was taking a toll, draining him of his strength. When he thought back to the day she had touched him while on his motorcycle, the torment still hit him like lightning.

The pain. That probably explained why he lost control of his motorcycle the first time he saw her. And that had been the only reason he had stopped and looked back.

Despite the hot shower, Payton had goose bumps. When had he last had goose bumps, he asked himself. 1740?

He soaped up vigorously, trying to scrub off the confusion flowing through him. Earlier, when he saw her climb up the monument, he had wondered whether he could stand being so near to her. He had climbed up after her, shaking and afraid.

$$\sim$$

She was standing in the sun. Her hair was shining golden and her face was in the shadows. Although he'd been following her for days, he had never really seen her properly. And now her back was to him again. He was grateful for that because the hot pain that seared through his body seemed to be increasing, like he might suddenly explode. He took several deep breaths before he regained control. His hands curled into fists. After a few minutes, he could breathe a little more easily, and he knew he could bear the pain—if only for a short time. But she mustn't, for God's sake, come any closer. Then something unexpected—but he supposed, inevitable—happened. She looked at him, and she laughed.

That face, he thought. Could it really be true?

No, he said to himself. He had to be mistaken. That was impossible—absolutely impossible! And yet, it would explain everything.

~

So from then on, there had only been one option for him: stand up to fate and find out everything he could about her.

Payton turned off the water and wrapped a towel around his hips.

She had also felt something, he was sure. Something more than pure curiosity. That had become clear when she agreed to take a walk with him, and later when she decided he could drive her home.

He went through all the times they had touched that day. The first time, on the monument, it was like brushing against a hot iron, and he had instinctively pulled his hand back. Even long after she let go, his skin still burned where her fingers had been. But if he moved back a little, the burning died down and became more of a steady pressure on his body instead. As long as he kept a safe distance, he thought he could be close to her. Sitting near her on the rock was warm, but not burning. Actual contact, though—like when she'd taken his hand at the stream—that was too much. Even the icy water didn't ease the painful scorch of her touch.

He was almost crazy with fear when he'd imagined sitting in his car with her. He wasn't sure why he'd offered her a ride.

But during the drive, he conjured up almost superhuman strength, so much so that he'd actually enjoyed it.

Other than his family, she was the first person he had talked to in a long time. And he'd been ridiculously happy when she asked whether they would see each other again.

He would gladly see her—for a number of reasons. But most importantly, he needed to answer one question: What the hell was wrong with him?

Payton saw her stumble. Just like in his memory. She wobbled backward. He wanted to act, but he was paralyzed. He needed to move, to help her, but his body would simply not obey. Reaching out too late, he grabbed desperately for her falling body. Her scream penetrated his whole body. At the last second, he caught her arm. He saw her panic, the fear of death in her eyes. Green eyes, like emeralds, opened so wide with fear. He could feel her fingers slip through his hands. He tried to pull her back over the balustrade. Inch by inch, she slid out of his grasp, and with a sudden release, she lost her hold and fell into the depths.

His own tormented yell woke him, shaking from the nightmare. He sat in his bed, trembling. He had known it. The similarity was unbelievable—obviously more than a coincidence. He really was damned.

~

My neck crawled with a shivery feeling. I couldn't believe I was betraying Alison and Roy. They hadn't reacted that well the night before, when they found out I'd gotten a ride from Payton instead of taking the bus. Alison, in particular, seemed to know something was up. She kept prodding, despite my explanations. Who was this friend, she wanted to know, and how had I met him? She wondered if she should allow me to go on the tour the next day. It was an overnight trip, she pointed out, and she wasn't sure she fully trusted me.

"Don't you realize that we are responsible for your safety?" she asked. "We'd never forgive ourselves if something should happen to you."

In the end, I managed to convince them that it wouldn't happen again. I swore that I'd be fine on the two-day excursion, that they had nothing to fear.

So the next morning I got on the bus, waved out the window like a good girl, and waited until we were several miles down the road.

It was time to improvise.

"Oh no . . ." I moaned. I held my stomach with one hand and put the other hand in front of my mouth. "I feel like I'm going to be sick."

I put a lot of effort into the show, making some realistic gagging sounds. A woman two seats in front of me looked around, alarmed, and called out to the driver to stop the bus.

Trying to look exhausted and weak, I put my head back against my seat. Another woman offered me something to drink and stroked my head. I ramped up the gagging sounds, and when the bus finally stopped, I hurried outside.

The driver, our tour guide, and the lady with the soda all followed right behind me.

"What shall we do?" Soda Lady wanted to know.

"Turn back," the driver said drily.

"But we'll miss the ferry!" the tour guide said.

"Yes, but I'd rather that than have her vomit all over my bus."

Crying, I bent farther over the bush, which I was apparently going to throw up into any second now.

"Oh, please. I don't want all of you to miss the ferry to the Isle of Harris because of me." I tried to make my voice sound as sincere as possible. I looked sadly at the woman, and I could tell she didn't want to wait for the next ferry.

"You certainly cannot come along on an overnight trip if you are feeling unwell," said my tour guide. "What if you get worse?"

"No, of course. You should go without me. I'll call home to get someone to come and pick me up."

I rummaged around in my backpack.

My three guardians looked at each other slightly confused until Soda Lady nodded decisively.

"Do you want me to make the call to your parents, love?" she asked. "You'll be better off at home resting, and we could still make it for the ferry in time."

I opened up my phone and typed in a number. After a few seconds, my bank's automatic account information system started talking to me.

"Welcome to . . ."

"Hello, Alison?" I put on my best I'm-not-feeling-well voice. "I'm so sorry to bother you. I started to feel sick on the bus, and I need to come home. Can you pick me up? I'm only at the next village."

"To check your account balance, please press . . ."

"Thanks, Alison. I'm really sorry about this . . . I'm standing right by the main road . . . Yes, see you soon."

I put the phone back in my bag.

"My host family is coming to get me. You can go on. I'll be fine."

"Is it really OK to leave you here?" the bus driver asked. He seemed worried that it might be against company policy.

"Sure, Alison will be here in about twenty minutes." I held my hand in front of my mouth again and pulled out one last gagging fit, for good measure.

"Please, go," I pleaded. "I really don't want you all to see what I had for breakfast."

"Get well soon, love." The woman patted me on the back before she hurried toward the bus. "Come on," she said to the others. "Let's go or we'll miss the ferry."

A minute later the bus disappeared around the corner.

I got out my phone again and tapped in different numbers. My fingers were shaking. That had been more difficult than I had anticipated.

"Hi! I've escaped. Are you ready to pick me up?"

Even through the telephone, the sound of Payton's voice had me spellbound.

My heart was beating wildly and I was delighted when he promised to be with me in a moment. I giggled. Yes, Scotland was definitely piquing my interest—even if it wasn't in the way my parents and Mr. Schneider had hoped.

～

The white SUV came around the corner. The night before, in the dark, I hadn't realized what an expensive car it was. A tinted window rolled down, and Payton gave me a little smile. He had dark rings under his eyes, and looked almost . . . well, normal.

"*Madain math!*"

"What?"

His smile got broader. "I said, 'Good morning. That was in Gaelic."

"Oh . . . Good morning to you, too."

As soon as I sat beside him, I felt like the air got a little clearer, the sky a bit bluer. He made everything seem so intense.

"Tell me, how does a regular Scot like you come to have a fancy car like this?"

"What do you mean, a regular Scot? You don't even know me."

"True, but I intend to change that today. So then . . . tell me . . . are you by any chance a billionaire?"

"My family's been in the wool business for hundreds of years. But don't be so nosy. And anyway, one doesn't ask someone about his income. Isn't that also considered rude in America?"

"Well, at least I didn't ask for your bank balance," I said. "It doesn't matter to me anyway." His income was totally beside the point.

I looked out the window at the countryside passing by—a pleasant smear of green and sheep and hills.

"Where are we going?"

"So impatient! You'll have to wait and see." Payton grinned.

I leaned back and relaxed. As we drove along the road toward the Western Isles, winding through the Highlands, we started to catch glimpses of the spectacular coastline.

My guilty conscience about lying to Alison was beginning to fade. Still, I was surprised by my own boldness.

Skipping the two-day excursion meant I would be spending the night with Payton—one way or another—or that I'd have to pay for somewhere to stay on my own. Either way, Alison wouldn't start missing me for more than twenty-four hours. It was the first time in my life I'd done something so crazy. I knew Kim would freak out when I told her.

I glanced over at my handsome driver. He looked really hot. His hair was tousled from the air blowing through the cracked-open window. Black sunglasses covered his eyes—and those circles. Maybe he was out late partying, I thought.

When he noticed me staring, he smiled and turned on the radio. "Get the Party Started" by Pink was on, one of my favorites, so I turned it up and laughed. Oh yeah, I said to myself. The party was starting.

Payton raised his eyebrows. "You're in a good mood."

"Well, yeah. Aren't you?"

"Yes, but I'm not exactly the get-the-party-started kind of personality. Though, I must admit, my mood has improved since you've been sitting next to me."

We smiled at each other.

We made one more twisty turn, and suddenly, we had left the hills behind us. To the left was the crystal clear Loch Duich. And right in the middle of the lake, to my great surprise, was a castle, accessible only by a footbridge.

"Right, then. Here we are." Payton pulled into a parking spot and got out. "Do you know where we are?"

I shook my head and shut the door behind me. "No, but it's amazing!"

"You've never seen the film *Highlander* then?"

"No, when it comes to eighties movies, I'm more of an *Indiana Jones* fan."

"Well, anyway, this is the famous Eilean Donan Castle. And some of the movie *Highlander* was filmed here."

I stood still and looked around. The scenery was so pretty, it was overpowering. I couldn't imagine a more beautiful setting for a castle.

"Come on, let's go in," I said, pulling my smartphone out of my bag and getting the camera ready. I had to document this day for posterity, for sure. Payton paid the entrance fee, waving off my offer to pay my own way.

"Listen, I have more or less abducted you. Nobody knows where you are, and therefore, you are helplessly bound to my will. I think you should just obey me."

"Obey you? You're crazy! But all right, I'll pay for our food then."

I reached for his arm to lead him toward the entrance, but he immediately moved away. Man, I thought, for a cool guy, he was awfully stiff. Every time I touched him, whether coincidentally or on purpose, he pulled back.

Grumpily, I went on ahead. "Are you coming?"

My good mood—and ego—had been given a huge blow. But in just a few minutes, I wasn't mad anymore. The castle was fantastic. The grounds were much smaller than around the ruins near Loch Ness, but inside this castle, the rooms were partially furnished. I tried to imagine what life must have been like back then. If I'd had Payton by my side, I fantasized, I would have been well protected.

"How old are you?" I suddenly asked him.

He took a long time to answer.

"Nineteen. May I also ask questions of you, or am I the only one to be interrogated?"

"That, in itself, is already a question."

He arched an eyebrow.

"All right, I have an idea," I told him. "Today you answer all of my questions, and then I'll answer three of your questions." I gave him my best smile and batted my eyelashes.

"Three doesn't seem very many," Payton said. "But I will agree under one condition. I will try to answer all of your questions, but your three answers must be the absolute truth."

I was silent for a moment, wondering why he would think I wouldn't tell him the truth in the first place. It didn't matter, though. I didn't have any secrets to keep.

"Deal!" I stuck out my hand to him. And after a brief hesitation, he shook it.

I leapt at my opportunity, peppering him with questions for nearly a half hour. As promised, he answered them all. I heard about his brothers Sean and Blair. I learned that his childhood dog was a giant wolfhound named Lou. I found out that he loved the beach at night.

"Same here," I told him. "I live at a place called Silver Lake. There's nothing more beautiful than a summer night by the water!"

Suddenly, I felt very homesick. I'd been away from home for almost two weeks. I missed my parents and my friends—especially Kim. Was she still seeing Justin? I wondered. I decided I'd definitely call her in a day or two.

Payton lifted my chin with a fingertip.

"Are you OK? You look so sad." His voice was soft and concerned.

"I'm fine. It's just . . . I've never been so far away from home before."

"I could help cure your homesickness. There are plenty of beautiful beaches here, and I could take you to one later."

"That would be great. As long as I'm back in Aviemore by tomorrow night."

For a long time Payton didn't say a word, he just looked deep into my eyes. I started to get nervous. Did I say something wrong, I wondered. Did he want to get rid of me sooner?

He sighed, then laughed and said, "I really haven't the foggiest how I am to survive, but it's worth a try."

I was confused. Did he think I was dangerous? I chalked it up to another language difference. Even though we were both supposedly speaking English, he often said things that didn't make any sense to me.

"You can take me to a motel or something later on. We don't have to spend the whole time together," I said, trying to apologize.

"No, it's fine." He looked down at me. "I just hadn't realized that you were intending to spend the night with me."

My cheeks turned scarlet.

"Oh, that's not what I meant!" I sputtered, and Payton started laughing. When he laughed, he looked so different. The serious, closed-off face disappeared, and instead I caught a glimpse of a funny, sweet side. My heart started to beat faster.

I wondered, was I falling in love?

Still embarrassed, I mumbled, "Well, then, are we going to the beach now or not?"

Payton nodded but made no sign of leaving. "Now answer one of my questions."

I'd wanted the carefree moment to last a little longer, but the seriousness of his tone made me listen up.

"Go for it. What do you want to know?"

"Why are you here? Why are you in Scotland, and why are you here with me?"

"First off, that was actually three questions, but I don't want to be nitpicky about it. Second, you're wasting one of your questions. I already told you I'm here on a student exchange."

"But why here? Why are you with me?"

He gave me a piercing look, but I had no idea what he was getting at.

"Well . . ." I wasn't sure how to answer. "You're nice and definitely not as boring as the tour group. You've shown me some beautiful views and given me history lessons . . . I like your company." It crossed my mind that maybe he thought I was just there in search of a summer fling. "Spending the night together wasn't meant like . . . uh . . ."

I didn't know how to go on. I wasn't about to tell him that I'd never even been kissed. Fortunately, Payton seemed to have gotten the answer he'd been looking for.

"I just wanted to know if there was another reason for you to come to Scotland. Friends, or family, for example. I knew we wouldn't . . . you know . . . spend the night together."

He said it so calmly that his words pained me.

I guess I wasn't his type, since he obviously had no intention of making any moves on me. Although I had only just that moment made sure he knew nothing serious was going to happen between us, I still somehow hoped he might try.

"No, I don't know anyone in Scotland. Or Great Britain, France, Spain . . ."

I couldn't understand why he'd had to go and spoil the atmosphere with such a stupid question.

"Let's go," I said.

The white beach of Mallaig was breathtaking. Cobalt water lapped in small waves on the fine sand, washing away our footprints as we went. We had already walked quite a way along the coast when Payton pulled a picnic blanket out of his backpack and spread it out behind a dune. We had already eaten dinner, but it was a nice place to rest. Payton lay down on his back, tucked his arms behind his head, and closed his eyes.

How could he be so relaxed while my heart was constantly tapping at top speed? Trying to appear as collected as he was, I lay down next to him. Seagulls circled the water, calling out in their shrill voices. I closed my eyes, too. My skin tingled. I hoped with all my might that he would take my hand . . . Then I quickly opened my eyes again.

"Payton, seriously. Where are we going to sleep tonight? Can't I stay at your place?"

At first I thought he had fallen asleep because it took him such a long time to answer.

"No, that is not a good idea." He sat up and drew a pattern in the sand with a stick. "I was thinking we could stay here." He doodled some circles, waves, zigzags, and flowers. He seemed immersed in his sand creations—or maybe he was just pretending.

"Sleep here? On the beach?"

"If you want. We could make a fire, and I have some drinks in the car. And blankets."

I'd been thinking I'd sleep on a bed, or at least a couch. Then again, the idea of sleeping on the beach was extremely romantic. Well, I figured, I'd lost my good sense, and now I was losing my heart to this inscrutable Scot, so I might as well go for it. As least when I got back to Delaware, I'd have a fantastic memory.

"OK." I made a split-second decision. "That sounds good." I gave him my most beautiful smile. "But if we're going to be here for a while, then I'm going for a swim."

Now, I thought, let's just see if there really was nothing about me that would appeal to this nineteen-year-old boy. I whipped off my jeans and pulled my shirt over my head. In just my bra and underwear, I ran into the ice-cold water.

Before I could think about it, I dove right in, swimming and swimming until I felt numb.

Payton sat on the beach and watched me.

CHAPTER 7

Payton watched Sam, feeling like he could hardly breathe. The pain was almost unbearable. She was really pushing him toward his limit. Yet still he needed to be near her, almost more than he needed air to breathe. She made him feel more alive than anything else in the last 270 years. But he knew he couldn't carry on like this for much longer. He would have to talk to Sean.

All day, Payton had tried to ignore the pain. He'd even reached out to touch her when she told him she was feeling homesick. Seeing her upset was almost as bad as touching her. He wasn't sure he could survive a full night of torment. He'd probably collapse. But he didn't want her to see what she did to him— at least not yet.

Payton couldn't lie to her, and he couldn't explain anything without frightening her. And that, he definitely did not want to do. Since they'd arrived at the beach, he had felt something besides the pain. Warmth! He had felt the warm sun on his skin. He knew it was impossible. There was no such thing as warm or cold for him. And yet, he knew he was being warmed all the same.

All this has to mean something, he told himself. He wished that he could concentrate, but his eyes kept turning to the water. That crazy girl had jumped into the water wearing only her purple underwear.

His reaction to her body surprised him. He had found her pretty beforehand, true, yet her looks had held as little importance to him as all the other beautiful things he perceived but was unaffected by.

Payton desperately waited to see her come out of the water. The pain was slightly milder since she had gone swimming. Still, he wished he could have gone in after her.

Sam was walking toward him, dripping wet. Her hair clung to her shoulders and back, and goose bumps covered her entire body. She wrapped her arms around herself and started running. Payton couldn't take his eyes off her. He got up and handed the blanket to her, his eyes taking in her slender body. Feelings arose in him, feelings that he had long forgotten.

Sam's icy, wet fingers brushed Payton's arm, and he flinched in pain. And that was the first moment he was able to fully comprehend the force of the curse. Up until then, there hadn't been anyone in his life he wanted to be close to. Feeling desire for the first time, Payton could hardly bear to be in the same town as Sam.

But he swore to himself that he would no longer let the curse rule his life. Something would have to change.

~

An entire night and a full day of searing pain and burning torture later, Payton had dropped Sam off in Aviemore. Since her package of sightseeing tours was over, she wouldn't be able to meet up with him as easily. The next few days, she was scheduled to accompany her host dad to his class, and she also had to write up a history report for her teacher back in the States. But she had promised get in touch with Payton just as soon as she could.

He was torn. On the one hand, he was very happy when the burning died down. Yet on the other hand, he believed more and more that this girl was meant for him. Why else would fate have led him to her? Why would he have almost run her over on her first day in Scotland? Why had he happened to drive by when she'd missed the bus? And why did she look so much like the woman he hadn't been able to save? For whose death he was, in fact, responsible? Had the curse led her to him? To punish him even more? It had been such a long time already.

His SUV left the main road and bumped over a rarely used field to a lonely cottage. He'd been intending to talk to Sean at home, but the last two days had just been too much. His desire to be close to Sam was so strong. And somewhere, deep down, underneath the red-hot pain that poured over everything like a river of lava, he could feel tenderness. The desire to be close to someone, and to be loved—he'd never known it before. And damn it, if it meant pain, then bring on the pain. He wanted to bear it, so he could feel the indescribable feeling of her skin on his.

He felt as if he were being torn into pieces. Never in the past centuries had he thought he was capable of it. Of falling in love!

That's why he'd gone to his secret refuge. If he'd gone home, Sean would have known something was up, and he certainly wouldn't have been happy. And the others? To tell the truth, he didn't really care about them. But he had sworn his brother Blair an oath, and was therefore forced to obey him. He decided to keep his secret for a bit, at least until he really knew what was going on.

CHAPTER 8

The sun reflected off the dark-gray hood as Blair McLean rubbed the milky polish in circles. He was in the courtyard, surrounded by a row of special cleaners and waxes to burnish his Bentley to a high sheen, when Sean came racing up the gravel path on his motorcycle.

Dust sprayed into the air as Sean tried to skid his way to a stop, barely three feet in front of Blair, but his rear wheel slipped, and he landed with a crash under his Moto Guzzi.

Strangely—and against all the experience he'd gained in the last 270 years—Sean found he wasn't protected from injury. On the contrary. The gravel tore open his skin, leaving a three-inch gash. The power of the pain when he hit the ground took his breath away. His heavy bike squashed his foot, and he yelled out in surprise.

He crawled out from under his bike, gasping, his usual cocky composure completely shot. When he tried to walk, he was shocked to find that he could hardly put any weight on his ankle.

"*Bas mallaichte!* Bloody hell," Sean said. "What on earth is going on?" He lifted his head and looked at his older brother.

Blair was grinning, his chest quivering from trying to suppress his laughter. "What is it? Don't you like your motorcycle?"

"Are you nuts? I hurt myself, and you're laughing?"

Blair stopped laughing. "Hurt yourself? How could that be?"

Sean would have really liked to punch his brother at this moment, but it hurt too much to move his shoulder. After so many years of feeling nothing at all, the pain was intensified and unexpected.

"No really . . . I hurt myself. I can hardly bear it. *Ifrinn*," Sean gasped angrily.

Blair stared into his brother's face, contorted by pain. Then it seemed he couldn't help it; he started laughing again, so loudly he startled a family of red-throated divers right out of a tree. He couldn't stop. He hadn't laughed that hard in a very long time. He sank to the ground, leaned his broad back on his freshly polished tire rim, and rubbed the tears out of his eyes.

Sean's crash had no doubt looked spectacular, but he'd always been a daredevil and he'd always gotten up without batting an eyelid—probably thousands of times. Blair had seen at least half of these wipeouts with his own eyes, and he'd never before laughed about them. Or anything else. No pain, no joy. That's the way it had always been.

Sean was still rubbing his ankle and holding his bruised side.

"You have to admit, it's kind of funny, isn't it?" Blair asked.

"What?" Sean didn't see anything funny.

"That you should finally feel something, now, only after a crash! Not when you bite your tongue or eat soup that's too hot, but when you land under your bike while going forty miles an hour."

Blair reached his arm around his brother's shoulders to support him. Sean was laughing now, too, and together they swayed into the hall.

Nathaira Stuart looked up from her herbal dictionary in surprise when the two of them burst in. Blair dumped Sean onto a high-backed chair with a thud. Sean reached down and pulled a piece of gravel out of his knee, dropping it onto the floor in disgust. Nathaira put down the book crossly. She slowly shook her head at them and frowned.

"And what is going on here?" Her voice echoed through the silence of the great hall.

Blair and Sean looked at each other briefly before they both burst out laughing again.

"Stop snorting, you idiots!"

Nathaira tossed back her black hair, her green eyes sparking with annoyance. She looked confused. And she was not used to being confused. She took in the scene with marked disbelief, glancing from one face to the other. Her fiancé, Blair, was leaning on the back of the chair, trying to hold in his laughter and stand up straight. She had still not received an answer, so she stamped her foot angrily.

"Blair! Answer me! What is going on?"

He pointed at Sean and blurted, "He's hurt himself. He was crying like a child!"

Nathaira spun around with a jerk to face Sean. "Hurt? What does that mean?"

She rushed to Sean's side, looking at his leg with alarm and pulling away the fabric of his ripped pants.

"Blair, tell your fiancée to stop trying to get into my pants!" Sean, still laughing, twisted away from her.

She batted at him. "Shut up! This is serious! How could you be in pain?"

Blair put his hand on Nathaira's hip. "Calm down. There's bound to be a logical explanation."

Sean nodded. He certainly didn't want her to keep poking at his sore spots. Nathaira paced the floor, agitated, mumbling something incomprehensible. Then she rushed out of the hall.

Blair and Sean stared after her, surprised.

"'Tis funny, isn't it?" Sean wondered aloud.

"I agree with you that it's odd, but I don't think it means anything special."

"Why would you say that? Nothing like this has ever happened before."

Blair wasn't one for thinking too hard with no real reason. "Doesn't matter. Nothing bad happened."

"Yes, but don't you want to know why this is going on?" said Sean. "I certainly do. Because if this is the way the winds are now blowing, then I think I might have to start driving a little bit more carefully."

Nathaira came back into the room with a stack of books piled high in her arms. She dropped them on the table and pushed them around until she found the one she must have been looking for. All the books had one very thing in common. They were old. Very old.

"A long time ago, I read something in one of these books, something that can help us. Where is it?"

Blair seemed to be losing interest. He probably wanted to finish detailing his car before the typical Scottish weather would spoil his efforts. "*Mo luaidh*," he said to Nathaira, "why don't you look at your books in peace and we'll all talk this over later. We should probably tell Cathal and Payton, too."

Sean agreed. "Exactly. Give it some time. It doesn't look like Payton's going to be back this evening, anyway, and Cathal isn't due back for a week. Let's just see what happens."

Nathaira sighed. "All right, but if something like this happens again in the meantime, I want to hear about it im-mediately. And as soon as Cathal is back, we will call the clan together!"

CHAPTER 9

I was not happy. I hadn't seen Payton for several days, but my thoughts were constantly circling around him, like the seagulls we'd seen at the beach. That night had been incredible. Payton hadn't tried anything, but I could tell he liked me from the way he'd looked at me. We talked for ages, and later, after it got dark, we lay next to each other on the blanket and looked up at the stars. Even when we were silent, we seemed to get along.

At one point in the middle of the night, I woke up to find Payton watching me. He smiled when he realized that I was watching him right back. Bravely, I had reached out for his hand. He stopped short, but after a second, he squeezed my hand, and held it the rest of the night.

And then, nothing.

To be fair, I had been the one to say I'd let him know when we could get together next. But deep down, I'd hoped he wouldn't wait for me to call. It was impossible to concentrate on my report for school when I didn't know how, when, or even if things would proceed with Payton. My head told my heart—unsuccessfully—to calm down and forget about the Scot. After all, I'd be returning to Milford in a few weeks and I'd never see him again.

I put down my pen and went to find to Alison. She was washing the dinner dishes.

"Hey, Alison. Do you think I could take the bus to Inverness tomorrow? I want to get a souvenir for my friend, Kim. And . . . I'm kind of embarrassed to say . . . but I've really been craving a Big Mac."

Alison laughed. "And I thought you liked my cooking! Of course you can go to Inverness. If you want, I can drive you."

That was exactly what I didn't want.

"Nah, I can take the bus. You have enough to do as it is. But thanks for the offer."

I sauntered back to my room and called Payton's number. It rang and rang, but he didn't answer, and I couldn't help being upset.

I finished my paper, in a funk, and stared dolefully around my room. I switched the radio on and threw myself onto the bed. Maybe I should try again, I thought. But maybe he didn't answer on purpose. Would he call me back? Did I even get the number right? I grabbed my phone and double-checked the number, and then felt even sadder than before.

The self-doubts kept rolling in: Maybe he didn't have a good time with me. Maybe he'd expected more. No, he'd been the one holding back. Ryan would have tried all kinds of maneuvers with a cute girl alone at the beach. But Payton was different. Which was exactly why I had fallen for him.

I closed my eyes. Ronan Keating's song "When You Say Nothing at All" was running through my head. The words described how I felt about Payton perfectly. Even when we didn't talk, our hearts had a connection.

Yes, that was exactly it. It may sound completely crazy, but the first moment I saw him, my heart leapt in recognition. It knew he was something special. My heart understood everything. And when I had reached out for his hand in the middle of the night, I knew he needed me just as much as I needed him.

I jumped. My cell phone was ringing. I scrambled up and took a few deep breaths.

"Hello?"

"Hello, Sam. I saw that you called, and I called back as soon as I could. Unfortunately, there's no reception in parts of the Highlands. What are you up to?"

I felt a huge relief. He didn't have cell-phone coverage!

"Nothing special. I was just hanging out, listening to music, feeling kind of bored."

The other end of the phone was quiet, and then Payton said in a serious voice, "I would like to ask you my second question now."

"Which second question?"

"I answered all your questions, and you promised to give me three honest answers in return. Am I going to get my second answer now?"

"Of course. I had completely forgotten about that. What do you want to know?"

"You said you were bored. Is that the only reason you called me?"

He sounded serious; he didn't seem to be playing with me. I thought about lying, but I had sworn to tell him the truth.

So softly that I almost hoped he wouldn't hear, I mumbled, "No, that's not the reason I called. The main thing is, I can't get you out of my head."

More silence. Then Payton's tone of voice changed, and he sounded far more relaxed. "Fine. What do you want to do?"

I was stunned. I had just more or less confessed that I loved him, and his only reaction was "Fine"? You'd think he might have said something like "Yeah, I think about you a lot too," or "I feel the same way." Just about anything would have been more romantic than "Fine."

I tried not to sound hurt. "Whatever. I'm up for anything. We don't have to meet if you don't want to."

I decided that was the last time I'd give him a call. Until what he said next, that is.

"Well, of course, I want to see you," he said. "I just don't have time today. And tomorrow during the day I have to meet my brother. There seem to be some problems at home. I will have time tomorrow evening, though."

"In the evening . . . OK." I was glad to hear that he wanted to meet up with me, but disappointed that my McDonald's ruse might go to waste. "So what do you want to do?"

"Surely you're not planning to leave Scotland without having been to a pub? How about this—I'll pick you up at the bus stop around eight."

A pub wasn't exactly what I had in mind. I didn't know what Alison would think about that either. But I told myself it would work out somehow.

"OK. See you tomorrow," I said.

"Yes, see you tomorrow, *mo luaidh.*"

Mo luaidh? What did that mean? Payton had said it so tenderly before we hung up. Good thing I was going to Inverness. I wanted to buy a Gaelic dictionary as soon as possible.

That made me think of my grandma's pendant, and I reached up to my neck. After the night on the beach, my skin had showed clear red marks where the pendant had been. I didn't think it was an allergy because the burning sensation didn't last. It was odd, though; it always came on at the most inconvenient of times. Like every time the thought of Payton crossed my mind, or when I tried to get close to him. I still wore the necklace every day. The burning feeling wasn't as bad as it had been at the beginning—or maybe I'd gotten used to it.

I took it off and cradled it in my hands. Then I picked up the souvenir version, the one I'd bought at the tourist trap. I still couldn't figure out why a pendant with a Scottish clan's coat of arms was in Grandma's attic. And a very old one, at that. An old pendant with strange features, like, oh, burning me at its whim. Maybe I could find out something about it in Inverness.

Ugh, enough thinking for today, I said to myself. I put the antique and the souvenir on my desk and thought about calling Kim. The five-hour time difference made it so tricky to call; I was always either interrupting Kim's dinner or having to stay up really late. Instead, I threw myself in front of the TV and surfed around until I found a rerun of *Mr. Bean.*

An hour later, I turned the TV off, put my pajamas on, and slipped under the covers. I fell asleep almost immediately.

I was scared. "You must face your destiny! You cannot run away!" The old woman's words echoed endlessly in my head.

"What destiny?" I wanted to ask, but the old lady had disappeared.

Sharp gravel was digging into my skin. I was kneeling on the ground and didn't have the energy to rise. The wind was pulling at me, as if wanting me to move on. But where to? In desperation, I buried my head in my hands and hoped for help.

Then something gently brushed my head. The old woman was standing directly in front of me.

"Who are you?"

I hadn't asked the question out loud, but I could read the answer in her thoughts: "Vanora."

"Vanora? But what do you want from me? What's going on? I'm scared!"

Her hand was resting on my head, as if she were blessing me. And just as before, she answered silently: "Face your destiny. Remember those you are a descendant of. Fear not. The pendant will protect you."

She put the pendant around my neck. It looked new and shiny. The metal was warm, and I immediately felt safe.

The wind died down, and the dark clouds disappeared. And like the clouds, Vanora vanished. Only her voice was still echoing in my head.

The last thing she said was, "Beware of the fall."

With a start, I sat straight up in bed, feeling terribly afraid. My heart was racing and a layer of sweat covered my skin. I switched on the lamp next to my bed. Seeing the cozy room in the light, peaceful and tidy as usual, helped to push the nightmare to the back of my thoughts.

That stupid pendant was even haunting me in my dreams. I looked for it on the desk, but it wasn't there; it was around my neck. That was impossible! I was certain I'd taken it off. Then I took a closer look and saw that the pendant had changed. It was no longer old and tarnished. It was shining like new—and the engraved writing was clearly legible. I was starting to freak out when a quiet whisper made its way to my ear. The words sounded strange, but I could understand everything:

"Face your destiny. Fear not."

The woman in my dream seemed so real, and I wondered who she was, this Vanora, and why her words actually made me feel safe. I wanted to be brave for her, to face my destiny. But what was my destiny? Would she come back and tell me?

Then I remembered that Roy was an expert in Scottish history and legends. I had discussed my first dream with him, and he was open-minded about it. Maybe he could help me decode this one. Disturbed by such a vivid dream, I lay awake for a long time, stewing things over in my mind.

~

Although I didn't have anywhere to go in the morning, I got up early to talk to Roy. I wanted to get his opinion as soon as I could. When I went down to the kitchen, he was already sitting at the table, engrossed in his newspaper and slurping his coffee. The fantastic smell of baked biscuits was in the air, but Alison was nowhere to be seen. That was good because she was far more skeptical than Roy when it came to myths and legends. Without her practical influence, I could talk to Roy without any inhibitions.

"Good morning, Roy."

I sat down next to him and poured myself a cup of coffee.

"Aye, good morning. Did you sleep well?"

"To be honest, no. And that's exactly what I want to talk to you about. Do you have a moment?"

Roy laid the paper aside, pushed the plate with biscuits toward me, and leaned back in his chair.

"What's up?"

I picked up a biscuit and broke off a little piece.

"I had another strange dream. It was similar to the one I had before. But this time, something else, something kind of weird, happened."

Roy waited for me to continue, but suddenly I felt insecure. It was absurd to believe that a woman from my dreams had come into my room and put my pendant around my neck. My newly spruced-up pendant, no less.

"Sam, look, I'm from Fair Isle. A tiny island, far north, between the Orkneys and the Shetlands. There are things there that many people, including those here, would not believe. I have seen things that aren't supposed to exist. But I did see them, aye? So you don't need to worry. I will believe you, whatever you tell me."

I could tell he meant what he said. And so I told him everything. In between sentences, I paused to put pieces of biscuit into my mouth. The warmth and sweetness of Alison's baking felt like my connection to reality. Like a soft, safe anchor in this whole muddle of dreams.

When I had finished, Roy shook his head. "Astonishing. Really astonishing. Do you mind if I look at the necklace?"

He held the pendant with strong fingers, and brushed over the engraving.

"*Cuimhnich air na daoine o'n d' thanig thu.* I know that motto, it's the—"

"The Camerons' motto, I know."

"Aye, right. It means, 'Remember those . . .'"

"'. . . you are a descendant of.'" I completed his sentence. Goose bumps covered my body, and I had to swallow several times to fight the lump in my throat.

Roy nodded. "But how did you know?"

"From my dream. There was a woman, and her name is Vanora. In my dream, she said that to me."

Roy laughed out loud. "Aye, in your shoes I would also be feeling alarmed. But remember, it is only a necklace. Vanora means "white wave," and that tells me she must be an old woman, one of the Island Folk. I am sure she is of no danger to you."

"But Roy, how do you explain why I am dreaming of island women I didn't even know existed?" I brushed up the last crumb from my plate and stuck it in my mouth.

"I think she wants to reveal herself to you. She wants you to understand what she is trying to tell you."

Roy had a strange expression on his face. I didn't know who I thought was crazier—me for telling him all this or him for believing me.

"Let's assume you're right," I said. "How do you know this stuff?"

"For thousands of years, the people on Fair Isle have been living there in peace, without any influence from outside civilizations. The people are fishermen, simple people. The Wise Women of Fair Isle made sure everything was in order. They spoke the law. They were the leaders of the tribe. It was a responsibility they passed down to their daughters and granddaughters. And because everyone was so dependent on the sea and its moods, all the Wise Women were named in honor of the water. Like White Wave or Peaceful Current. But also Raging Lake."

I leaned forward in my chair, nearly knocking over my coffee.

"These women," Roy said, "could also connect to the powers of nature, or at least, so it is said. Their supernatural powers and abilities became famous. At one point, some of the mighty Scottish clan leaders sent ships to the island with the intention of stealing one of the Fair Witches—that's what they called the Wise Women. They thought the witches could help bring them more power and wealth."

I imagined how terrible it must have been, to be taken forcibly from your family and home, to face an unsure destiny at the hands of people who wanted to steal your powers.

"The Wise Women saw the warships coming," said Roy. "And they gave the men of the island an order—to bid farewell to one of their daughters each. The men wanted to fight and defend their island, but they followed the instructions of the Wise Women, and soon eight girls stood waiting on the beach in their white gowns. As the heavily armed warriors streamed by the dozens onto land, they heard the voice of the eldest Wise Woman, a voice carried right up to them by the wind.

"Take these powerful children of our folk. To maintain the peace, they will obey you. Never again will you return to Fair Isle. The sea would devour you. Now go."

This was something the warriors hadn't expected at all, and there was disagreement among some of the men, who were determined to have a battle. Then the skies darkened. Lightning flashed over the wild sea. The clansmen took it as a sign. They grabbed the eight girls, dragged them to their ships, and left the island."

"Wow, what a story!" I couldn't wait to hear more.

Roy laughed. "I hate to do this to you, but I have to get going or I'll be late to work. We'll talk more later." He got up, folded his newspaper, and put his jacket on.

I don't know how he could so easily leave the story and return to the present day. I could still see the frightened girls in front of me, whose fate had been to leave their home to protect their families' lives. Face your destiny. These girls had done just that. But if that's what it had meant for them, I wondered, what could it mean for me?

Roy already had his bag under his arm. He stuck his head through the door and said, "I'm off, then. Have a good day."

"Roy? What does *mo luaidh* mean?"

"*Mo luaidh?* That means 'my darling' in Gaelic. Just how many necklaces do you have?" he joked.

I blushed. "It wasn't from a necklace."

"Aye." Roy grinned knowingly.

Then he was out the door, and I started grinning, too.

CHAPTER 10

Payton raced behind his brother, both of them flying along the wind-buffeted road on their motorcycles. Sean took a turn so low his knee almost touched the ground. Payton accelerated and followed suit. They'd been on the road together since the break of dawn, but they hadn't spoken a single word. Payton had almost caught up with Sean. When he reached him, he pulled up his handlebars and zoomed past him on his back wheel. Then he turned into a parking lot and stopped.

Sean pulled in and got off his bike. "Not bad. If you practice another hundred years, you might get as good as me." He patted his little brother on the back.

"And in another hundred years, you might finally notice that I've been letting you win."

The brothers were very competitive; it seemed every ride they did together ended up as a race. But there was no more time for that—it was almost noon, and Payton had quite a lot to discuss with Sean.

"So what's so important that Nathaira has called the whole clan together?"

"Something strange happened," said Sean. He paused. He seemed to be having a hard time putting it into words.

"I was hoping to annoy Blair. He was polishing his Bentley, and I thought a little gravel shower would do the trick. Unfortunately, my stupid prank backfired on me. I slipped and landed under the bike."

Payton lifted an eyebrow. "As I said, I let you win. You really are a pathetic driver."

"No, seriously. When I fell off, I actually got hurt. I felt pain. Terrible pain."

Payton paled. "Pain?"

"Yes! Ask Blair. He thought it was so funny he nearly fell over laughing. Don't you think that's strange, too?"

"That is strange. I wonder if this is all connected." Payton rubbed his forehead.

Sean watched his brother briefly. "If what is all connected?"

"Everything. I think everything is connected."

"Really, Payton. Could you please be a bit more precise? I have no bloody idea what you're talking about."

"I'd better start at the beginning." He leaned against his bike. "I was driving along one evening, and I saw this girl next to the road. I suddenly felt incredible pain. Pain so bad I couldn't even see. I rammed straight into her suitcase. Thank God I didn't kill her."

Tensely, Sean urged his brother to go on. "Well, what happened then?"

"Then, boom, I see her again, not even a week later. It was raining, she missed her bus, and she needed help. I almost rode past her, but then my curiosity got the better of me. I gave her a ride to Aviemore, and the whole time I thought I was going to die any minute. When she touched me, it felt as if I were burning."

Sean was paying very close attention.

"Since then, I've been following her. At a certain distance, the pain is bearable, but the closer I get to her, the worse it gets."

"What do you mean, the closer you get to her?" Sean asked. "How close have you been?"

It was clear from Sean's voice that he was not at all pleased, but Payton couldn't do anything about that at this point. His words tumbled out.

"I talked to her. Then we took a walk, and the next time we spent a whole day together. I'm supposed to see her again tomorrow. She's beautiful, and kind, and . . . well, it's hard to explain. I feel like I need her. I even need the pain! I haven't felt anything in so long that I now crave pain. I need to find out what is going on, why I react to her that way. I think it must have to do with the resemblance she has to—"

"Wait, what resemblance?" Sean still didn't quite seem to understand what his brother was talking about, but he couldn't miss the passion in Payton's voice.

"This sounds crazy, but when I first saw her, I thought one of the Cameron women was standing in front of me."

Now it was Sean's turn to go pale.

"Payton, for God's sake! Why didn't you tell me any of this earlier? She's a Cameron? Do you think this has anything to do with the curse?"

Payton felt cornered, but since when was it up to Sean who he spent time with?

"*Sguir!*" He warned his brother to stop.

As often happened when they fought, they had switched to Gaelic.

"I am to stop?" countered Sean. "With what? You are the one who needs to stop seeing that girl. It is far too dangerous."

"You can't tell me what to do. *Pog mo thon!*" Payton turned and stormed off, onto a footpath that led away from the parking lot, out into a park along the cliffs.

"No, I will not kiss your arse," Sean yelled before running after him. "And what do you think Cathal will say to this?" He tried to calm himself down, knowing that otherwise Payton would end the conversation for good.

"It's not up to Cathal, either," Payton said, slowing.

"But what about Blair? You swore an oath to him. And Blair will, as always, be of the same opinion as Cathal."

Rotten wooden planks led up to a scenic viewing area. Payton leaned his back against the fence, crossing his arms in front of his chest. "We don't have to tell them."

Sean didn't say a word for several minutes.

"All right, then," he finally said, "tell me the rest of the story, and we'll figure out what's best, together. What's important to the clan and what's not."

Payton shrugged, like he might be amenable.

"So she looks like a Cameron," Sean said. "But is she a Cameron?"

"I haven't any idea. Her name is Samantha Watts. She's American. But I doubt she's a Cameron. How could she be?"

"We have to find out. And if she is, we must tell Cathal."

"*Ifrinn!* I will not tell him! He hates the Camerons. I will not put her into danger."

"Why is this Samantha so important to you? You keep reverting back into Gaelic. That shows me how much you care."

Payton turned away. He felt caught. Sean always seemed to know his thoughts; it didn't seem fair. If only he knew himself what he should do. He briefly closed his eyes and breathed in the salty sea air.

Sean shook his head in disbelief. His question was hardly more than a whisper.

"You think I love her? How could that be possible? Have you forgotten that we are cursed?" Payton shoved his hands into his face, running them up and over his hair.

"Yes, I think that you love her. And the curse, for whatever reason, seems to be changing. Your feelings for this girl, the fact that I felt pain, the fact that we're all laughing so much more readily. These are all signs that something is happening. Nathaira is very unsettled, too."

Payton made a dismissive gesture. "We have only the Stuarts to thank—and their ancient fight—for this infernal curse. Had I known that night what a price we would all have to pay for it, I would have turned against Cathal."

They had talked about that night many times since. The McLean family had joined together with the Stuarts, and had sworn to support Cathal, the chieftain of the Stuarts, and his people. So like Payton, Sean had followed Cathal into battle. Blair, Cathal's childhood friend, had joined with them, too. Sean and Payton had trusted Blair and chose to ride with him. But Blair's youngest brother, Kyle, had secretly followed their group, hoping to stop them. When they spotted his horse, on a hill far behind them, Nathaira had ridden back to tell Kyle to go home. But it was too late. By the time she galloped up to him, he was already dying. A stab in the back had dug deeply into his lung, and the enemy had fled. Nathaira had returned to the group, smeared all over with Kyle's blood, and had told them about the Camerons' treacherous murder of innocent Kyle. Beside himself with anger, Blair swore he would take revenge.

Payton had always wondered how things between the Stuarts and Camerons would have been different if the Camerons had left Kyle in peace.

"Payton, we've talked this over for hundreds of years, and you know there's no sense in talking about it again. It's over."

"You know nothing! I let Isobel Cameron die. And because I wanted to save her, Kenzie Stuart died. For that alone I deserve purgatory. And now, almost three hundred years later, I meet this girl. I even dreamed I would let her fall. Just like Isobel!"

Sean couldn't answer to that. He himself was not free of guilt. But he had learned to live with it.

Payton sighed. "Sean, please understand. I have to protect her. And I must find out what is happening to me."

He kicked at the ground, knocking a few pebbles over the cliff. "Do you know what else? I felt the warmth of the sun."

"And what does it feel like? I can't even remember."

"*Och*, it was unbelievable. I also had goose bumps because I was cold."

"God, I would risk everything to have feelings, too."

Payton nodded. "So what shall we do now?"

Sean rubbed his chin, thinking, "We will wait to see what the meeting brings."

Payton was relieved. "Thanks, brother."

"Don't thank me too early," he warned. "I want to meet this girl."

"What? No way!"

"That's my condition. Otherwise, I'll tell the others everything."

Payton's jaw muscles twitched angrily.

"No!" he growled. "You will stay away from her, or there will be trouble."

Sean did not seem the slightest bit impressed by Payton's warning. "I'll have time on Friday. Think on this, brother. I will stand true to the oath that I swore Blair. I will not stand against the clan just because of some girl you told me about. I want to see her for myself."

With that, he left Payton standing on the cliff. With the engine of his motorcycle running, he yelled, "If you want another race, then you'll have to come now. Maybe I'll let you win this time!"

Then he sped off with screaming tires. Payton stared at his disappearing brother, and stayed right where he was. He didn't want to race. He felt the calamity that was brewing for them all.

CHAPTER 11

It was just before eight. I stood at the bus stop, full of anticipation, wearing a brown suede miniskirt that I felt slightly ridiculous in. I'd bought the skirt in Inverness to impress Payton, because all I'd packed for my trip were jeans, shorts, and casual tops—and one nice dress, just in case I had to go to church. But I desperately wanted to look good, so I splurged on the skirt. I paired it with a low-cut black sweater and hid the not-enough-cleavage problem with a cute scarf.

I had missed Payton. I'd been glowing all day since he'd called me darling. My thoughts were whirling: Was I really in love? Could he actually be in love with me? Maybe in a few hours, I'd get my first kiss. I was dizzy just thinking about the possibility.

His white SUV turned the corner and stopped next to me.

Payton looked even better than in my memory. His light-brown hair was casually ruffled, and his eyes had a sparkle like the sunlight I'd seen on the lochs. I'd barely buckled my seat belt when he hit the gas and the car took off.

"What story did you have to make up so you could see me?"

"None. I just told Roy that a really great guy had invited me to go to a pub, and he was totally cool about it. He just said that I should resist the urge to find out what Scots wear under their kilt on a first date."

Payton laughed. "Oh, if I had realized that you'd been wondering about that, I would've worn my kilt."

It felt like my heart might actually beat out of my chest. Thank God I was sitting down.

We had been driving for only about five minutes when Payton steered into a parking space and we crossed the street to a pub. From outside, I could already hear the sound of amplified guitar. Payton politely held the door for me. I was surprised how many people were packed into the place. I tried to push through the crowd but didn't get very far, so I was glad when I suddenly felt Payton's hand on my shoulder. He guided me to an empty table in the corner, where it was a bit quieter.

Most of the patrons were thronged around the bar while up on stage, two guys were playing guitar and singing rowdy folk songs. I yanked my miniskirt down a bit and slid into a chair. It was hot inside and a lot livelier than most parties Kim dragged me to back home. I was kind of excited to be in a pub to begin with. I was surprised that no one checked my ID.

A stocky waitress made her way skillfully through the crowd to take our order: two ales and two fish suppers. Payton had told me I needed to get to know the local food, and it was either that or the haggis. And when he revealed that haggis is sheep's stomach filled with offal, I chose the fish dish, no further questions asked.

The music was fabulous, but you had to shout to have a conversation. I leaned over to Payton, quite close to him.

"How was your meeting with your brother?"

Payton drew away from me a little bit and shrugged.

"Eh, it went OK. He's kind of a pain in the neck. He wants to meet you."

"Me? Why? You told him about me?"

"Yes, and now he's curious."

It suddenly got quieter. The musicians climbed off-stage for a break and headed for the bar. A few people made toasts to them, merrily clinking glasses together. One of the musicians shouted something, and everyone laughed.

"What did he say?" I asked.

"He said that there are two empty guitars, and that any-one is welcome to go up and play while they enjoy a few beers. Would you like to?"

Actually, I could play guitar fairly well, but I didn't want to make a fool of myself in front of Payton, much less a pub full of strangers.

"No way. But what about you?"

He thought about it briefly, and then, to my surprise, he nodded.

"You know what? I haven't played for ages, but why not?"

He took my hand and pulled me toward the stage. He nodded at the smiling musicians, bowed to the other guests, and sat down on the stool. The crowd quieted, expectantly. Then Payton began to sing in Gaelic. Although I couldn't understand the words, the tune was beautiful.

Payton plucked at the strings of the guitar at the exact same speed as the beating of my heart. His eyes were locked on me. My vision narrowed, and it was as if we were alone.

The world around us had stopped turning. Only he and I and this old song existed.

After the last chords died away, there was a burst of applause and a free whiskey from the crowd.

"And now you," he demanded, shoving the instrument into my hands. Everyone clapped encouragingly, so even though I was sweating, I gave in. Just as seriously and thoughtfully as Payton, I sat down on the stool. I bowed slightly. Then I launched into "I Gotta Feeling"—strumming and singing way more energetically than the crowd was expecting.

I immediately won the audience over. They laughed, and in a flash they were all singing along with the Black Eyed Peas song. That was excellent because my voice is only so-so.

I searched for Payton's eyes. He wasn't singing, but he was smiling. Better than nothing. The last verse of the song was completely drowned out by the clapping and chanting of the crowd. When I climbed off the stage, I was handed a glass of whiskey of my own. Payton and I squeezed our way back to our table through the jubilant crowd.

"That was excellent. You were great! My mushy love song was no match."

I was still quite breathless and really hot. Without thinking, I pulled off my scarf and wiped the thin layer of sweat from my face.

Suddenly, Payton froze. He stared at my neckline and looked totally crushed. He grabbed me roughly by the arm, pulled me toward him, and took my pendant into his hand.

"What. Is. That?" His voice was dangerously quiet. He held my arm in a viselike grip and fixed me with an icy-cold stare.

"Nothing . . . What do you mean? Ow, let go of me!"

I tried to free myself, but he yanked me even closer.

"Sam"—the way he said my name sounded almost like a threat—"tell me where you got this pendant, immediately!"

I had no idea what was going on. His fingers dug painfully into my skin, and his face had clouded. His cheekbones were standing out as he clenched his jaw, and his lips were bloodless and tightly shut.

"Let go of me! What are you doing?"

I jerked away, horrified, and rubbed my arm.

Payton practically knocked the table over as he abruptly left the pub. Not sure what to do, I stood there a moment. Our order hadn't even arrived yet. I pulled a ten-pound note from my purse and put it on the table, and then I followed my strange companion outside.

He wasn't in front of the pub, so I crossed the road and looked around. His car was still there, and Payton was behind it, just standing there.

"What's wrong with you?" I was furious. The evening wasn't turning out at all like I'd hoped.

"With me? You're asking me?"

Payton was shouting so loud I jumped.

"Yes, I'm asking you! What was that, back in the pub, with the necklace? I'm really getting fed up with your mood swings!"

"I need to know what that is." He motioned at my necklace in disgust.

"It's called jewelry! I inherited it, if you really want to know. But I don't know how that's any of your business." I wrapped my scarf around my neck again and crossed my arms in front of my chest.

"You inherited it? A Cameron heirloom? That actually explains quite a lot!"

Well, good for you, I thought, because I didn't understand a thing, except that every time I was about to kiss a boy, something went terribly wrong. I was close to tears. Just minutes before, everything had been perfect. Then suddenly we were facing each other like enemies. And I didn't even know why. I didn't want things between us to end like this. Carefully, I reached out my hand.

"Payton, please. Tell me what's going on. I really don't understand why you're so upset."

A single tear rolled down my cheek, but he seemed made of stone. He didn't answer.

I yelled his name one more time. I wanted to hit or shake him, just to get him to react. But he shook his head and lowered his eyes.

"I have to go," he said. "We shouldn't meet again."

Without looking at me, he got into his car and started the engine. I was trembling and tears were streaming down my face, but I didn't care. I helplessly stood watching the taillights of his car get smaller and smaller.

A bunch of people came out of the pub laughing and disappeared down the road. I stood there dumbstruck. Then I wiped the tears off my face and started to walk home. Thankfully, we had stayed in Aviemore and I was home within ten minutes.

As I passed through the living room, Alison looked concerned, but she was polite enough not to question me. I was relieved when she didn't follow me up the stairs.

I banged the door behind me and threw myself onto the bed, sobbing into my pillow until I could hardly breathe. I hated Payton. I hated Scotland. I hated Mr. Schneider for getting me into this mess. I hated my parents for agreeing to his plan. And most of all, I hated most this stupid, stupid pendant!

I tore the necklace from my neck and flung it away. It slid over the wooden floor and wrapped itself around a table leg. I didn't care. I didn't plan to ever touch that thing again.

I decided I had to talk to Kim and tell her everything. It was only five thirty in Delaware, so hopefully Kim would be around. She answered after only three rings. I was so happy to hear her voice that I couldn't speak right away; I had too many tears in my throat.

"Sam? Is that you? What's wrong?"

"Oh God, Kim, everything is terrible!" I sobbed and sniffed into my cell phone.

"Oh no, sweetie. Do you want me to fly over and kick some English butt?"

"Scots. They're called Scots here. I'm in Scotland, Kim." But her reaction made me feel better, and I could at least put together a complete sentence. I told her about Payton, how much I liked him and how mysterious he was. Then I told her about his scary behavior that evening.

"Wow, I don't know what to say," Kim said. "But this I do know. Your Prince Charming seems to be totally insane. You should just forget about him."

That pissed me off. It was easy for her to say. After all, she was constantly falling in love, but when it didn't work out, she found a replacement right away. But this was the first time I had ever been in love. Completely. The full package. And I knew I'd never find someone like Payton again. I didn't want to forget about him.

"Oh, Kim. It's not that easy! I love him!"

Silence.

"Uh, hello?" she said. "Your exchange program is going to be over in two weeks. You're still coming home, no? It's not exactly convenient to be in love with someone who lives on the other side of the world."

That was Kim. Tell it like it is.

"I think I'll die if I can't see him again," I wailed, trying to imagine a future without his sparkling eyes.

"Well, don't die immediately. There's still Ryan . . ."

"Hmph! That conceited idiot. I couldn't care less about him."

"Oh really? Maybe I should fill you in on what's been going on here in Milford. I'm still seeing Justin, by the way—not that you asked—and things are going really well. Your hoochie cousin Ashley got here right after you left, and sure enough she started chasing Ryan, and I guess he was desperate for some consolation after you broke his heart, poor guy. Anyway, they were spotted together a few times, but all of a sudden, no longer. Justin thinks Ryan got tired of her because he's actually totally fallen for you."

"Ryan is in love with one person, and that's himself. Surely Ashley isn't going to give up that easily. And you know yourself what Ryan is like. He's not exactly picky."

"Yes, but he told Justin that he thinks about you all the time. And he keeps asking me if I've talked to you and how you're doing."

I didn't want to talk about Ryan anymore. Kim obviously didn't understand my situation. No matter what happened with Payton and me, I could never get over him so easily.

"Listen Kim, I have to get going, can you do me a small favor?"

"Sure, what is it?"

"Be nice to Ashley? I don't really like her either, but don't forget she's kind of messed up because her mom died when she was so young. It's got to be hard. And she's probably not doing too well if she had an argument with Ryan."

"Oh, Sam! Ashley wouldn't talk to me anyway. I'm sure she's doing just fine."

"Kim, please. Just go by the house and say hi. And while you're there, you can do me another favor."

"No way, José. I am not going to talk to Ashley, and you can forget the second thing, too!"

"Please . . . It's for school," I lied. "There's a book in my bedroom, a red book. I just need you to look and see if there's anything in it about a Scottish clan by the name of Cameron. I'll call you again tomorrow night, OK?"

I put the phone down on the bedside table and slid under the covers, too tired to undress.

I longed to talk to Payton, to tell him how much I loved him, and to find out why the necklace had made him so upset. Tears ran down my cheeks and onto my pillow. The hands of the clock crawled on relentlessly, and I tossed and turned from side to side. With Payton's Gaelic song running through my head, I eventually cried myself to sleep.

Chapter 12

Payton bashed the steering wheel as he raced out of Aviemore onto a deserted street. He floored it and tried to recapture the lack of feeling that came with being immortal. Speed had no meaning; no adrenaline pumped through his veins. His pulse remained steady and the passing landscape may as well have been in black-and-white. It was better this way, he thought. Everything was back to dull, as dull as his life had been until he met Sam.

Still, it was impossible to pretend that he had no feelings for her. And now he knew she could make him human again. She had changed the curse! Because she was a Cameron. She wore the Cameron coat of arms. She looked like the women of the clan. She had crept into his heart. And if she was who he assumed her to be, then she would hate him if she found out what he had done.

There shouldn't actually be any more Camerons. He and his family had exterminated her ancestors. They had spared no one.

But he wished things had turned out differently.

≈

Payton clearly remembered that day. His little brother, Kyle, had spilled a bucket of milk while playing with their giant wolfhound, Lou. Payton and his father were teasing him about it over a mug of ale. Kyle was a strong boy, who had just turned sixteen, and it was already obvious that he would be a strong man. Nevertheless, Lou was a massive dog, reaching up to Kyle's waist. When Lou had lunged for the bucket of milk, Kyle dove for it, keeping the bucket from the dog. But the cook had slapped Kyle for spilling nearly all of the milk, and while Kyle held his buzzing head, Lou had greedily licked up the milk from the ground.

Kyle had come to Payton for consolation. The two youngest brothers were very close. Their older siblings were seldom at home, but Payton and Kyle actually liked to spend their time around the castle. Their talk soon turned to the family's cows. Sheep and cattle were the family's main source of income, and recently there had been a lot of cattle theft. It was normal in the Highlands for a few cows to go missing, but in the last weeks, dozens of cows had disappeared.

"There are two more cows missing," their father, Fingal, reported.

This topic always upset the old man. He often told them he felt like he'd spent his whole life on fights and disagreements with the neighboring clans. And as he got older, he didn't want anything to do with that sort of game. Immersed in thought, he combed his fingers through his shoulder-length snow-white hair.

"I have been thinking about a solution for this problem for quite a while now," said Fingal. "I would like to hear your opinion."

Payton directed all his attention to his father, wondering what his father intended to do. Kyle grew more serious, too.

"We joined forces with the Stuarts many years ago because it was only together that we were strong enough to protect ourselves from attacks by the other clans. That agreement made sense. Even after the old Stuart died, Cathal and I renewed our oath. Your brother Blair, my successor, is surely just as interested in keeping peace with Cathal as I always have been."

This was all common knowledge to Payton and Kyle, and they nodded.

"One could say that I am getting sentimental in my old age, but I would like to leave my sons with a way to have a more peaceful life than I had. The old feud between the Stuarts and the Camerons is a thorn in my side. It often pulls us into trouble, needlessly. That is why I have decided to join forces with the Camerons."

Payton looked from his father to Kyle and back. He liked the idea of settling the situation between the clans, true, but he couldn't imagine that the Stuarts would be satisfied with this plan.

"Father, how do you think this will work? Are we to just forget the constant robbery and no longer defend ourselves?" he asked.

Fingal shook his head.

"No, of course not. We must stop stealing one another's cattle and start protecting our herds together. Thus we could keep almost double the amount of cattle on the same land. The borderlands would be safe, too."

"That is good. But how?"

"A bond that is stronger than an oath." Fingal looked at the two questioning faces. "A marriage. I have already talked to Blair about it, but he didn't like the idea."

Hidden by his beer mug, Kyle giggled. "And it's pretty clear that Nathaira Stuart will like your idea even less!"

Fingal nodded. "Yes, that's what I fear, too, but these decisions are not for the women to make. No, Blair will do what I demand of him. He knows what he has to do for his clan."

Payton remained skeptical. Kyle, on the other hand, grinned. "Father, if Blair refuses, then I'll marry a Cameron."

Payton laughed. "You?"

"Yes! Have you ever had a good look at the Cameron women? Each one is prettier than the next. I wouldn't say no to such a union!"

Fingal clapped his hands on his legs, roaring with laughter, too.

They were still laughing when Blair, Cathal Stuart, and his sister, Nathaira, joined them in the hall. All three seemed to be in a bad mood, and their angry words echoed through the room. Fingal asked them to join them at the table, but only Cathal pulled up a chair. Blair stayed standing with Nathaira by his side, as always.

"Cathal, *ciamar a tha thu?*" Fingal asked.

"I am not well. There have been more raids. This time one of my shepherds was killed," Cathal said angrily. "I can't tolerate these thefts any longer. Tonight I am going to the Camerons. We will see whether they have our cattle standing in their stables!"

Everyone could see how upset the young chieftain was. And he did have to prove himself in front of his people, to not appear weak. Cathal could no longer ignore the voices in the clan who were demanding revenge, but Fingal did not want to fight anymore.

"I can understand that, but this time you will have to do without my support."

"Father," Blair cried out, "what are you saying? Of course we are going to stand by our friend!"

"No," Fingal thundered, "we are staying out of this!"

"Father, you can't mean that. I am not going to obey you. Cathal needs our help!"

Cathal himself had gotten up, too, and shot an angry look across the table. "Fingal, for all the Saints' sakes! You can't refuse to support me. We have an oath sealed with blood."

The old McLean chieftain stood up slowly, leaned on the table, and declared with more determination than expected, "Cathal, *mo charaid,* I understand why you are so upset, but confrontation is not the only way. At my age, one wants to have one's inheritance safe. And I do not wish to start a revolt during my last days. I will not lose good men in a fight, nor will I expose my people to arbitrary revenge. No, this is a path we are not going to tread again. An allegiance is what will bring us all a lasting peace."

Silently, the men stared at Fingal. Only Nathaira couldn't hold herself back. She went on the attack.

"You old coward! Just because you have no more guts. The clan will refuse to support Cathal if he doesn't care for their safety!" She had placed herself directly in front of Fingal.

Kyle grabbed her arm and pulled her away. "What are you thinking, you stupid woman? Go! Don't interfere in men's business."

He pushed Nathaira toward the door and threw a warning look at Blair. "Maybe you should marry a Cameron woman instead, as that girl only means trouble."

Blair, who often acted on impulse, grabbed Kyle's collar and pushed him against the table. With a loud crash, two chairs fell over and wood splintered. Quickly, Payton ran to help his little brother, but Fingal was already banging his fist on the table.

"*Seas!* Stop this, immediately!"

He glared in warning from one to the other as he spoke. "Cathal, take your sister and leave! You heard my answer. And you, Blair, join me in my quarters. We have much to discuss."

With that, Fingal turned around and left the hall. Payton was standing between Kyle and Nathaira, who lingered in the door. They both looked like they still wanted to fight.

"Calm down," Payton said.

"Blair," Nathaira whined, "what does Kyle mean, that you should marry a Cameron? You are marrying me, I believe."

"Yes, of course. There is nothing for you to get upset about."

Blair had good reason to be angry. His father had humiliated him in front of his best friend, treating him like a child. And on top of that, his fiancée was acting up.

But Kyle also still hadn't cooled down. "You idiot! You can't put that *nighean na galladh* above the interests of your own clan!"

Now Cathal joined in again. "No one—and certainly not a half child like yourself—calls my sister a dog's daughter! Away with you or you will get to know me!"

"I am only saying that if I were the chieftain of the clan I would realize how beneficial a marriage with the Camerons could be. I wouldn't think purely with my pecker!" Kyle whirled around and stomped out of the room. Just in time, too, as Payton would have been hard-pressed to stop Blair from throttling his little brother.

"Blair, you are soon to be the head of this clan. I demand your help tonight, or I will consider our oath to be voided." Cathal's words echoed through the high hall.

"Of course, *mo charaid.* You can count on me. Sean, Payton, and I will accompany you."

When Cathal was in a mood like this, Payton preferred not to say anything. It wasn't advisable to fight with him. He would argue with Blair later that their father had explicitly forbidden joining the attack.

But Payton also knew that he didn't really have a choice. When their father had been very ill a few months before, he had demanded that his sons swear loyalty to Blair. He wanted to prevent any quarrels between his sons after his death. Shortly afterward, Fingal's health improved, and no one doubted who still was the McLeans' chieftain. But there had never been such a fight as this.

Cathal and Nathaira left, and Blair went to his father's quarters. Payton stayed back alone to finish his ale. Just as he put his beer mug to his mouth, Sean came into the hall.

"What's been going on in here? Cathal and his sister just stormed right past me without even a nod."

He sat down on a chair next to Payton, pulled up Kyle's half-empty mug, and took a big gulp.

Payton was giving Sean a blow-by-blow account when they heard shouting coming from the living quarters. Finally, a door banged and Blair appeared in the hall, his face bright red.

"Don't just sit around—get ready! We are riding with Cathal in an hour."

On his way out, he bumped into Kyle, who was just returning.

"And you—get out of my way," Blair said, pushing Kyle out the door.

Sean, who hadn't witnessed his siblings' fight, asked, "Is Kyle not coming with us?"

Blair looked scornfully at his youngest brother.

"No, I have no need for disloyal, impertinent children."

~

A car was coming toward him. Payton took his foot off the gas and breathed deeply. The memory of that fateful day had burned itself into his mind. The guilt he felt weighed just as heavily now as it had then.

All the Camerons are dead, he said to himself. But one question after another popped into his head: How come Sam looked so much like a Cameron? And where did she get that coat of arms? Could it be that someone truly had managed to escape?

He thought back to how young and stupid he'd been. He didn't know how many people were supposed to have been in the castle at the time. Nor had he bothered to ask how many had been killed. Cathal had claimed there were no more Camerons, and everyone believed it.

But Payton's heart recognized Sam for what she was. A living, breathing Cameron. When he'd left her there at the pub, she was crying. He had made her cry—and he hated himself for that. And now the toughest questions came to him: Could he ever make up for what he'd done to her ancestors? Could he tell her the truth?

He would ask her to forgive him. Then he would leave her in peace, never see her again—and love her for the rest of his endless life. His immortal heart lay in the hands of a woman who would never forgive him if she ever found out what he had done. Still, he had to see her one more time.

CHAPTER 13

I put my cell phone away. I had just talked to Kim. She was still a little mad at me, so she kept the conversation short, using a date with Justin as an excuse. But she had done what I asked and looked through my grandma's diary. There were dozens of things about Scottish clans written in the book, but she wasn't sure what I was looking for. The first pages said something about keeping up the family legacy, though, and I knew that meant I really did have something to do with these Camerons. I thought of the message on Grandma's pendant: Remember those you are a descendant of. What was I supposed to do with that?

Even though Payton had acted like a jerk, I wanted to talk to him. I found myself dialing his number, and then quickly hanging up. No, I tried to convince myself, I wouldn't run after him. He was the one who had behaved so stupidly. He should be the one to apologize.

But, I thought, what if he didn't apologize? What if he never talked to me again? With shaking fingers, I tried his number again. I was waiting for it to connect when all of a sudden my phone rang. I jumped, and my phone fell out of my hand and slid under the bed. I groped around until I found it, and thankfully, it was still ringing. "Payton," my phone display read. I took a deep breath and said hello, but I was too late. Damn!

Then I decided that since he had taken the first step, it was all right to call him back. Quickly, I typed his number, and on the first ring he picked up.

"Hello, Sam," Payton said quietly. He sounded contrite.

"Hi! What's up?" I asked pertly, trying to act like it was no big deal.

"Sam, listen, I'm so sorry about yesterday. I wish I could explain better, but suffice it to say, I am an idiot."

"My thoughts exactly," I said, just as perkily as I could.

"Can I make it up to you? I don't know what got into me."

I was unbelievably relieved. What Kim had said about me returning home in a few weeks was in the back of my mind, but I had fallen in love. And I wanted to enjoy every moment of it.

"Just promise me you won't be an idiot in the future?"

Payton exhaled. "Promise. Listen, I could come and pick you up . . . We could get some ice cream or something?"

"Sounds great!"

"Right, I'll see you soon."

Quickly, I got myself ready, deliberately leaving the stupid necklace behind. And the short skirt. It certainly hadn't brought me good luck, and besides, jeans made more sense for an ice cream date.

Fifteen minutes later, I heard a car outside, but when I pulled back the curtain, I saw a red Mini Cooper instead of a white SUV. And when I opened the door, curious, I found two good-looking men.

Payton shrugged.

"Sorry. My dear brother Sean"—Payton motioned grandly to his brother while speaking—"couldn't be persuaded not to join us."

Sean bowed to me, a cheeky smile on his lips. He looked like Payton, with slightly darker hair, but he was taller and thinner as well. That wasn't the only difference. Their manners were almost opposite; while Payton was introverted and pensive, Sean was a giant flirt.

"My lady, I'm pleased to meet you," he said, grabbing my hand.

I blushed as he pressed a kiss on it.

"But I can't stop asking myself why you spend all your time with him," Sean said, laughing, as he pointed a thumb at his brother.

"Shut up," Payton muttered. He was smiling at me, but I could tell he was annoyed. He led the way to the car, threw a faux nasty glance at his grinning brother, and held the door open for me. In the meantime, Sean went around to the driver's seat, whistling a jaunty tune.

On the way to Inverness, Sean asked me hundreds of questions—or so it seemed. He was very childish, despite his age; he seemed to always be joking around.

"Sam, honestly. You came all this way, and you spend all your free time with my brother? All the men in the United Kingdom, and you settled for this guy?"

"Well," I said, "the selection of eligible bachelors isn't that big, you know. And Payton can be very entertaining, when he is not behaving like an idiot."

A grunt from the passenger seat let me know that Payton was listening, and I winked at Sean, who was peeking at me in the rearview mirror. Sean was perfect for getting even with Payton. He seemed to find it highly entertaining to make fun of him.

After we parked, we wandered through the town, and somehow Sean kept managing to squeeze in between Payton and me. He threw an arm around me.

"What would you like to do now, my sweet lady? Shall we leave this man to brood alone? A fair maiden like you deserves only the best."

I glanced over my shoulder, searching for help, but there was none coming from Payton. I knew that Sean was only trying to pull his leg—and I wanted a little bit of revenge—but Payton looked positively glum. I needed a few seconds to think about what I should do.

"Well, first of all, I need to find a bathroom." I pointed to a nearby fast-food restaurant and said, "I'll just pop in here."

"We'll wait here for you," Payton said, and the doors closed behind me.

I was relieved to have escaped the two of them for a moment. I didn't want to hurt Sean's feelings, but I was annoyed he'd come along. It was nice to meet him and all, but it was terrible timing. All I really wanted was to be alone with Payton and throw myself into his arms.

Before I walked back, I had managed to sort through some of my confused thoughts. Through the glass door, I could see the two of them standing opposite each other, immersed in a heated debate. Somehow I knew I was the reason for that.

"Hi, boys, I'm back," I trilled, trying to sound happy.

Immediately, they both smiled. This time, Payton was the one to put his arm possessively around me. He seemed more than a bit tense, but his hand tenderly stroked my upper arm.

"You and I are going to go have an ice cream now, while Sean gets some stuff done. We'll meet up with him again later."

That surprised me. Sean smiled apologetically.

"Sorry, I have some errands I really should tend to. I had completely forgotten, but you two carry on. You'll manage without me."

He threw me a kiss and headed off toward the town center. Payton led me in the opposite direction. We walked side by side, silently taking in the view of Inverness Castle, perched on a nearby hill. Payton bought ice cream from a van that touted gourmet varieties. I decided on a scoop of chocolate–salted caramel and a scoop of lemon meringue; Payton got raspberry–dark chocolate. We wandered farther down Castle Road. To our left was the sandstone castle and to our right, the expansive Moray Firth. We sat down on a bench on the riverbank and licked our cones.

"Sam, I wanted to apologize again. When it comes to you, I am just not myself." He was staring at the river with such a serious look on his face. "It's just, there are so many things I would like to tell you, or should tell you, but I can't," he said.

"It's OK, Payton—I'm not very good at talking about my feelings either. And anyway, I can tell how you feel. You can't hide it from me!"

He liked me, and I knew it, whether he could tell me or not. And I loved him. Nothing else mattered.

At last, Payton looked me in the eye. His gaze slid down my face to my neckline, where the pendant used to be.

"Yes, you are right. I can't hide it. It's just that this has never happened to me before. I am scared," he whispered in my ear. My entire body felt electric. His finger gently drew a line from my ear to my chin. Then he turned my face to his and smiled. Oh, that smile! My heart started to race, and my knees would surely have buckled if I hadn't already been sitting. He brushed his finger slowly over my lip.

Then he grinned even wider when his finger came away with a bit of ice cream.

"You should let them give you a napkin next time." He stuck his finger in his mouth to lick off the chocolaty drop, and I turned bright red. Food on my face—how embarrassing!

I tried to hit him playfully, but he jumped up, running away from me. I ran after him, laughing, as he zigzagged down the sidewalk. We were completely out of breath when we met up with Sean at the corner. He was on the way to the parking lot, just like us. When he saw us coming, he shook his head, pretending to be devastated.

"Poor Sam, you needn't run after that idiot. I would be happy to offer myself as a replacement. And I guarantee that I wouldn't run away from you, regardless of what you were to do."

"You had better run," Payton said. "Otherwise, I'll make you!"

Oh no, I thought, was the sibling rivalry flaring up again? Laughing, I put my hands on my hips and said, "If you two can't get along, then I'm running away from both of you!"

The brothers showed only a tiny hint of remorse, but they were on their best behavior from then on. Half an hour later, I waved at the Mini Cooper as they drove away. Payton left with a promise to take me on a special outing. Unfortunately, I'd have to wait for two days because he had family business to take care of first. What that was all about, I was very curious to know.

~

"You are an arse," Payton started the conversation, as soon as Sam left the car. "What the hell was all that about?"

"Simple, I wanted a reaction. Unlike you, I feel fine when I'm close to Sam."

"What? You don't feel that awful burning, the tormenting pressure on your body?"

"Not at all. Otherwise, I wouldn't have touched her, now would I?"

"I thought you wanted to see how high of a threshold you could stand."

Sean shook his head.

"No, whatever it is you can feel, it seems to be something special between you and Sam, because I didn't feel anything. I must admit, though, that her looking so much like Isobel Cameron did take me aback."

"Crazy, isn't it? How many generations must there be between Isobel and Sam?"

"I would guess at least ten. But are you really sure about the Cameron connection?"

"Yes, definitely. And I think that is exactly the point. There was a reason why she met me. I am convinced of it."

"One thing's for sure: you are clearly in love."

"If you say so," Payton mumbled.

"You don't know this? You almost freaked out just because I made a few joking remarks to her."

"A few remarks! You were hitting on her!"

"Well, she is quite lovely."

"Yes, and she's not for you!"

Then Sean turned more serious. "About the clan gathering tomorrow . . . I am not going to say anything about Sam, even though I believe that she may be a key to this puzzle. I like her, and she doesn't seem to have any idea who we are. I don't think she poses any danger." His voice became much stronger now. "However, as a result of some tests I performed while you were eating your ice cream, I must demand that you end this affair."

"What?" Payton said, glaring at his brother. "What kind of tests? And I can't end it. Believe me, I wanted to, but it just isn't possible!"

Sean pushed one of his sleeves up to his elbows, revealing that his arm was covered in a bandage.

"What is that?" Payton asked.

Sean held his arm out while hanging on to the steering wheel with his other hand.

"Unwrap it," he said.

Wrinkling his forehead, Payton did as he was told and then drew in a quick breath.

"What have you done?" he whispered.

Sean shrugged. His lower arm was covered in deep, bloody cuts. The gauze was sticking to the crusty parts and fresh blood was still seeping out of the deepest wound.

"After I fell off my motorcycle, I realized that I didn't heal as quickly as usual. Our self-healing ability has been compromised by the changing conditions."

"You did this to yourself?"

"Like I said, a few tests. Sam is easing the curse . . . We are becoming more human." "Could you feel the pain?"

"Why do you think I made so many cuts? You were right. After such a long time without feeling anything, even pain is intoxicating."

Payton struggled to make sense of it.

"We are becoming vulnerable, Payton. That is why you must end it!"

"Why? Do you want to carry on like this? You want to live through eternity like this? Without feelings? Without love?"

Payton thought he'd rather die than go on living like that, especially since he'd been shown so vividly what he'd been missing all these years. His hand was still burning from where he had touched Sam's shoulders. No, he knew he couldn't return to that darkness again, when he couldn't feel at all.

"You can't make a decision on your own that will put us all at risk," Sean said quietly as he turned into their driveway and rolled slowly to a stop.

"Yes, I can . . . No one asked me if I wanted to have this life!"

Payton tore open the door. But instead of going inside, he jumped straight onto his Ducati and sped off.

∽

Sean stayed in the car, puzzled. He understood Payton, but an oath bound him to the clan. If Payton didn't show responsibility, well, Sean would have to step in himself. He rolled down his sleeve and stroked the bandaged area carefully.

He'd meant to test his theory with only a single cut. But when the silver blade had marked its bloody trace through his skin, a powerful sensation had flooded his brain. He'd pressed the blade into his arm again and again, devouring the pain.

Yes, just like Payton, he too had been starved.

CHAPTER 14

Tensely, Sean looked at the doorway. He was waiting for Payton. The room was filling up, and in a few minutes Cathal would formally greet the clan. Everyone was there. Seventeen men had been affected by the curse, and all of them were still the same ages they'd been 270 years before. As time went on, other people they'd been close to had gotten older and died, and this group had banded together so as not to be alone. But as the centuries ground on, the group gradually started to spread out. Cathal had let them go—under one condition. They still had to swear loyalty to him. Only a small core of them lived with him now, including his sister, Nathaira, and the three McLean brothers.

Sean's eyes followed Blair, who was greeting a few men. But still no Payton. What was he going to do, he wondered, if Payton didn't turn up? He let out his breath when he saw that he wouldn't need to worry about that—Payton had walked into the hall. He was obviously stressed out. He made a beeline for the empty seat beside Sean, where he sat without even saying hello.

The group was settling in now. Chairs were pushed around as everyone found a place to sit. Nathaira, clad in a bloodred dress, stepped into the room. The coldness in her eyes silenced the men. Holding her head high, she walked through the hall to the head of the long table. The seat next to her was still empty. Everyone waited without a word.

When the door opened a short time later, Cathal strode in wearing his chieftain's robes. But even without the robes, Cathal was impressive. A born leader—proud, strong, and used to ordering people around. He took his place behind his chair and nodded to his attendants in respect. He raised his full glass and started his speech:

"Friends, companions, and family. It has been a long time since we last met and it feels good to know that you still answer to my call. Our meeting today is for a good reason: my sister fears for our safety. But we will come to that in a moment. Let us first raise our glasses. To our community, our clan, and our loyalty to one another. *Slàinte mhath!*"

Everyone raised their glasses and drank to their leader.

When things had quieted down again, Cathal asked Sean to rise and tell of his experience with the motorcycle crash. Murmurs went around the room, with the men frowning and looking at each other questioningly. It was undoubtedly hard for them to comprehend what they were hearing.

Then it was Nathaira's turn. Like a sorceress about to cast a spell, she solemnly placed a large leather book on the table in front of her. She started to read in a clear voice, seemingly oblivious to those around her.

"A curse's power may never change, as the cursed are not to have a chance to escape their destiny. But should the destiny change and its determination be fulfilled, then all of nature's powers may combine and free the cursed hearts at last. The cursed souls can then lightly and freely leave their old life behind them."

Nathaira looked up at the men, standing mute for several moments. Then she shut the book and said, in a much louder voice, "Do you understand? Do you know what this means? We are all going to die!"

Everyone started to talk at once. Cathal banged his fist on the table and yelled, "Quiet! Listen. Everyone will get his chance to say something, but only later!"

Slowly, the questions ebbed, and the impatient, scared eyes turned to the only woman in the room. Nathaira took a deep breath before she spoke.

"If we want to save ourselves, we must find out what is strong enough to weaken the curse. Sean's accident showed us that we are now no longer invincible. We must take care now and be alert. And we must prevent the curse from being broken. I don't want to die. And who knows what will happen? We could just start to get older now, or we may just disintegrate into ashes on the spot. We simply don't know. But you," she looked urgently at the group, "you must find the cause of this change—and destroy it!"

Everyone seemed to agree with Nathaira. Angry faces looked around. Sean observed that Payton sat rigid with fear. Sean knew exactly what was going on in his brother's head: he wasn't fearful for himself, but for Sam. Still, he had a responsibility toward the others. So he got up and started to speak.

"Men, calm down. I don't think we are all going to drop dead tomorrow. There is probably some explanation, and I have no doubt that things will be fine."

Nathaira cast him a dubious look.

"What?" she snarled. "Were you not listening? And since when have you become an expert on curses?"

"I think the fact that I have been cursed for nearly three centuries qualifies me just as much as your books." Sean was waiting for Payton to speak out, but when he was sure he wasn't going to get any help from him, he continued. "I believe I know the cause of what happened."

The room went dead quiet. Cathal and Nathaira jumped up, and Blair glared across the table. But before even one of them could say or do anything, Payton stood up, grabbed Sean, and threw him to the ground. He bent close to Sean's ear and dangerously rasped, "*Bas mallaichte*, Sean, *sguir*!"

A few men took hold of Payton and shoved him back onto his chair. Sean was brought to the head of the table, to Cathal, who demanded, "Well, what do you mean? Say what you know!"

Others echoed him just as vociferously.

"There is a girl who seems to be a Cameron descendant," says Sean. "But I think it's a coincidence that she is here, and she is only here in Scotland for a short time. She hasn't any idea of her ancestry, and she certainly doesn't know who we are. She is definitely not a danger to us."

Again, chaos broke loose. Cathal silenced the room with an upraised hand. He stood menacingly close to Sean.

"It is not for you to decide what is safe. Tell us this girl's name!"

Payton leapt to his feet. "No, Sean, don't do it! They will kill her!"

All eyes turned to Payton.

Blair grabbed his little brother by the shirt and said, "What do you know about this?"

"The question is, what has this got to do with you," Payton said. "She is no danger to you."

Sean spoke out in support. "I don't think it's a big risk. Let's wait and see what happens when she leaves Scotland. We can always act then, if we need to. The last thing we want to do is be rash and draw attention to ourselves."

Cathal nodded his approval. "We shall think about what we heard today and give it proper consideration. Payton, Sean, you are not to leave the castle."

He nodded to two of his men, who grabbed the brothers by their arms.

"For the sake of peace, of course I will stay here," says Sean. "Just like Payton. You can call off your dogs!"

After a moment, Cathal nodded again, and the two soldiers stepped back.

"Yes then, we'll wait and see. But should the situation change, then Payton, God be with you if I find out you have gone against me."

With that, the meeting was over. Slowly the crowd dissolved, and each and every one of them left.

~

Payton went to his room to think about what he should do. He was under observation, and most definitely didn't want to lead anyone to Sam. But he had to see her. He knew he'd find a way to slip away unnoticed in the next few days.

~

Nathaira glanced over her shoulder. Nobody was following her or paying any attention to her. Of course not, she thought—she was only a woman. Quickly, she dashed across the courtyard and knocked at a door. It opened a crack, and she slipped in. Relieved, she pushed the bolt in place and leaned against the doorframe.

Then she looked closely at the man in front of her. Tall, strong, and attractive. Just like so many years ago, he still wore his blond hair at shoulder length, and a reddish beard covered his cheeks. Alasdair Buchanan seemed surprised by her presence.

"Nathaira, what are you doing here?"

"Am I not allowed to visit an old friend?"

Alasdair raised an eyebrow and tilted his head to one side. He didn't believe a word the black-haired beauty in front of him was saying.

"No, really. What do you want here, what is the reason for your visit?"

Confidently, Nathaira took off her cloak and shook her long hair. She watched Alasdair carefully and saw his mistrust—but mixed in, something else. He still desired her, as he always had. She, though, hadn't felt passion for him for a very, very long time. Still, like a cat, she crept around the man, her hand brushing softly over his shirt.

"But darling, don't be so doubting. I am only here to ask you for a little favor."

It took Alasdair a lot of effort to fight for composure. Nathaira drove him crazy, but he would not make the mistake of giving in to her again.

"I think you now have your fiancé to ask for small favors."

He wriggled out of her fingers and crossed his arms in front of his chest.

"No, I need a real man on this. Blair is only my brother's lapdog!"

Alasdair laughed out loud. "So you would rather have a lapdog for a husband than me?"

"Oh, really, Alasdair, don't be ridiculous. You know why I had to choose Blair back then: Cathal had not been chieftain for long and his position was more than endangered. He needed this alliance."

"Yes, I know. But that didn't make things easier, especially after the—"

"And you still can't forgive me, can you?"

"No."

Without a word, they glared at each other. Then Nathaira's posture changed, and she shoved her chin forward.

"Fine. Then don't forgive me. But you will nevertheless help me. You owe me!"

"I owe you? Ha! You killed my unborn child, and you think I owe you something? I loved you. I wanted the child just as much as I wanted you!" He turned his back on Nathaira.

"Yes, but my brother would have killed you if he had found out about us. You know that. And I almost died! You can't imagine the pain I was in. You don't know how close it was for me."

"So what do you want?" Alasdair asked, without emotion.

"Follow Payton I will give him an opportunity to disappear from here, and I am sure that he will go to the girl. Follow him."

"And then? What will you do then?"

"Me? Nothing. But you will act. You will kill her. Before she undoes us all."

"But Cathal said we should wait."

"Cathal is stupid. Why wait? Don't you see the danger we are in? I almost died for you once. This time, I don't want things to go so far!"

Alasdair paced around the room, brooding. He felt uncomfortable killing a defenseless girl. After all, times had changed.

"Nathaira, I am sorry, but I can't do that. I will respect what Cathal said."

"You dog! You are making a huge mistake! You think you have a choice? Wrong! You will do what I tell you. Otherwise, I will tell my brother what you did to me."

"Did to you? And what is that supposed to mean?"

"You raped me, took me against my will."

"But that isn't true!"

"Yes, but who will he believe? You or me? And think about it: thanks to this girl, you are now again capable of feeling pain. How must an eternity full of pain and torment feel?"

Nathaira scowled at him. Alasdair knew she was right. Cathal adored his little sister and would punish him with all his might if Nathaira were to incriminate him. Even if everything she said was a lie.

"I think you should go now," he said, and he held the door open.

"Are you going to do it?" Nathaira had no intention of leaving until she got what she wanted.

Icy silence filled the room between them. They looked at each other with cold eyes, yet the wounds they had inflicted on each other such a long time ago were still clearly fresh.

Alasdair finally mumbled, "Yes. And now away with you!"

Content, Nathaira reached for her cloak and slid it on. At the door she stopped and looked at the man in front of her, and a sad smile stole its way across her face.

"Alasdair, if you can ever forgive me, then—"

"I will never do that," he said, as cold as a rock. Not a spark of pity was visible in his green eyes.

Nathaira lifted her chin, looked to make sure no one was coming, and stepped back out into the courtyard. It was late, but the sun had yet to set. It cast an uneasy salmon-colored glow over everything, a washed-out light that had overstayed its welcome. She wasn't ready to return to the closeness of the castle, so she walked to the fortified wall instead.

She sat down on a ledge to think: Why was her life so complicated? Before the curse, she had loved Alasdair Buchanan, her father's handsome warrior with northern roots. His strength and his courage had impressed her when she sat opposite him at the table at a party in honor of her father. She remembered the way he had looked at her then: so full of admiration and passion.

After the meal, he had led her by the arm, and while everyone was talking and drinking, they left the room. In the half light of the stairwell, they didn't waste a second but followed their feelings and kissed.

They had managed to keep their romance a secret for a long time, but then Nathaira's father died and Alasdair couldn't be near her during the mourning period. Then only a few days later, her brother, Cathal, in his new role as chieftain, had ordered Alasdair to go with the other warriors to stop the robberies on the borders. He left without knowing that she was carrying his baby under her heart.

Two months he had been away. Two months during which she had realized, to her shock, that she was with child.

She had feared Cathal's reaction. At that time, her brother was new to his power. And she knew he wanted to arrange her marriage to his best friend and partner, Blair McLean. A thousand questions had raced through her head: What would he do to her if he found out she was pregnant? Would he banish her? Would he kill Alasdair? Cathal would never agree to a marriage between her and Alasdair. He would accuse her of soiling the family and of deceiving him.

Nathaira had done the only thing possible: she had crept away. She rode north for two days, hoping to find the Wise Woman who lived in the hills. She had almost given up hope when something strange happened.

There were no clouds in the sky—none at all—when blue flashes of lightning ripped through the sky, so bright they blinded her. When she could see again, a small woman, bent over and white-haired, was coming toward her. Nathaira was scared, shaking at the knees, but she followed the witch silently, deeper into the hills. Hours later, they arrived at a lonely hut.

"I am Brèagha-muir. You were looking for me. I know what you want of me, but I am telling you, it is dangerous. If you nevertheless want it, then follow me." The old woman croaked with a voice that set Nathaira's teeth on edge.

Without another word, the witch disappeared into her hut. Nathaira rubbed her arms, trying to chase the cold out of her limbs. If she were to think about it for much longer, she knew she would change her mind, so she took a last deep breath and followed the woman. The hut was dark, the wooden planks of the walls blackened from the soot of the fireplace in the middle of the room. Herbs and sacks hung from the ceiling, giving off a tart smell. A boiling pot hung over the fire. Onions and a skinned rabbit lay next to a large knife.

"Sit down and drink this," Brèagha-muir demanded. Nathaira hesitated only for a moment when she held the beaker with the murky liquid to her lips. The potion was bitter, and her tongue immediately went numb. Tears shot into her eyes, and she coughed, but she forced the last drop down her throat. Slowly, the old woman came around to her and put a gnarled, onion-scented hand on her forehead.

"Girl, getting rid of the fruit of the womb isn't a child's game. But you are strong. You may manage. Take off your clothes, and lie down over there."

Nathaira swayed on her stool as the room started to spin. The straw-filled mattress that Brèagha-muir had pointed out was dirty and damp. It smelled like decay. But already, Nathaira's limbs were no longer obeying her, so she glided helplessly over and undressed. A rough woolen blanket was spread over her. Then Brèagha-muir went back to the table, took up the knife, and with one strong blow, cut off the rabbit's head.

Nathaira lay there feeling as if a poisonous snake were winding through her insides, digging its teeth into her flesh, oozing venom into her blood and her thoughts. As if from a distance, her own screams reached her ears. When the witch fed her more of the vile drink, Nathaira didn't think she could tolerate it. She willed herself to spit it out, but her paralyzed muscles disobeyed. She felt as if she were burning— that no more air could get into her lungs—and she thought she might throw up. Then she sank into a deep, merciful darkness.

Feverish dreams tormented her while the warm blood ran out between her legs.

~

Brèagha-muir would change the blood-soaked blankets, she thought, but she couldn't do much else for the young woman. The treatment was working, but survival of the patient was less than sure. Many a woman in the same situation had died.

In the middle of the night, the old woman gave the girl some water and checked the bleeding. She furrowed her brow. She knew if the bleeding didn't stop soon, the girl didn't stand much of a chance. The metallic smell of warm blood filled the hut. Brèagha-muir sat down and prayed.

As she called her powers to stand by the young woman in danger, the wind picked up and rain drummed on the roof. Nodding contently, Brèagha-muir stood and lifted the body of her patient. With astonishing strength, she cradled the girl as she carried her out into the rain.

On a flat rock, almost like an altar, she lay her down, freed her from her bloody blanket, and stepped back. The icy rain fell onto the girl's naked body. Like red paint, the blood was washed away.

~

Nathaira opened her eyes. She saw boiling skies above her, flashing lightning, and rain. Then the world around her went black again.

When she woke up four days later, she was lying in a woolen dress on a clean straw mat. Her hair had been combed and bound up tightly in a braid. She smelled of rose petals. Although the hut looked familiar, she still wasn't sure where she was. The hut was empty. No pot was hanging over the cold, dusty fireplace. Not a single herbal sack was hanging from the ceiling. And from the dust on the table, it looked like no one had lived here for years.

Nathaira stood up, light-headed and weak. Everything around her was turning. She groped her way to the door unsteadily. Her lower abdomen was in great pain. After only a few steps, she was exhausted; she desperately needed help—and something to drink.

She pushed the door open, squinting when the bright sunlight hit her eyes. She felt as if she had died and had just returned from the kingdom of darkness. She fell to her knees and wept.

She was alive. Now she just needed to go home.

Her horse's warm muzzle poked gently at her shoulder. The animal was well fed and already saddled. A full water bottle was in one of the saddlebags. Greedily and crying with relief, she downed the cool drink.

The day after next, she reached the safe grounds of her homeland. The tower of her family castle stood out against the horizon to greet her.

What exactly had happened in the hut, Nathaira couldn't say in retrospect. She wasn't even sure if Brèagha-muir was real or if it was all a dream.

But one thing she did know: Alasdair would come back from the borderlands, and she had killed his child.

~

A sound tore Nathaira out of her thoughts. A car door slammed, and someone was driving away. The glow of head-lights brushed by her momentarily.

Quickly, she wiped the tears from her face. Tears? How useless feelings were, she thought. How much easier it had been in the last few centuries. Without pain and without tormenting memories.

~

"Psst . . . Payton," Sean whispered. "Nathaira just told me to go shopping in town. She even handed me a list. I reminded her that I wasn't supposed to leave, but all she did was shrug. And then it occurred to me that maybe you would like to go on a little trip."

Sean grinned at his brother and held the list out to him.

Payton shook his head. "We are not allowed to leave the castle."

"Yes, but Nathaira said it's all right. She will take care of Cathal. She said she wants me to go deal with the shopping."

"All right, then, but I hope she will not get into too much trouble if I'm not back by this evening."

"What are you going to do?"

"I don't know yet, but I am not going to leave Sam unprotected."

"Cathal will not go back on his word. He will wait."

"I don't think that everyone else is so beholden to that long-ago oath."

"Don't get me wrong—I like Sam, and I'd like to help her, too. But I am bound to my oath. I don't think you'll have to worry. Cathal doesn't think much of anyone who undermines his authority. Still, if you get into trouble, let me know. I am on your side."

"Thanks, Sean. But I'll make sure Sam is safe. She needs me. And I need her."

CHAPTER 15

I was surprised to find Payton suddenly standing in front of me. Quickly, I slid out the front door, pulling it shut behind me, before anyone at home found out who had rung the bell.

"Come with me." I tugged on his sleeve, leading him past several trees.

I hadn't actually been counting on Payton to show up, but I was very happy to see him. In the last few days I hadn't heard anything from him and I'd missed him awfully. I leaned against a tree trunk and looked my gorgeous visitor up and down.

Payton was pale. The expression on his face was a mystery, as usual, but he was holding my hand, which I took as a good sign.

"I missed you," he said, though he glanced hastily over his shoulder.

"I missed you, too. Should we go somewhere else?"

He really didn't seem comfortable here. And I didn't want Alison or Roy to catch me with him. But I definitely did want to kiss this boy. I didn't think I could wait much longer.

As we drove down the road, I regretted that I hadn't asked him where he wanted to go.

"Ben Nevis?" I could hardly believe my ears. "Are you insane?"

There are several high hills in Scotland. If it's higher than three thousand feet, the Scots call it a *munro*. At just over four thousand feet, Ben Nevis is not only the highest munro, but also the highest mountain in the British Isles.

"Come on, the hike takes only about four hours. You can do it!"

Not only was I completely out of shape for such a hike, but I wasn't dressed for it—or the famously unsteady Scottish weather. On the other hand, I'd been wishing for some alone time with Payton. And counting the drive to and from Ben Nevis, we'd be together all day.

"OK," I said hesitantly. "But we don't have to go all the way to the top, do we?"

Payton laughed and reached for my hand.

"No, but did you know that it's almost more difficult to get down than to go up?"

"What? Oh my God, why can't we just go to a movie? That's what the kids in the US do, you know?"

"Yes, I know. And that's exactly why we are not going to do that," he said. "I want your time in Scotland to be unforgettable. I want you to think of me every single day of your life. You have no idea how much I am dreading the day when you go back. I want to show you all my favorite places and then, when you are no longer here with me, I will at least remember where you laughed. Where you took my hand. Where your eyes lit up."

I didn't know what to say. He was right. I wanted to see his favorite spots. Wanted him always to think of me. I hated to watch the calendar, seeing my departure date constantly looming closer. So off we went. For a little hike.

~

After two hours of steep climbing, the view was spectacular. The town of Fort William was below us. On the horizon, the massive Highlands jutted upward to the sky. We were alone—just as I'd hoped—having not seen another hiker since our first twenty minutes in. At first, Payton and I talked as we went, but as the climb got more rigorous, our conversation stopped. Still, we maintained a wonderful feeling of connectedness.

"Payton, I need a rest."

The muscles in my upper legs were burning. I sank into the grass and stretched out my arms and legs. Payton sat down next to me. He pushed a bottle of water into my hand and took off my shoes and socks.

"You are really doing well. We can take a break and keep going or just stay here. As you wish."

I shut my eyes. The damp grass tickled my bare feet, Payton's voice was like music, and the sun stroked my face. I had never been so happy in my entire life.

"I love you," I murmured.

Oh my God, I thought. Did I really just say that out loud?

I opened my eyes a crack to check whether Payton had heard me. He looked happy, but he didn't say anything. Then he grinned. He picked a long blade of grass and tickled my feet.

I laughed, opened my eyes the whole way, and sat up. Payton stroked my ear with the blade of grass, then along my cheek to my chin, and down my throat to my collarbone. His eyes were locked on mine the entire time.

I wasn't laughing anymore. Instead, I was holding my breath and I felt very hot. I licked my lips. Payton's eyes were full of passion. The blade of grass trembled as Payton brushed it past my neckline and over the soft curve of my chest. Then he bent over, brushed my hair out of my face, and brought his lips close to mine.

Suddenly, he jumped up. He pounded his feet into the ground and let out a string of snarling Gaelic sounds.

I was flustered—still confused about not receiving a kiss. But when he let out a pained cry and showed me his arm, I understood. Blood was running all over the place from a deep gash across his wrist. He had leaned onto a stray piece of broken glass.

"We need to apply pressure to that," I said, jumping up and digging through his backpack.

"It's not that bad. I'm sure it will stop in a moment."

"No . . . it won't. That cut is too deep."

There was no way I'd let him resist. Since my mom is a nurse, I didn't fool around when it came to first aid. I cleaned the wound with mineral water, put a clean tissue over the cut, and bound up his arm with my scarf. I knew he needed to get to a doctor as soon as possible. He was going to need a few stitches. And maybe a tetanus shot.

"Can you walk? Or are you dizzy?" I asked.

"Why?" Payton looked up, surprised. "Do you want to go up to the top after all?"

"Of course not! We're going back. You have to go to the doctor!"

"You're sweet, Sam, but I don't need to go to the doctor for something minor like this."

"Payton, you really don't have to act cool around me."

"I have gotten over far worse injuries before, believe me."

Payton sat down. He was twisting a blade of grass between his fingers again. My cheeks turned scarlet when I thought about the feelings he had awakened in me using one tiny blade of grass. He rolled the grass between his fingers absentmindedly, and I was unable to think a single normal thought.

"We're not going any further, OK?" I said when I'd recovered. "We are going to go back down, slowly."

Payton nodded, but his thoughts seemed elsewhere.

"Sam, if I were to tell you something unbelievable, would you still believe me?"

"It depends on what it is. Try me."

"No, it doesn't work like that."

He lay back in the grass and said nothing. Now I was really curious.

"Well, I don't think you have any reason to lie to me," I said, "so I would assume that you were telling the truth. Am I making any sense?"

Payton grinned, but he still remained silent.

"So . . ." I tried to gather my thoughts. "I guess that means I trust you, and I'll believe anything you tell me."

His smile got bigger.

"If I had proof," he said, "then it would be even better. Someone like you, someone who analyzes everything so logically, would have no doubts at all when presented with proof."

"Well, sure, proof would definitely be helpful, but I trust you to begin with." Ceremoniously, I raised my hand as if swearing an oath.

Payton sat up and laid his bandaged arm in my lap.

Then he nodded. "Take it off."

"What?"

"The scarf. Take it off."

"No, we need to keep pressure on it."

"Sam, I thought you said you trusted me. Take it off!"

Startled by his tone, I fumbled as I unknotted the scarf and unwound it layer by layer. The tissue I had put over the cut was only slightly bloody in the center.

"Carry on!"

Payton kept his eyes on me. My fingers shaking, I carefully lifted the tissue. I looked at his arm in disbelief as my fingers gently touched the rapidly healing cut.

"How is that possible?"

He draped his healthy arm over mine and shrugged.

"Payton, how . . . ?" I didn't know what it was I wanted to ask. What I could see was absolutely impossible.

He lifted my face with one fingertip and looked me in the eye. His eyes were full of pain when he asked uncertainly, "Do you want me to tell you a story?"

I nodded and knew that what was to come next would change everything.

~

Payton closed his eyes. He didn't know where to begin. He wanted Sam to understand why he couldn't kiss her, although there was nothing else he would rather do. His voice trembling, he began to tell her his story.

"It was the year 1740. A group of young Scots went out one evening to take revenge for cattle theft. In the Highlands, the clans had been fighting for ages; sadly, this type of thing was common, particularly if one clan felt another clan had grown weaker.

"At age sixteen, the boys were already men, working, going to battle, or dying in fights. But at that time, the Stuart clan was weak. Their chieftain had recently died, and it wasn't clear who was to be his successor. The eldest son would not necessarily make the best chieftain, so there were bitter fights within the clan—even between siblings—over who should be the next leader.

"The Stuarts' eldest son, Cathal, was elected."

Payton looked into Sam's eyes. Her hand was still lying on his arm, covering the wound. He continued.

"Cathal knew that allowing the cattle thefts on his borderlands was making him appear to be a weak leader. That kind of thing could split the clan apart, and he couldn't allow that to happen. So that is why about twenty men went to the neighboring enemy clan—to take back their cattle."

He paused. "But right from the start this venture was doomed."

"Why?" asked Sam.

"Let's just say that it would have been better had Cathal not acted so rashly. The warrior's intention was to let the enemy clan know that they would use violence if necessary to settle the damages. And surely everything would have turned out differently if . . ."

Payton swallowed. Even after all these years, it was hard to report the death of his youngest brother. He cleared his throat and squeezed Sam's hand. "If Kyle hadn't died!"

"Kyle?"

"Yes, the youngest of the alliance. He wasn't supposed to be there at all that night, but he rode after the others, secretly following them. Cathal had spotted him in the distance and immediately sent someone back to take Kyle home. But it was already too late. Kyle had been attacked—stabbed from behind with a short dagger. He had drowned in his own blood.

"That cowardly and perfidious attack changed everything. Now everyone wanted to take revenge. No one stopped to consider the consequences. Within a few minutes, they had charged the enemy's castle. It was the middle of the night, and most of the inhabitants were asleep."

"What happened then?" Sam asked.

The terrible pictures raced around in Payton's head. He couldn't stop the images, but he couldn't tell Sam what he saw. Couldn't explain his guilt or what he had done.

"Payton . . . what happened?"

"It doesn't matter. The only thing that is important is that fate was determined by that moment. A curse was laid on Cathal and the warriors with him that night. A curse that took everything away from them."

"A curse? Did the men believe in things like that?"

"It has nothing to do with believing. You don't have to believe something or want to acknowledge it if you have to live with it every day."

"Well, what kind of curse was it?"

"The worst. Each and every one of them was cursed to live a life without any feeling—without love, without warmth, without pain. Only emptiness. And they would suffer that for all eternity, because they were never going to die."

CHAPTER 16

Delaware

R yan was sitting in his dad's police car. The window was down, but there wasn't much of a breeze in the sticky summer heat.

"Dad, do we really need to deal with this now? I have a whole year to figure this out."

"If you're going to want to attend the police academy—"

"Yeah, I know. I need to take some community college classes first. But I'm not a hundred percent sure whether I even want to be a cop."

"I think you need to give it serious consideration. It's a family tradition—starting with your grandfather—and I always thought you'd make a great cop. You've been talking about it ever since you were a kid."

"Yeah, but every little boy wants to be a policeman or a fireman. That doesn't mean it actually happens when he grows up."

Ryan stuffed his earphones in to indicate that the conversation was over. He bobbed his head to the music.

His father shook his head.

"Hey, Dad, stop the car. I'll get out here."

Ryan pointed to two of his friends on the sidewalk. He snagged his backpack out of the backseat.

"Fine, but we'll talk more tonight. You need to have a plan."

"Yeah, OK. Bye!" Ryan slammed the door and ran after his friends.

~

"Hey, Justin. Wait!"

They thumped each other on the back, and Kim asked herself how the coolest guys in the school could behave so idiotically without being laughed out of town. Then again, she wasn't exactly calling them out.

"Greetings, Ms. Journalist," Ryan said when he finally acknowledged that she was there.

"Hi, Ryan," Kim said.

"Say, have you heard from Sam? Does she miss me?"

"I don't think so. I think she's been a little distracted."

"What do you mean? She's not seeing some guy in a skirt, is she?"

Ryan seemed a little shaken by the idea. Perhaps to boost his self-esteem, he whistled at two fifteen-year-old girls on the other side of the road.

Kim snuggled up to Justin, smiling to herself. "Well, from what she said, she seems to really like what she's found under the skirt."

"What? Is she crazy?"

"Ryan, Ryan . . . Have you forgotten Ashley already? Why should you be the only one to have fun this summer?"

~

They arrived at the lake. Kim spread out her towel and Justin lay down next to her. Ryan rolled up his jeans and sat down in the sand. Kim took off her T-shirt, and Justin zealously rubbed sunscreen onto her back. The black bikini really looked good on her, Ryan had to admit. He wondered why it had taken him so long to notice Kim and Sam. They were both pretty cute. Oh well, better late than never, he thought.

"The thing with Ashley is over, by the way," Ryan said. "That was so last year."

"Last year? The first week Ashley was here, you were glued together," Kim retorted. She was, after all, the editor for the school paper; she noticed everything.

"I thought that would help me forget about Sam, but trust me, it just made everything worse. Please, Kim . . . Sam really means a lot to me. Can't you try to put in a good word?"

"All right, you idiot. But if you screw up again, even I won't be able to help you anymore."

Kim turned onto her stomach and dug a magazine out of her bag. Justin trickled some sand onto her back until she jabbed him in his side.

"Stop it!"

"And what if I kiss every single speck of sand off your skin later?"

That was too much romance for Ryan. He jumped up and pretended to gag.

"God, you two are disgusting! I'm off, see you later."

Chapter 17

Scotland

Wow!"

Slowly, my fingers brushed over Payton's fully healed wound as we sat next to the trail. His skin was even. Only a milky-white line betrayed where the piece of glass had dug into his wrist. At the most, it now looked like an old, faded scar.

Everything was starting to come together in my mind. I looked into Payton's eyes. I saw love, hope, and something dark. I stroked the delicate scar again and hesitantly asked, "And what would happen, for example, if one of these cursed men got hurt?"

I was afraid of the answer, and I started to shake, but Payton's strong hand calmed me.

"Well, the wound would heal within a very short time."

Payton held my hands tight.

"So," I asked, "you can't feel anything?"

My fear of this second answer was even greater: I loved him, and he couldn't feel anything? Although I had promised to believe whatever he told me, I hoped that couldn't be true.

"Sam, do you understand what I've been telling you? Do you understand that I am one of the cursed?"

"Yes," I said softly. No wonder he'd been such a mystery to me. "But I can't quite wrap my head around how that can be—or what it means for me. You're telling me that you're actually immortal?"

"I haven't aged a day in two hundred seventy years."

"Isn't that a good thing? Doesn't everyone want to stay young and live forever?"

Payton grabbed my upper arms.

"You know absolutely nothing! How can you even think that?" He was so mad he was almost shaking me.

"Have you been listening to me at all?" he growled. "What kind of life do you think it is, to live without feeling? When you wake up and know exactly what your day is going to be like. Colorless, cold, no pain, no joy. What it can be like to live far longer than all your family and friends, to stand at their graves and not even be able to shed a single tear of sorrow. Not even be able to mourn when your parents die, or your nieces and nephews. What it's like to have to hide, because you don't change, because you'll always be nineteen."

He let his arms drop.

"I'm sorry. I wasn't thinking." I felt bad about what I'd said, and I felt terrible that he was suffering so much. "Please, Payton, sit down with me and explain everything to me. I want to understand. I want to understand you."

He was obviously tortured by this curse.

"Can you imagine what it is like to be dead? That's what it is like for me. But yet, I'm alive. I taste nothing. The best food is the same as a handful of dirt for me. None of the world's alcohol can make me drunk, and not even the most beautiful song can reach my innermost. I would rather be dead than live like this—you can take my word on that. Imagine the most beautiful sunset you have ever seen, the fantastic colors, the warm glow on your skin. The feelings that spread inside you in such a moment. Happiness, contentedness, or admiration. That's what my life was like. But once I was cursed, that all changed. I can see the colors, but I feel nothing."

"But that doesn't make sense. I've seen you fighting with your feelings. Now, for example. You're suffering, you're tormenting yourself, and you're relieved to have told me your secret. That's feeling!"

Payton knelt down in front of me, took my hands, and said, "Yes, that's exactly it. You are changing everything . . . I can't tell you how much you're turning my life upside down. Since I first saw you, I can't be without you. And ever since I met you, I am starting to be able to feel again."

"Why? And why me?"

"I don't know."

"What do you feel?"

"Pain!" He laughed.

"Pain? That's awful!"

"No . . . I mean . . . yes. It is awful, but I am so glad to feel anything at all. You're like a drug to me. I need to have more and more of you."

"Is that good or bad?"

"When I am really close to you, like now, it feels terrible, as if I were burning. At first, the pain took my breath away, but now I'm getting used to it and can cope with it quite well. When it gets too much, I move away from you, and then it gets better again. Sometimes, it's as if I were caught between two concrete blocks that are pressing on my lungs, just strongly enough not to squeeze me to death."

"You call that coping?" Instinctively, I stepped back a few feet, but he pulled me back toward him.

"I have everything more or less under control now. Trust me."

I nodded. How insane! And the craziest thing about it was that I hadn't the slightest doubt that Payton was telling me the truth. Scotland did seem magical, and if I were ever to meet a cursed person, Scotland seemed like a logical place. Plus, I had seen his miraculous healing process with my own eyes.

"Payton, I need to ask you something."

"Yes, what?"

I knew I was about to make a fool of myself, but I really wanted to know. "Two hundred years is a long time. How many women did you have?"

Payton looked at me, somewhat dazed. Then he fell back into the grass and laughed. He pulled me down and brushed a lock of hair off my forehead.

"Silly girl! I've been telling you how lonely and empty my life has been up until now. I tell you that I burn when I'm near you, and you ask me something like that . . . What would I want with a woman? I couldn't feel anything before!"

I blushed. "I mean . . . it's none of my business anyway."

"If I could, I would shut you up by kissing you, just to make you stop asking such stupid questions!"

I wondered if I'd heard him right. Had he said kiss? Did that mean he would never be able to kiss me?

"What would it feel like for you if we were to kiss?" I asked. "Just in theory?"

Payton grinned cheekily.

"Well, theoretically, I would probably die doing so, because a mere touch of yours feels like a burning-hot poker drilling into my skin. But I will only know for sure when I have tried it."

"No, no, no," I said. "That's out of the question. I am not going to do that to you!" I slid farther away from him.

"Sam, please understand. I am hungering for more. I want more. I just have to know what it's like to be even closer to you. I would rather die than not know. I can't breathe when you touch me, but I don't want to breathe anymore if you can't touch me. I don't know what we can do, but I can't let you go. I actually hope that the pain will last the next thousand years. Then I will at least know that I am still a human. Sam, please, stay with me today. Don't go away. I want to feel you!"

"Oh, Payton!"

I wanted to throw myself into his arms, to kiss him and stroke him, but I was so scared. Then he took my hand and placed it on his heart. It was pounding against my fingers, and he stiffened, but he held my hand there. He put his own hand shakily around my waist and pulled me even closer.

"Dear God, please give me strength," he prayed. Our lips touched. He briefly twitched back. Then he didn't resist.

We were both trembling. His lips were soft and tender. Very slowly, I opened my mouth, and my tongue stroked his lip. He sighed in pain, but then he kissed me back. His hands caressed my neck and my back. He wouldn't let me go. Our kiss, which at first had been very careful, became more and more passionate.

Then he pushed me away, smiled happily—and stepped back a good ten feet.

"God, Sam, you are killing me!"

I couldn't say a thing. I could barely hear. My lips felt swollen, and my blood was racing around in my ears.

"How long will you need until we can repeat that?" I asked breathlessly.

"Well, I guess I should be ready in . . . about a hundred years!"

While we were still laughing at his answer, there was a roll of thunder in the distance. Dark clouds had gathered, and it was obvious we were in for a storm.

"We have to hurry down," I called through the rising wind. "Or can we find shelter somewhere up here?"

"No, we have to go back. Now!"

I couldn't imagine that we could make it the whole way before the storm hit.

"Come on!" he said. "When everything gets wet, it'll be much more difficult."

We were almost back to our starting place when the first raindrops started to blot the ground. I'd been hiking down so fast I figured I probably wouldn't be able to walk a single step the next day. My legs were aching already. Payton seemed to be having less trouble. Naturally, I thought. Again and again he kissed my hand, while keeping a close eye on the sky.

We had made it. I could finally see Payton's SUV, when he suddenly grabbed my arm. He had stopped walking and was staring warily at the almost-empty parking lot. He growled something in Gaelic and then pushed himself in front of me, as if shielding me.

I was seriously freaked out. Over his shoulder, I could see a man, casually walking toward us. He didn't seem to even notice the pouring rain.

"Payton, what a coincidence. And here I thought you weren't supposed to leave the castle?"

"Alasdair, my friend, you are mistaken. I'm doing business for Nathaira."

Alasdair was standing just an arm's length away. And although Payton was tall, the other man was several inches taller.

"What a surprise," Alasdair said. "I'm also doing some business for Nathaira."

Payton stiffened. He reached behind his back and pressed something into my hand. His car keys.

"Still chasing after her?" Payton said. "You still haven't got the message, after all this time, that Nathaira belongs to someone else."

Alasdair snorted angrily. "Shut your mouth! Do you think I am her dog? No, you all only see the tip of the iceberg. I, on the other hand, know that under the surface of the water, there's massive trouble. More iceberg. You never know what kind of trouble is lurking under the surface. Trouble that will be your undoing."

"Fascinating. Have you become a sailor?"

"Don't worry, I just want the girl to reveal to me what else is lurking under the surface."

"What do you mean?"

"She didn't come out of nowhere, now did she? She has a family—Camerons, to be precise. I want to know who, where, and especially, how many!"

Payton stayed in front of Sam, blocking Alasdair from seeing her.

"Alasdair, I am warning you, leave us in peace!"

"Us? Are you already so beholden to this Cameron bitch?"

"*A dhiobhail*," Payton growled, and then he attacked. Both men crashed to the ground, rolling around and throwing punches.

"Run, Sam," Payton gasped.

I didn't want to leave him. I didn't have the slightest idea what they had been fighting about, since they'd been speaking in Gaelic, but the hate-filled look in Alasdair's eyes said it all.

"Sam, now! Get away!"

Payton was struggling to keep his opponent under control. Unlike the silly boys who fought in the halls of our high school, this was not for show. Both men were hitting each other with all their might, and for Payton, it wasn't looking good. A strong hit to his temple made him lose his focus, and Alasdair took his opportunity. He ignored the man lying on the ground and pounced at me, as powerfully as a wildcat.

Images flashed before my eyes, pictures from my dream:

I was running. I was running as fast as I could, on stony, wet ground. I could see waves pounding against the cliffs in front of me, the churning gray waters swirling around the rocks below. A menacing curtain of clouds had pushed itself in front of the sun and I shivered, despite the sweat running down my back. On the mountaintop behind me was an old lady with white hair. It rose up off her like smoke, billowing around her wrinkled face. Only her eyes

*were young. And although she was speaking to me in a language I
didn't know, I could somehow understand every word she said:*

"You must face your destiny! You can't run away!"

*Goose bumps spread over my whole body. I looked for a way out.
In front of me, there was only the icy water, and behind me the terrifying apparition. But when I turned around again, she had disappeared. Where had she gone? I scanned the rocky, bare landscape.
She had vanished. Relieved, I breathed deeply and sank wearily to
my knees as a cold blast of air came down from the mountains.*

"Run!" Payton's shout brought me back to reality, and
I finally took off. I barely had a head start and knew the
giant behind me would easily catch up. Thankfully, Payton
was back on his feet. He was trying to get between me and
Alasdair. Against all odds, I managed to gain some ground. I
had almost reached the car when the keys slipped out of my
hand. I ducked behind another parked car and felt around
on the muddy ground.

The men were fighting again. Their muffled cries
weren't far away. Then it was quiet.

I could hear my own jagged breathing, which was bound
to betray me. I tried to hold my breath, but that made me
dizzy. I took a deep breath.

"Lose something?"

Grinning nastily, Alasdair held up the keys.

My mind was racing. What was I supposed to do now? I
couldn't outrun this guy, and Payton was nowhere in sight.
My legs were trembling with fear and exhaustion, but I refused to give up without a fight. I knew I had to buy some
time.

"Who are you? What do you want?" I said. I pushed myself farther back and brushed my wet hair out of my face.

"It's far more interesting who you are, isn't it? Maybe I will spare you, if you tell me all I want to know."

"What? There must be a misunderstanding. I have no idea what you're talking about."

"Liar! You must think I'm blind! You can't deny your descent."

In one swift motion, he pulled me up by my arms and raised me off the ground.

Suddenly, his eyes rolled back in his head, and he fell to the ground, pulling me down with him. Payton was standing there with an iron bar, breathing heavily. He heaved the unconscious body off me and helped me up.

"Quick, get to the car!"

But the giant was still clutching the car keys in his hand.

"Payton, the keys!" I motioned toward the huge hand.

Even though he didn't look too dangerous just then, I was definitely not going anywhere near that man. And sure enough, when Payton grabbed the keys, Alasdair came to and punched him in the gut. Payton threw the keys at me before attacking his opponent again. This time, I didn't wait to see how the fight would end.

I jumped behind the steering wheel, revved the engine, and locked the doors. I careened through the parking lot, wheels screeching. I couldn't see a thing. Frantically, I pushed and pulled at the controls on the steering wheel until I finally found the windshield wipers. Then something hit the passenger side, and I screamed. It was Payton. He was clinging to the car, hanging from the roof rack and trying to open the door. I quickly pressed the "unlock" button and hit the brakes.

"Go that way!" Payton pointed. "We'll turn off this road in about three miles."

"Who was that, and what did he want?" I was just about to have a panic attack, and my voice cracked.

"Later! We have to see whether he's following us first."

We raced along the country road, rain pounding on the windshield. It was hard to see, with the headlights of oncoming traffic, and I had to focus extrahard to stay on the left side of the road. All the while, I obsessively checked the rearview mirror. But apart from a red truck that had turned off at the last intersection, the road remained empty behind us.

Slowly, I started to relax, and my thoughts cleared. "We've lost him, haven't we?"

Payton's brow wrinkled, and then he nodded. "I think so. Keep going. It isn't far now." His face was cut all over the place, and he was holding his right side.

"Are you all right?" I asked hesitantly.

"Mmm, I think so. But I must admit that it would be nice if my self-healing capabilities weren't weakened now." Abruptly, he sat up straight. "Wait, right up there."

The entrance to the dirt road would have passed unnoticed if Payton hadn't told me to turn. An old oak hid the narrow lane from passing drivers. And it was good that we were driving an SUV as we bounced along the hardly visible track. I slowed down steadily to a stop.

To be safe, I left the engine on, but by now, I desperately needed some answers, and I was nearly hysterical.

"You have to tell me what's going on! Tell me the truth, now, or I'm going to the police."

Payton pressed his lips together and didn't say anything.

"Payton, I'm warning you. I have a right to know!"

He nodded. "You're right. You're going to find out anyway, so you may as well hear it from me. That was Alasdair
Buchanan, one of the other men who is cursed, just like me."

"I gathered that, but what does he want from me?"

"I should have told you long ago, but I didn't know how."

"Told me what?"

"I told you about the night we were cursed. And I told
you that we attacked our enemy's castle."

"Payton, please. What are you talking about? That was
hundreds of years ago. What does it have to do with me?"

"It's simple. You shouldn't exist."

"What?"

"The enemy was the Cameron clan. You are obviously
one of them."

"Me? As far as I know, I'm not even Scottish. My last
name is Watts! There aren't any Camerons in my family."

"Sam, you are definitely a Cameron. I could tell the first
moment I saw you. And then again at the Glenfinnan Monument. You look so much like the Camerons I knew, it took
my breath away, and I knew I had to find out who you are."

"Are you insane? You followed me just because I just
happen to look like someone who lived centuries ago?"

"Sam, listen. Try to understand. It wasn't just that you
look like a Cameron. The pain I feel when I'm near you, the
way you look, the pendant . . . I had to find out what that
meant for me, and for all of us. You are the reason the curse
is changing. Not only for me, but for all of us."

"The curse, the curse . . . I still don't get it. Can't you
make your people leave me in peace!"

"I can't promise you that. They're convinced that we're all going to die because of you."

"Well, that's just great," I grumbled. "So let's say I really am a Cameron. What did the Camerons ever do to you?"

"You're asking the wrong question. What you should ask is what we did to the Camerons."

"What you did? You had a fight. You said that it was normal at the time for the clans to fight."

"No, Sam. It wasn't just a fight." A tone of melancholy had entered his voice. "It was a massacre. We attacked the castle, and the Camerons were taken completely by surprise. Most of the inhabitants were murdered while they were sleeping in their beds. Cathal ordered us not to spare anybody—and we didn't. After that night, there were no more Camerons in the Highlands. None."

Everything started to spin inside my head. I felt like I was the one fighting now, my conflicting feelings rolling around and duking it out. My heart was breaking into a thousand pieces. I had fallen in love with a monster!

"You're saying that you killed my ancestors—all of them. That you killed sleeping people—young and old. Then you were cursed. And now you find one you apparently missed, and you have to get near me?" I was shouting, full of anger and hatred. "Well, what were you planning to do with me? Did you want to kill me? Why didn't you just do that? Why all these lies?"

"I didn't want to kill you! And I didn't want to lie to you. I didn't tell you about the massacre because I was scared that you'd never be able to forgive me!"

"Forgive you? You're a murderer, you killed innocent women and children, you wanted to destroy all of my ancestors, and you abused my feelings to satisfy your own curiosity. I don't know where to start, Payton, but I will never forgive you!"

"Sam, please, I didn't mean to hurt you. You look so much like Isobel Cameron, and I'll admit that was what attracted me to you at first. But not anymore."

"Who?"

"Isobel. I was trying to help her, to hide her. But she was so scared that she ran, and she stumbled backward off the parapet. I wanted to save her—I grabbed her arm—but instead of letting me help her, she fought against me and fell. You're right—she was innocent. And I am guilty of her death." He looked away and took a deep breath. "And while I was trying to save Isobel, I left a friend without protection. He paid for that with his life. I have more guilt than you can imagine, and I have to bear it for all time. But I tried to protect your family. And I still want to!"

"Liar!" I screamed. "I wasn't in danger until I met you. I have no idea how you can even look me in the eye. You should be ashamed of yourself! I hate you! Get out!"

"This is my car and I—"

"Get out! Get the hell out of the car! And get the hell out of my life!"

Tears streamed down my cheeks, my heart felt flattened, and everything hurt. Without taking his eyes off me, Payton slowly loosened his seat belt and got out of the car.

Without a backward glance, I revved the engine and sped off.

I imagined Payton standing there like a statue in the rain, looking after me.

I was sobbing uncontrollably, but I just went with it, crying myself hoarse. One thing was clear: I had to leave

Scotland. I couldn't stay here a moment longer. Alison and Roy were bound to understand.

CHAPTER 18

The flight attendant pushed the refreshment cart up the aisle, and I ordered a ginger ale. I was feeling sick from the stress, the worry, and the recirculated air. I turned toward the window. Unfortunately, I didn't have a window seat, but I was able to catch a glimpse past my neighbor's shoulder. The Atlantic was spread out beneath us like an endless blue carpet. I was on my way home, leaving Scotland and Payton behind me.

The thought of never coming back made my stomach lurch. Thinking about Payton was so painful. I'd left his car at the airport. Would he ever pick it up, I wondered. I told myself I didn't care. I had enough to do just trying to breathe in and out—the pain was that deep.

Never before had I been in love, never had I kissed a boy. I'd wanted to wait for that right person at just the right moment. What a stupid idiot I'd been! Payton had lied to me the whole time, right from the moment we met. And when I found out what he'd done—who he'd been, and worst of all, who he still was—my beautiful memories were destroyed in one blow. I had been so naive.

I wiped away my tears, and the elderly woman next to me patted my hand soothingly. "Oh, sweetie, you don't need to worry. Flying is the safest way to travel!"

I sniffed and nodded. Then I closed my eyes and pretended to sleep. The other passengers' quiet conversations would normally have comforted me, but on this flight they were driving me crazy. I tossed and turned, trying unsuccessfully to forget that handsome Scottish face with the crescent-shaped scar on his chin.

Mo luaidh. My darling. That's what he had called me. Without anticipating that I would get Roy to tell me what it meant. I wondered why he had said that to me, if he didn't really care.

I shook my head. It didn't matter; I could never forgive him.

Thankfully, Roy and Alison had bought my story: some urgent family business had come up, something about my grandma's estate and a pack of lawyers. Sadly, I had to go back home a week earlier than expected. I changed my flight, packed up my suitcase, and said my heartfelt goodbyes. Roy had offered to drive me to the airport, but I declined. I desperately wanted to spend those last few moments in Payton's car, to feel him close to me, to smell his scent.

Uncomfortably dry air blew down on me. I reached for my scarf, but it had disappeared. Oh, that's right, I recalled—I'd stuffed it into Payton's backpack after I'd taken it off his wound. I vaguely remembered that his backpack was still in his car.

That really sucked. It had been my favorite scarf.

CHAPTER 19

Payton unlocked the door and slid into his car. Her scent was barely noticeable. The chilly morning air had crept inside and wiped away any trace of Sam. He put his hands on the steering wheel, just as she had done, trying to will her back.

His eyes dropped to his backpack. He opened it, and there it was: Sam's scarf. Payton pressed the soft material to his chest and again tried to draw her back to him. The liveliness of travelers in front of the airport terminal was in stark contrast to the loneliness in his car. Payton couldn't believe that he had lost her. The one who had given him his life back. The only person he'd ever encountered who was capable of weakening the curse.

Without knowing why, he started the engine and drove to Avicmore. Maybe he would feel something of her presence there.

Payton wasn't in pain, but he was almost dying. His heart was breaking; he just couldn't feel it.

~

It was still early in the morning when he pulled in across the street from the cottage. He sat there completely still—quiet and tense. He hoped, by some miracle, that she'd suddenly come out the door, but of course she didn't. Sam was gone. A tear rolled down Payton's cheek as he imagined her there: she had slept behind that window, lay there on her bed, and thought about him. He had followed her to this place, hidden in the darkness, and tried to understand what it was she triggered in him. He'd felt the pain and even welcomed it, understood that she was to play an important part in his life. But he'd had no idea that he would fall in love with her.

He was wiser now. He knew that his heart would beat only for her—as long as he lived, for all eternity.

∼

Suddenly, the front door opened and a giant stepped out. The man seemed to immediately notice him. He stopped for a moment, as if unsure, and then set his shoulders determinedly and came straight for the car. Just as Payton was wondering whether he should drive off, the big man knocked on his window.

"I'm Roy. You must be Sam's friend, aye?" The way he stressed friend told Payton that Roy wasn't quite sure how close the two were to each other. But at least he was smiling.

"Yes, I'm Payton."

"Payton, Sam has left."

"Yes, I know. I was just about to go. Sorry to bother you."

"Wait, wait. Not so quickly."

A short glance to the house, and then he went on. "Come with me. I think I ought to tell you something."

Roy walked a little way down the road and turned the next corner. Not sure what to do, Payton just watched before he got out of the car and followed him. Roy was sitting on a garden wall, waiting. When Payton sat down next to him, Roy looked at him, as if assessing him.

"Payton, huh. Will you not tell me something about yerself?"

"There isn't anything to tell. I only stopped here briefly . . . I think I should leave now."

"Aye, of course you can do that, but maybe I can help you."

"Help me? With what?"

"Maybe it'll help to talk about destiny. Do you think that Sam was destined to meet you?"

"What do you mean?"

"On the first day after she arrived here, she told me about a dream she had. She said a white-haired woman named Vanora had told her she should mind those she was a descendant of, and that she couldn't run away from her destiny."

Payton was dumbstruck. Questions tumbled through his head: Sam had dreamed of Vanora? How could she know that name? Why would the woman who had cursed them all have appeared to Sam in her dreams?

He thought of explaining what he knew about Vanora, but Roy would probably have him institutionalized.

So he played it cool. "All right, then, she had a dream, and what else?"

"Aye, listen, boy. You don't have to talk to me, but you can trust me. I am a descendant of the women of Fair Isle and I recognize you for what you are, even if you're not going to tell me."

Payton wasn't sure what to make of this. The Fair Witches—Vanora had been one of them. And yet . . . What could this man know about him?

"I see."

"I know a lot about Vanora, too," Roy said.

"What about?"

"Her life, her powers, and her death, aye?"

"Then tell me about it."

"How about this—I can give you some advice. On Fair Isle lives a woman called Uisgeliath. She keeps the old writings. There you will find your answers."

The doubting look in Payton's eyes made Roy reveal one last thing. "Payton, listen to me. It is possible!"

Roy got up and sauntered off. His briefcase swung along, accompanying each step, his tweed jacket a bit dusty from the wall.

Payton called after him. "What is possible? Roy, what do you mean?"

The big man turned around once more. He smiled and said, "The curse, Payton. It is possible to lift the curse. It is possible!"

Then he raised his hand in farewell and disappeared. Payton rushed after him, but when he reached the corner, there was no sign of Roy.

Payton couldn't imagine how Roy could possibly know anything about the curse, never mind the solution for breaking it. He combed his fingers through his hair, not sure how much to believe.

But if there was even the slightest chance Roy was right, the course of action was clear. First, he would need to talk to Cathal about what Alasdair had done, and then he'd go to Fair Isle.

∽

"No, Cathal. You gave me your word," Payton boomed. "You said that the girl was safe. If you can't control your men any longer, then I will no longer abide by your orders!"

"*Sguir!* You're one to speak. I told you to stay here in the castle, and instead you crept off like a rat, escaping to find your little girl."

Cathal was lording over the table of gathered clan members. He knew his time as clan leader was almost over, but he did not want to accept that truth.

"If everyone here only does what they damn well want to do, we are all at risk of being discovered," Cathal said. "What do you think they'll do to us if they find out that we are immortal? At best, they will think we're some wacko group and send us off to a loony bin. At worst, they'll lock us up and experiment on us. I have not been watching out for this clan this long to have everything fall apart now!"

"But Cathal, I was only trying to protect us," whined Alasdair.

"By fighting in public, acting as if you were at the battlefield at Culloden?"

"There's nothing to protect us from anyway," Payton said. "The girl has gone, and she isn't coming back."

"Girl? Ha!" Alasdair balled his hands into fists. It was obvious that he hadn't yet forgiven Payton for the knockout.

"You can maybe convince the others that she is a child, but she is a woman. I've seen you with her, and it's obvious: you have chosen her over us."

"Our side, your side, my side." Payton shook his head. "Have you forgotten that we are no longer in the year 1740? Back then, we all behaved like that because we were angry and didn't know any better. Had I the choice again today, I wouldn't have taken part in that massacre. We murdered innocent people, and we have paid the price ever since." He lowered his voice, but spoke with even greater intensity. "But I swear, you will not touch Sam. She has nothing to do with the change to the curse, and I will do whatever it takes to prove it to you."

"Prove it?" Cathal was getting angry. He had noticed that some of his people were nodding in agreement with Payton.

"Yes, I have found out that there is a way to lift the curse. But I need to go on a journey to find out more about it, to find a solution. And for as long as it'll take me to do so, I want you to leave Sam in peace."

"How sweet, the bold knight wants to save the maiden," Nathaira mocked.

"Shut up, Nathaira," Sean said. "I'm with Payton on this. And Cathal, you shouldn't forget that we McLeans are not bound to you by an oath, but only to our brother."

Blair shifted in his seat and lifted his eyes.

Payton walked toward his older brother. "Blair, I swore you a holy oath that I would trust and follow you. But today, brother"—he knelt at his feet—"today, I would like to beg you to trust and follow me. I know what I am doing. And I will do nothing that will put you in danger or harm you in any way. Remember that our oath is sealed with our blood.

Our blood! Please, Blair. Stand with those who are of your own blood. Don't oppose me."

He got to his feet again. "Have you all forgotten what honor is? Can you upon your honor really hunt that woman? That innocent girl? When there are other options? Blair, I beg you. Grant me some time to solve this. Afterward, I will surrender to you, and to Cathal's wishes, but you must give me this one chance, if you are really my brother!"

"Well then," Blair said, "my brother is right. This truce is something that must be granted him. Cathal, can you get your men to wait for Payton's return?"

Cathal, who would have loved to interrupt Payton's speech, was now also very annoyed at Blair, for questioning whether he had control over his men.

"Of course! My men will do whatever I tell them to. Go then, don't lose any time! But if you can't deliver any results in one week's time, our agreement will become invalid and I will decide on the correct solution with the Stuart people."

With that, he rose from the head of the table and left the room. Blair quickly pushed back his chair and hurried after his angry friend. Nathaira stayed back, white with rage. She glared maliciously at Payton, Sean, and Alasdair.

Without another word, Payton left the castle, and the people he had known his whole life.

CHAPTER 20

Delaware

I should have known. Running back home wasn't all that it was cracked up to be.

Ashley was still there—and mad at me. As if it were my fault that Ryan had dumped her. Hello? I wasn't even on the continent when he broke her heart. I wondered what had suffered more: Ashley's heart or her pride.

So I was forced to spend the last days of my summer vacation with Blonde Poison, Kim's nickname for Ashley. And she was always home. My parents had grounded her after they had caught her smoking, but it seemed to me that the rest of us were being punished, too. My parents had to bear Ashley moping around, and I couldn't count on having my room to myself for a single minute of the day; my dear cousin grouchily spent all of her time staring at the small TV in my room. Well, not all of her time. She'd look up on occasion to shoot me a nasty look.

My poor parents. They were dying to hear about my trip to Scotland. And I didn't want to think or talk about it at all. Certainly not with Mom and Dad. I tried to fake enthusiasm, babbling about this monument or that castle, but it was hard to keep up the ruse. I told them I was jetlagged and needed a nap, grabbed my phone, and called Kim. I hoped she could take a break from smooching Justin to give some sympathy to her best friend.

"Kim. It's me. I'm back."

"Oh my God! I missed you so much. We have to meet up right away. I have so much to tell you. You won't believe what happened to me!"

Ah, Kim. I had flown halfway around the world, met an immortal, gotten my heart broken, partially lifted a curse, and fled from a murdering Highlander. But before I could tell her anything, I'd first have to listen to what she'd been up to—even though I doubted that she'd set foot outside Milford even for a day. Still, you had to give her credit; she was utterly honest. And I knew eventually she'd listen to me, using her reporter's instincts to pepper me with questions until she knew every single detail of my story.

"Do you have time today? I can come over," I said.

"Pick me up at three, and we'll go to the beach. That way we can be alone. My mom is off work this week, so if you come here, she'll drive you crazy with a million questions."

Hmm, I thought. I wonder where Kim gets it from.

"All right, see you in a little while."

∼

To kill time before going by Kim's, I unpacked my suitcase. I put all my dirty clothes into the laundry bag, which was hardly able to hold the gigantic load. Then I came across the suede skirt I'd bought in Inverness—the one I'd worn to seduce Payton—and I threw it onto my bed in disgust.

Ashley looked up from the TV. "Wow, that's hot! Wouldn't have thought you would wear anything like that."

"Actually, I don't think I'll ever wear it again."

Ashley muted the sound and sat down backward in her chair to watch me. "Why did you buy it then?"

"A mistake, I guess. I thought it might be 'me,' but it really isn't."

"Can I try it on?" Ashley picked up the skirt without waiting for an answer and held it up to her hips.

"Go for it. You can have it if it fits."

I pulled out a few more socks and some shoes. Then my hand touched something cold and metal. Grandma's pendant. The piece of jewelry lay in my hand, looking shiny and new. I still didn't understand how that was possible. But as I'd learned in Scotland, things that can't exist . . . well, they do exist.

In the meantime, Ashley had squeezed into the skirt, but she couldn't fasten it. "Almost! But it's cute. Let me see what it looks like on you."

"No."

"Oh come on. Please?"

"No."

"Hey, Sam, what did I ever do to you? If I can forgive you for taking Ryan away from me, then you can stop treating me like I don't exist."

"What are you talking about? I didn't take Ryan away from you. I'm not even interested in him. In fact, I think he's kind of a jerk. You are welcome to him."

"Really? But Ryan said there's something going on with you two."

"Yeah, right—in his dreams."

Ashley laughed, and even I couldn't stop smiling a little.

"OK, give me the skirt," I said, pulling it on.

"Wow, Sam, that looks awesome! Don't give it away. You should totally wear it."

"Nah, I don't think so."

I quickly took it off, but Ashley's admiration had made me feel a lot better. Maybe I would wear the skirt again someday. I would definitely wear the necklace. I had missed it. When I put it on, I immediately felt better.

Ashley turned back to her show, and I watched her for a moment, wondering if we would ever manage to be friends.

When I shut my now-empty suitcase, I suddenly felt like crying. I missed Payton so much that everything hurt. I sank onto my bed, trying not to hold it in.

I must have been tearing up, though, because Ashley switched the TV off and asked, "Hey, is everything OK? Are you crying?"

"No." My voice was breaking. "Just leave me alone."

And, to my great surprise, she did.

Quietly, she shut the door behind her, and I didn't have to hold back anymore. Sobbing loudly and releasing a real flood of tears, I mourned the lost love of my life. Again and again, I thought about that wonderful first kiss. It had seemed like the beginning, but it was actually the beginning of the end.

~

It was unbearably hot here compared to Scotland. I kicked off my shoes and walked the short distance to Kim's house in my bare feet. My jeans shorts, frayed at the bottom where I'd cut them off, were sticking to my legs, and I was sweating through my gray tank top. Ick. The humidity made me feel like I was being steamed alive. What wouldn't I give for a brisk Scottish breeze in my face.

Deep in my thoughts, I didn't notice that someone was walking behind me. So when I felt a tap on my shoulder, I shrieked, jumped sideways, and landed in a bush.

"Ow! Damn!"

"Sorry! Oh my God, I really am sorry." It was Ryan. "Sit down, you're bleeding."

Ryan put an arm around me, and I hopped on one leg to the curb. I took a seat while Ryan looked at my ankle. It was all scratched up.

"I really didn't mean to scare you, Sam. I thought you had heard me. I called your name a couple of times."

"Ow!"

Ryan was gently prodding my injury.

"If I had heard you, then why would I have gone on walking and not turned around to talk to you?"

"Well," he mumbled and looked uncertainly at me, "after our last conversation, I thought you maybe didn't want to talk to me."

If I hadn't known Ryan for such a long time, I would surely have been won over by his big blue eyes, but I wasn't falling for it.

"No, it's fine. I just don't really know what we have to talk about. I'm not sure we have all that much in common."

My newly straightforward, confident manner seemed to throw Ryan off track.

"Um . . . well, I just wanted to apologize . . . Somehow everything seems to go wrong when I talk to you. And I feel really bad about that."

"Here's an idea—just stop talking to me. Maybe then things will work out better."

I determined that my foot would probably not have to be amputated, so I stood up and hobbled on. I didn't mean to be harsh, but I figured the only reason Ryan wanted me was because I was hard to get.

"I'm not sure that would make a difference." He put his arm around me again. "Here, let me help you. Where are you going? To Kim's?"

I would have declined his assistance, but it really was very sore when I put any weight on my leg. On the other hand, I felt extremely stupid to be dependent on Mr. Perfect's help.

"Fine, help me. But only because it's your fault that I hurt myself!"

Before I knew what was happening, Ryan pulled my legs out from underneath me, like a groom carrying his bride over the threshold. He was laughing. "If this is all my fault, then I guess I'd better carry you the whole way. As compensation, so to speak."

"Ryan! Put me down! Seriously, let me go! Oh my God, this is so embarrassing."

"What? Normally, girls like it when I scoop them up like this."

"Yes, so now you see the problem. I don't go for players. Put me down!"

"I'm not a player. And anyway, I like carrying you."

"Please stop. You know, it might actually be possible to like you if you weren't always showing off!"

We had arrived at Kim's fence, and he gently set me down onto my feet. I felt a little guilty. I wasn't trying to hurt him, and I felt like maybe I'd been a little harsh.

"Listen, I'm sorry," I said. "I really mean that. I know your awesomeness would radiate upon me if we were a couple. But I'm just not into you that way."

He looked crestfallen, but he didn't say a thing. Instead, he turned slowly and walked away.

Irritated, I watched him go, wondering why I couldn't seem to stop myself from being rude to him.

But as I pushed open the gate to the fence, he turned around, smiling, and yelled, "You never know, things may change. Someday you might be into me!"

I hadn't even knocked on the door when Kim tore it open. "Can I believe my eyes? Did I just see Ryan carrying you down the sidewalk? How long has this been going on?"

Annoyed, I pushed my gossip-loving friend to one side and stepped into the hall.

"Kim, please, ugh, no. Why is it that everyone wants me to hook up with that idiot?"

Kim stuffed her towel into her bag, and then dug through the closet in search of sunscreen.

"I don't want you to hook up with him. I was just surprised . . . you know . . . because you don't usually let boys carry you through town."

"Yeah, well, I hadn't planned that out or anything. He snuck up on me, and I fell. I think I may have sprained my ankle."

"Are you all right? Will you be able to walk to the beach or do you just want to hang here?" Kim's worried voice reminded me why I loved her.

"Oh, it's not that bad. I can go, just as long as . . ."

"As long as?

"You carry me!" We both burst out laughing.

∾

I limped the short distance to the beach as inconspicuously as possible. The whole time, she sang Justin's praises.

"Oh, Sam, you can't imagine how sweet he is. He has little dimples when he laughs, and he's so thoughtful. He even calls when he says he'll call. And his kisses . . . I have never experienced anything like kissing him. He can really kiss!"

The more Kim went on, the sadder I became. She was so happy, and my heart was broken. With difficulty, I swallowed down the lump that had formed in my throat and tried to put on a happy face.

In my mind, I could see Payton wading through the icy river, sitting on the rock. His eyes had invited me to follow him. Back then, I thought that I was going to have the most exciting summer of my life. Well, it had definitely been exciting—but also so unbelievably painful! I couldn't stop thinking about him: that enigmatic Scot with his gold-tipped hair, that voice that went right into my soul, and his kiss that had moved the ground. How had he managed to first win my heart, then to tear it out of my chest and trample on it, all in such a short time?

I must have looked upset, because Kim's speech came to an end. "Oh, sweetie. How stupid of me. I'm going on and on, and you look miserable. What's wrong?"

I collected my thoughts while Kim laid out a blanket. When we sat down next to each other, she gave me her full attention. "Tell me everything. Start from the beginning. What did that Scottish guy do to you? Should I ask Justin to beat him up? He'd do it, you know."

There was no way Justin could strike down an almost invincible, immortal Highlander, and as I imagined the fight, I couldn't stop myself from letting out a little laugh. I didn't know what I'd do without Kim. She always managed to say something to make me feel better.

"It's a very long and very complicated story," I began.

And so I told her everything.

We were only interrupted once, when Lisa's crowd paraded past us and let out a few nasty remarks. But Kim, whose self-confidence had risen dramatically, shot back with a barbed joke, and the Barbies quickly went on their way.

When I'd finished, tears were running freely down my face and I had to blow my nose.

Afternoon had slid into evening, but the sun was still high and hot. The sky was so different here than in Scotland. Although it was often cloudy in Scotland, the sky radiated such a bright blue that you felt you could see all the way into space. Above Milford, there wasn't a cloud to be seen, but the blue seemed washed-out and milky. I wondered if that meant the air in Scotland was cleaner, with less smog. I was so wrapped up in my thoughts that I missed what Kim had just said.

A jab in my ribs catapulted me back to reality.

"Ow! What?"

"Are you listening to me at all? I said, I'm finding it difficult to believe all this stuff about a real curse. Could it be that they were only pulling your leg?"

That thought had occurred to me, too, but I couldn't deny what I had seen.

"No, I saw myself how quickly Payton's cut healed. That isn't something you can fake. And that guy, Alasdair, you should have seen how he looked at me. I don't doubt for a second that he wanted me dead." I wiped my eyes. "So what do you think I should do?"

Kim shrugged.

"I don't think there is anything you can do. You're back home now, where you're safe. Maybe you can just forget about everything. School's going to start soon, and that should help."

She was right—I had to move on. But my heart tightened, and all I could think was, How can I forget?

"Sam," Kim whispered, "let go. Forget Payton. Don't think about him anymore."

"But I love him! I can't breathe, I can't sleep, I don't want to live without him. Something connects us. The amount of pain he felt when he was close to me, I think it's a punishment for what he did. And I am sure that fate led me to him!"

Oh brother, I sounded just like Roy. Did I believe in fate? Destiny? There was only one logical explanation: I was losing my mind. That thought must have just occurred to Kim, too, because she was giving me a strange look.

"Sam, seriously, calm down. You're beginning to sound a little out there. Try to do normal things. Go on a date with Ryan. Go to the mall. Jeez."

This wasn't helping. Of course she couldn't understand. She didn't have weird dreams or magic necklaces to contend with.

I stood up. "I think I'd better go home. I need to clear my thoughts." I started walking away.

"Hey, Sam, don't be mad. I'm sorry—mentioning Ryan again was a stupid idea. Hey, wait," Kim yelled, stuffing everything back into her bag. She rushed after me.

I didn't feel like fighting with my best friend, but I certainly wasn't going to wait for her. I was still limping, though, so within moments she had caught up with me.

"I told you I was sorry!"

"I know. I'm sorry, too. I don't know what's wrong with me. There have just been so many crazy things happening lately. I do need to go, though. My dad said he has something important he wants to talk about. With my luck, he probably wants to let Ashley live in my room forever!"

"No way. They wouldn't do that to you. You'll have your little empire back to yourself very soon."

"Yeah, fortunately . . . See you!"

"Bye. I'll call you tomorrow!"

~

When I got home, my parents and Ashley were already having dinner. I grabbed a plate, served myself a large helping of chicken and corn on the cob, and sat down with them. The atmosphere between Ashley and my parents was still pretty chilly. They had the right to ground her, but I know she felt they were being unnecessarily harsh.

"Well, what did you want to talk about?" I asked with my mouth full, looking expectantly at the grumpy faces surrounding me.

My mom pushed her empty plate slightly away and smiled.

"Daddy and I have decided to go away for a few days. Alone. By ourselves!"

I stopped eating and waited for an explanation. Ashley looked up, too.

"As you know, it's our twentieth anniversary," my dad said. "And we have decided we deserve a little vacation splurge. That is, if we can rely on the two of you."

His eyes drilled their way first into Ashley, and then into me. What did he think we would do, I wondered. Burn the house down?

"We can't possibly leave until you two promise to get along. And that you will behave well. That means no cigarettes, no alcohol, and no boys. Is that clear?"

Ashley shrugged disinterestedly, as if this part of the speech weren't meant especially for her.

I nodded demurely. I wasn't planning to smoke or drink—and boys, well, I'd had enough of them anyway.

"Good. Then it's settled," Mom said. "We're leaving in two days."

CHAPTER 21

Sean stormed into Payton's room, knowing full well that he would find it empty. But when he saw for sure that his brother had already left, he lost his courage. He pushed his hair out of his eyes and looked around the room while he considered what to do next.

The bed was untouched, the door of the wardrobe was wide open, and several shirts were strewn carelessly on the floor. Payton's cell phone was on the table. He hadn't taken it with him deliberately, Sean realized. He'd shut his family out of his life.

Sean swore. Perplexed, he paced around the room, lifting up a few things here and there, trying to think what he would have done had he been in Payton's shoes. Where should he start looking for him? He'd said something about Fair Isle; maybe he was on his way there? He just couldn't believe that his brother, who had always been so close to him, had left without saying a word. He couldn't have gotten very far yet, Sean thought. After all, he had seen a light in Payton's room during the night.

He desperately needed to warn him.

In the morning, Sean had been cleaning up some broken glass under the table when suddenly a group entered the big hall. He had been about to back out and say hello when something they said caught his attention, so he pressed himself farther under the table and tried not to make a sound.

"Nathaira, I gave the others my word and I don't intend to break it." Cathal's voice echoed through the quiet room.

"Brother, I am not demanding that you break your word, but it can't harm us to keep a closer eye on the girl. Alasdair sees it the same way."

"And what does your fiancé say about your and Alasdair's plan?"

"Cathal, are you our chieftain, or are we to now turn to Blair?"

Some men in the room also voiced their approval for Nathaira's proposition. Cathal seemed worried about losing his authority should he turn against his sister, and he reluctantly agreed.

"All right, then. Some of the clan will fly to Delaware and find the girl. And I will be among them. No one will act without my approval on this matter."

Sean, who couldn't believe his ears, clenched his fist. A shard of glass dug deeply into the palm of his hand, and a thick drop of blood oozed out.

Cathal left, and the hall started to empty out. Only Nathaira and Alasdair remained.

Sean shifted around on his knees, trying to quietly find a less uncomfortable position. His head was spinning with questions: Should he tell Blair? Should he try to warn Payton?

Nathaira started to speak again.

"Alasdair, I must say I am disappointed with you. I would have thought that a man like you would easily be able to deal with a fledgling like Payton. And the girl—how could she get away from you?"

"We have changed, Nathaira. Things aren't like they used to be. That fight was more difficult than you can imagine."

⚬

How different he was than Blair, Nathaira thought to herself. She was so confused. Her feelings were beginning to return, too, and she was starting to feel desire again. She wanted to throw herself into the strong arms of her former lover. To feel passion for the first time in 270 years.

She approached Alasdair and put her hands around his neck. Their faces almost touched.

"When I look at you, I can't see any change," she said. "You are still the most handsome man I have ever seen. No other man awakens the same desire within me. The nights I spent with you are the ones that I dream of. What was so bad about the old Alasdair that you had to change?"

Her green eyes fluttered as her lips brushed his.

⚬

Alasdair fought for his composure. He wasn't made of stone. The way Nathaira was pressing herself against him made him almost willing to forget what she had done. Tenderly, he stroked her back, her hips, and finally, her rear. He pulled her close, letting her know that he felt desire, too.

Nathaira gasped.

"Alasdair, let's just forget everything, leave everything behind and start over." She was nearly breathless. "You're right. Things have changed. Cathal no longer needs an alliance with the McLeans. There is barely even a clan any longer. His power is declining, and sooner or later each of us will go our own ways. It is time for me to leave Blair. You and I, we could have a second chance. Can't you see that?"

Alasdair didn't know what to say. He wondered if Nathaira really meant it or if she was only playing with him. At that moment, he couldn't care less. He wanted her and, whatever she was after, he would have her first. He clasped her willing body in his muscular arms, kissing her and lifting her up. Without interrupting their kiss, he carried her to the door, but Nathaira freed herself from his embrace.

"Darling," she murmured, "I am so happy that we have each other again. But you must promise me one thing: you mustn't let that girl live, under any circumstance. You mustn't allow her to destroy everything, now that we have finally reunited. Please."

Alasdair's heart sank. So that was what she was after.

Then again, he thought, what did it matter? Soon Nathaira would belong to him. Who cared what happened to some girl as a result?

"Whatever you wish, my heart," he said. "Let us now go to my chamber!" He opened the door and pulled the giggling Nathaira behind him.

~

Slowly, Sean crawled out from under the table and wrapped a napkin around his bleeding hand. There was no way he could report his latest discovery to Blair. His brother would never believe that his fiancée was so treacherous. He ran from the hall, determined to warn Payton.

But with Payton gone and no way to call him, Sean had to come up with a new plan. He would have to ensure Sam's safety himself. He couldn't rely on Blair for that job. His brother was too much under Nathaira's influence. He wasn't sure Cathal would invite Blair to go to America with him anyway. Sean decided he'd ask Blair to track down Payton, and he himself would follow Cathal. Striding quickly out of Payton's room, Sean went to look for Blair.

He found his older brother sitting in the hall, immersed in reading a car magazine. So typical of Blair, Sean thought. The clan is falling apart, the curse is changing, his fiancée is in some other guy's bed—and what is Blair focused on? Finding a new car to polish and admire.

Sean sat down next to his brother and stonily waited. Blair put down the magazine, looking annoyed.

"Hello, Sean. What do you want?"

"I need your help."

"You want me to help you after getting me into so much trouble at the clan gathering?"

"Now hold on. I didn't get you into trouble!"

"Yes, you did. Cathal isn't talking to me because you stood up against him."

"It's a fact that we owe our loyalty to you, and not to him. And when in the last two hundred seventy years have we demanded that you stand up against your friend? Never before! But this time, he is wrong. You have to trust us."

"Whatever you say. So what do you want?"

"I need you to find Payton. I think he is on his way to Fair Isle."

"Why will you not go yourself?"

Sean had been expecting that question, so he'd already thought up an answer.

"For two reasons. First, it'll get you out of the line of fire here, and Cathal will calm down more quickly once he realizes he actually needs you. Next, I think you should clear things up with Payton. He is your brother, after all, and he needs you. You only know half the story—the clan's half— and I think Payton has the right to tell you his view of things, too. Then you, as our leader, can make the right decisions."

Blair rubbed his chin in thought.

"All right, then," he said. "But I'm telling you right now that if I don't find him on Fair Isle, then he can bugger off. Why are you in such a hurry to find him anyway? He has to be back in a week at the latest, because that's the deadline Cathal gave him."

Sean sighed in frustration. He was convinced that Payton would never come back to the castle if he didn't find what he was looking for. And Sean knew that Cathal was already preparing his trip to the United States; he wasn't waiting for Payton's information.

"You have to give Payton a letter from me. It's really important that he get it. Please, Blair, you just have to trust me!"

Blair cast a final glance at his brother and stood up, planting his hands on his hips.

"Fair enough. I have to admit that I have probably gotten a little bit lazy in the past two hundred years or so. A little adventure is not going to hurt me."

Sean was relieved. He had expected that he would have to use stronger ammunition with Blair and was surprised that he had won him over so quickly.

"Payton left his phone here, obviously on purpose, but don't you dare do the same. Take your cell phone with you, and get in touch with me when you've found him." He started to go, and then turned back. "Oh, and if possible, could you not tell Nathaira anything?"

"Pah, she's just as pissed off as Cathal. I haven't seen her since the clan gathering. I don't think it'll harm her to wonder where I am. She's a little too used to always having me at her beck and call. I'll leave immediately."

Feeling slightly calmer, Sean walked his big brother to his room. Then he booked his flight to the States and packed his things. His suitcase was ready. He just had to wait.

He peered into an old chest that he hadn't opened for many years. On top, tidily folded, lay his kilt; a brooch with the McLean coat of arms, cut from the finest horn; and a dark-plaid-and-fur bag. Farther down, he found what he was looking for. His *sgian dhu*. Almost tenderly, he stroked the small knife. The blade was just as sharp as it had been on the day his father, Fingal, presented it to him. He had been ten years old at the time, and the day was still as vivid in his memory.

~

It was the day of the big hunt. All of the McLean clansmen arrived at the castle at dawn, and even before the mist that covered the valleys had vanished, they rode off. It was Sean's first time along, and he didn't leave his father's side.

The dogs ran off in pursuit, and the horses followed, their hooves churning up hunks of moss. The birds nesting in the nearby rocks were frightened, flying off, shrieking across the morning sky. The damp and chill of the air crept under Sean's clothes. But the goose bumps he felt on his body weren't from the cold so much as from the excitement, the feeling of expectation. Fingal's hair had still been brown back then, with only a few white streaks at his temples. He was middle-aged, but he still seemed young and strong that day. Sean admired the way his father steered his horse—so easily it seemed effortless—using just the pressure from his thighs.

Sean, on the other hand, was finding it enormously difficult to keep the horse he was riding under control. Encouraged by the other animals' energy, his steed also wanted to gallop off. Strained, Sean tried always to keep his father in sight.

In front of them, a broad piece of land stretched out. On the other side was the dense forest. At that time, there had still been many thick forests in that part of Scotland. Rich forests, full of wild animals.

Only many years later, after the terrible defeat at Culloden, had the Duke of Cumberland ordered that all the forests in Scotland be cut down. He earned the nickname "Butcher Cumberland," for hunting down the survivors of the Jacobite Rising—and butchering them. He demanded that the forests be cleared so that the rebels couldn't feed themselves with wild animals or keep their fires burning with the wood. Without the forests, a great famine spread, which took many more lives than the war had claimed.

But at that time, on the day of the hunt, the forest still existed. As Sean and his father entered into the woods, the shadows danced upon them eerily, and their horses seemed to meld into their surroundings, the browns and blacks matching the colors of the tree trunks. They could only ride at walking speed.

Sean felt as if he and his father were alone in the world. The other hunters had all disappeared, and only seldom did the sound of a barking dog come from far off. Fingal stopped his horse, stood up in his stirrups and peered to the west. Sean tried to see what had caught his father's attention, but as hard as he tried, he could see only trees standing tall in front of them.

Fingal pointed to a stand of young oaks. A single ray of light fell through the dense treetops, streaming straight down to the ground. The damp moss glittered under a thousand dewdrops, and the first insects to greet the morning danced in the golden ray. The forest floor was lit up a vivid green and partway up the tree trunks. And there, the warmth of that one ray of sunlight was enough to chase away the mist, while elsewhere the ground was still hidden by a silver veil.

And then, a small movement. Now Sean could make out the shape. It was the stag that his father had already spotted. The majestic animal slowly came out from behind the tree and reached its muzzle into the air. It seemed to smell their scent.

Fingal didn't delay. He stretched his bow back in one powerful motion. His arm was steady, his muscles taut, his knuckles white. Sean took everything in. He could play it all back detail by detail, as if it had been recorded in slow motion. He thought his father was just as graceful and glorious as the stag.

Then the animal looked in their direction. Purring quietly, the arrow cut through the air and found its target: the stag's trembling chest. The creature did not seem surprised. Its front legs buckled, and it slowly tumbled to the ground, without taking its eyes off Fingal and Sean. Quickly, they dismounted and closed in on their prey. The noble animal lay in front of them, its chest rising and sinking with each fading breath.

Together they knelt, and Fingal motioned to his son to cut the animal's throat, to relieve it quickly from pain. Sean could see his face mirrored in the stag's dark, shiny eyes, and his own eyes widened when his father gave him the *sgian dhu*. Although the silver blade was very sharp, Sean used all his might to press it against the animal's pulsating neck. With a quick, powerful cut, warm blood streamed over his hand and splashed onto his kilt.

Fingal noticed Sean was trembling, and put his hand on his son's small shoulder in praise. They stayed like that for a while next to the beautiful animal, neither of them speaking a word. Only when two other hunters turned up was the intimate moment over. Sean had taken an animal's life with his own hands for the first time.

The rest of the day was a blur, but by the time the day was over, they had not only the stag but also many rabbits and two deer to take back to the castle. Sean washed the blood from his hands at the well and cleansed his new knife. He admired the *sgian dhu*'s horn handle, lavishly decorated with carvings of a hunting scene. Proudly, Sean stroked the blade, still able to sense the feeling of the dying stag under his hands.

For many years after that, Sean had carried the knife daily, wearing it in a sheath on his boot. He had grown up feeling its weight, balance, and its blade, until it felt like a part of him. But then, times had changed; the knife had become less important. It was put away, together with a few other mementos of that lost era.

Sean held the knife again, his hand immediately melded with the handle. It was as if the years the knife had been stored away simply didn't exist. He wasn't sure why he felt compelled to take the knife with him now. What was awaiting him, he wondered, that he felt a deep desire not to face the future without the deadly blade?

Sean didn't have an answer to this question, but in all his time on earth, he had learned to trust his instincts. He shrugged and slid the *sgian dhu* into the leather belt on his boot.

Chapter 22

My parents were away. They had left on their trip the day before. Ashley and I had grudgingly agreed to get along with each other for the rest of the week, but I was hoping it wouldn't even be that long. Uncle Eddie had called to say that he'd be finished with his tour in the next few days and would come to pick Ashley up as soon as he was done. She wanted to enjoy her last few days in Silver Lake at the beach, so she headed there as soon as my parents left the house.

I, on the other hand, was thrilled to be left alone. I wanted some peace. I still couldn't get Payton out of my mind. On the contrary. Day by day, it was getting harder for me to concentrate. I was even having trouble with the easiest of tasks, such as breathing, eating, or sleeping. I missed him so much. It felt as if a gaping hole were burning in my chest, constantly calling for emotional fuel and using up all of my energy.

So I looked for a distraction, and I persuaded myself that reading Grandma's diary would take my mind off things.

Deep down, I knew I was still obsessed with Payton and Scotland. I needed to find answers to some of the questions that were constantly running through my mind. I hoped the book would tell me something, anything, about the Camerons.

When I opened it, I was surprised to find that it wasn't a diary at all. I didn't quite know what it was, but going by the age of the paper in this book, it couldn't possibly have been written by my grandma.

Carefully, I turned to the first page and held my breath:

France, 1748

Dear Muireall,

I, Marta McGabhan, am writing this because I do not have the time to pass all that I know on to you. I've been taking care of you since you were born, and hoped to pass this along all the time, but I fear that even at eight years of age, you cannot possibly understand what I have to leave to you.

Therefore, I am writing down my knowledge in the hope that you will one day be capable of understanding your history. In the hope that you may be able to go the right way by these lines, to master your life, to look ahead and to always remember those from whom you descend.

I do not know where I should start, there is so much to say and I have so little time left. It is true; I am dying. This sickness has clenched me in its deadly claw for so long, and now seems to be dragging me mercilessly into the dark. For days I have been waiting for an opportunity like this, a moment in which I should be strong enough to hold the pen so that I could fulfill my most important duty.

As I write this, dearest Muireall, you are lying in your bed, only a short distance from me. Your calm breathing proves to me that you were strong enough to survive the fever. The roses are returning to your cheeks, your hair is shiny again and your body feels pleasantly warm instead of burning hot. Luck does not seem to be on my side, and it pains me greatly that I will leave you here alone, much more than the fever's pain hurts me. I am an old woman and am not fighting for my fate, but it is different for you. You have to live. You have to stay safe. I have, therefore, arranged for you a crossing to America in the next few days. Here in France you will not be safe enough without me. But in the Colonies, you should have nothing more to fear. Take this decision I made for you as a blessing to you, and face your destiny.

You, Muireall Cameron, are the daughter of Tomas and Isobel Cameron. Your great-grandfather was Lachlann Cameron, who in his youth burned with passion for your great-grandmother, Caitlin Stuart, although the two clans had long been enemies. The Stuarts have never forgiven the Camerons for stealing one of their daughters. That is exactly what they accused your great-grandfather of. But everyone knew that your great-grandmother was very happy to be stolen by Lachlann. And after Caitlin had become pregnant, her family banished her. But worse was to come when Lachlann was found murdered only a few days after his son, Eideard, had been born. Caitlin knew exactly that her own family must have been responsible for the murder; and instead of returning to her deceitful family after this act of treachery, she shortly afterward married Lachlann's brother, Manus Cameron. Since then, there has not been a peaceful day between the neighboring clans. Manus raised his brother's son as his own, and Eideard grew up to be a strong man. His father's murder smoldered in the young man's chest. Manus, on the other hand, wanted to hear nothing of revenge.

But Eideard couldn't quite tame his anger, and so it came that again and again animals disappeared from the Stuarts' herds. Not so many that it was obvious, but enough to give Eideard a sense of revenge against his neighbors. At that time, it was not advisable to move around in the borderlands between the two clans without protection. Shepherds or farmers who were going about their work there, many a time they never returned home. The feud went so far that there were real battles when the two opposing clans met.

The Stuarts had no intention of ending the feud either, just like Eideard. On the contrary. To get themselves into a better position, the chieftain, Kinnon Stuart, participated in the attack on Fair Isle. He captured a Fair Witch, hoping she would make him more powerful—perhaps even invincible. Kinnon took the eldest of the Fair Lasses to his castle: Vanora. He hoped her powers would already be strong enough to fulfill his wishes. The twenty-year-old witch was to be his weapon.

"Hey."

I was so caught up in what I was reading that Ashley's sudden appearance in the doorway made me jump. Reluctantly, I put the book down and looked up at her. "Oh, hi. I thought you were down at the beach. Soaking up the sun and all that."

"I was. But I started to get hungry. How about you?"

Admittedly, my stomach was rumbling, and when Ashley mentioned food, its insistence got worse.

"Hmm, yes, I could use something to eat."

Casting a regretful glance at the book, I went downstairs with Ashley.

"You know, you're getting sunburned," I told her. "You might want to be careful. You don't want to get blisters."

Ashley shrugged. "I wanted to make sure I was really tan before I head back home."

When I opened the fridge door, I was discouraged by the almost-empty shelves.

"Oooh, gourmet offerings," I said. "We have some ham here, and two eggs."

"There's bread and ketchup in the pantry," Ashley said. "What can we make with that combination?"

"An egg sandwich," I suggested without enthusiasm. "We could fry these up."

Ashley wrinkled her nose, but she nodded and got out a pan.

"But let's order in Chinese or Thai tonight," she said. "I think we'll starve to death if we don't get some meals delivered."

"Sounds good. Or we could go to the supermarket later today and pick some stuff up."

"I'd rather go back down to the beach. Let's have something delivered tonight, and then go shopping first thing tomorrow morning. I'd hate to waste this beautiful day at some stupid grocery store."

While Ashley cracked the eggs into the pan, I spread ketchup on the slices of bread, added some ham, and then decided to spread on another layer of ketchup for good measure. Now all we needed was the egg. I wished we at least had some sliced cheese, but that would have to go on the shopping list.

"How are those eggs coming along?" I asked. It felt nice to get along with her for once.

"Coming!"

Ashley let the hot eggs glide directly from the pan onto the bread; then she plunked the pan into the sink, where it made a loud hissing sound. As usual, I had badly burned my mouth on the first bite. It seemed I would never learn to wait to let my food to cool. I had to admit that our meal of leftovers wasn't nearly as bad as I had feared. Ashley also nodded in approval, and we emptied our plates. Using the last piece of bread, I wiped up the ketchup and stuck it in my mouth. Ashley threw her plate into the already overflowing sink.

"I guess we'll have to deal with these dishes sometime, too." My parents would have been appalled if they ever saw the kitchen in such a mess.

Ashley grabbed a bag of potato chips from the pantry, sauntered out the door, and headed back to the beach. I prodded the roof of my mouth with my tongue, drank another glass of cold water, and added my plate to the jumble in the sink. I was in a hurry to get back upstairs to Grandma's book.

I plopped back onto my bed, savoring the peace and quiet, and flipped to the last page I'd read.

The twenty-year-old witch was to be his weapon.

During this time, Eideard married a dull girl called Aigneis. Their marriage was blessed with three children: Anna, Kyla, and Tomas—your father.

Having children made Eideard slightly calmer. His pushing desire for revenge started to fade as he grew a bit older and wiser, and his love for his children made him feel more whole.

Things quieted down for the Stuarts, too. The beautiful Fair Witch, Vanora, did not have the desired abilities that the clan had hoped for. Again and again, she claimed that she was only able to use nature's powers, and never with malicious intent. Kinnon, who did not want to believe her, kept the woman prisoner in his tower for

*many years. After about ten years, his son, Grant, started to show
an interest in the beautiful prisoner. And although Grant was already married and his wife, Una, had only just given him a son, he
fell in love with the witch.*

*Not even his father, Kinnon, had any idea that his son went to
the charming prisoner every evening.*

*Vanora would have had the power to protect herself from Grant's
advances, but then she would have had to reveal her powers. And
she never wanted to become a tool for these men. That is why she
put up with Grant's abuse. Only by her tears could she express that
Grant was taking her against her will. In the beginning, Vanora
thought about taking her own life, but she did not want to give her
torturer that victory. And later on, when she realized that she was
expecting a child, she wouldn't kill herself and take the child's life,
too.*

I could hardly believe what I was reading. The woman
who had come to me in my dreams had really lived? I hadn't
quite bought Roy's story, but now, with it all laid out in
black-and-white in front of me, my whole body was tingling.
I felt an odd recognition, a connection. Everything in me
seemed to leap.

And if Vanora really had existed, then it was possible
that everything Payton had told me was true as well. I had already seen his quickly healing wound with my own two eyes.
And the scary Alasdair was also very present in my memory.
Still, far away from Scotland and its legends, back on dull,
safe American ground, I didn't know what to believe: Could
my grandma's book give me all the answers I was looking
for? And if so, what would that change for me? Could I

maybe forgive Payton then? I doubted that; after all, he was still a murderer.

I hated to call him that, to lump the sweet Scot who had given me my first kiss in with an ice-cold, calculating killer. As I'd gotten to know him, I really had thought I could see into his soul. And what I had seen there was sadness, loneliness, and pain—not a murderous streak.

Oh, Payton, I thought . . . Why? Why was everything so desperately complicated? The more I thought about Payton, the more I felt despair. I was miserable, and I started to weep. When some of my tears dripped onto the old writing, I quickly wiped them away.

After Vanora had borne the child, she was chased away by Grant that same night. Weakened by the birth, without having seen her baby even once, she was dragged by the guards outside the front of the castle and was threatened: she was never again to be seen on the Stuarts' land.

So Vanora fled over the border to the land of the Camerons, where she was fortunately received mercifully and looked after. And although Vanora was now free and could have gone where she wanted, she spent the rest of her life there. She could not leave her child too far from her. She had no idea what had become of the baby, but she felt that the child was alive. That knowledge and the hope to one day see her child again was enough to bind her to her new home. But at least one thing she had managed: never had she revealed her powers.

Dear Muireall, I am sure you are asking yourself what the witch's story has to do with you. It's simple: the night that made you an orphan, Vanora saved both of our lives.

How Vanora knew what would happen, I cannot tell you, but she came storming into your parents' chamber only a few minutes before all hell broke loose in the castle courtyard. She wakened Tomas, told him that she had a vision of an impending attack. Quickly, Tomas was ready and at arms, but when he arrived in the courtyard, it was almost too late to defend the castle. The massive gate swung open and a group of heavily armed men pushed into the courtyard. Only a few Cameron guards were on duty at night, and they were either surprised in their sleep or were still weaponless when the fight started. Tomas ran to his men, and Isobel, his wife, held you, her crying daughter, in her arms. Vanora warned her to get herself and the child to safety, to leave the castle through the small corridor behind the kitchen building, and then to hide. The witch's words echoed like thunder through Isobel's chamber, but your mother was so frightened, it was as if she had turned to stone. As quickly as Vanora had arrived, she disappeared again. Only the truth of her words remained, and already the first shouts and loud sounds of fighting penetrated the corridors.

I, Marta McGabhan, tried to push your mother to the door, but fear paralyzed her body. In the end, I did not know how else to help, so I pulled you out of her arms and ran to the kitchen with you. Now, at last, life returned to Isobel, and while I was getting you to safety, I could hear steps behind us. She was following me. The castle was dark, it was in the middle of the night, and it was difficult to get to the kitchen. I was just about to turn the corner when I could hear weapons clashing in front of me. Quickly, I pressed myself into a corner, and held you tightly close to me to muffle your crying.

Then warriors came around the corner. Their weapons reflected the little light that found its way around the walls. Your mother ran directly at them. The men chuckled at their surprise, and drove Isobel in front of them with their swords, making it quite clear what they were intending to do with her before they would kill her, just like the rest of the inhabitants of the castle. With a last glance at the darkness of our hiding place, your mother crossed her heart and tore away. She ran along the path we had come and reached the stairs that led up to the tower. The men stormed after their victim.

I had no time to wait for your mother, and I certainly did not want to wait to see whether the warriors would come back. As fast as I could, I ran to the kitchen. For fear of fire, the kitchen in this castle, as in so many, stood slightly apart from the other buildings, directly at the castle wall. The fighting was barely audible here, and therefore I dared to catch my breath for a moment. There was no sign of your mother. I pressed myself as flat as I could against the outer wall of the kitchen, hiding us behind a pile of barrels. I did not know what to do or where I could hide us, when I heard Vanora's voice. Not out loud, but in my head: "Run! The fight is lost! You are not safe here any longer. Save the child, save the Cameron bloodline. Get away from here. I will help you. I will give you a chance and a magic pendant. It will always warn you if you are in danger. But now delay no longer. Run!"

And when the voice in my head had made room again for the sounds of the night, I found a necklace in my hand. I put it around your neck to protect you, and I crept into the dark kitchen. The smell of food was in the air, and in the fireplace there was still a little fire. I quickly knotted a tablecloth to a bag and filled it with a loaf of bread, a large piece of ham, and some apples. I didn't dare take any more, for fear someone might soon find us. Then I felt my way along the wall to the back door. But the door was locked. Desperately, I tried to think what I could do now. There weren't any more sounds from the castle. The fight was apparently over. Maybe, I thought, I could just hide here until everything had passed.

Suddenly, lightning struck in the sky. I could see through the window that the whole horizon was covered in powerful blue lightning. An icy wind blew through the kitchen, tore the locked door off of its hinges and pulled at my gown. The copper pots above the fireplace banged loudly against each other and crashed to the ground. That noise would undoubtedly lead the warriors here! I grabbed my bundle, pressed you close to me, and stepped through the door, out into the darkness of the night.

Not far from the wall, tied to a small tree, was a gray mare. Where it came from or who had tied it there, I cannot tell you, even today. I can only assume it was Vanora. I had never sat on a horse before, and my fear of the animal was almost as big as my fear of the warriors. But I had been given a task: to protect you. Therefore, I didn't delay, didn't look back, but rode off with you. I rode the whole night and the whole next day, stopping only to feed you or let the horse drink some water. As if on a string, I was pulled further and further, until we finally reached the border to England many days later. I would have thought us safe there, but the pendant burned hotly in my hand, and I remembered that this meant we were still in danger. So we prepared to keep moving, and leave England as well.

Many weeks passed—weeks during which we were so cold we almost froze, so hungry we almost starved, and so tired we could hardly stay on our feet. But when we rode over a hill one evening, instead of evergreen fields and dark forests, we finally instead saw water on the horizon. Behind that lay France, and for the first time since we had left our home did the pendant cool down.

I shut the book. With trembling fingers I put my hand up to my throat. The necklace lay cool and hard in my hand. I couldn't believe it. This was real life—my life. Was I going crazy? Everything in my world was turning upside down, and then around and around again.

It was difficult to summon the courage to keep on reading. The handwriting of the nanny, Marta, got weaker and weaker from line to line. Anxiously, I flipped ahead a few pages. This was obviously someone else's writing. The letters were no longer small and jagged but large, energetic, and strong.

Boston, 1760

I am Muireall Cameron. Twelve years ago I came here, to this beautiful country, with this book, my pendant, and only a handful of other belongings. My nanny, Marta, was unfortunately not able to live long enough to see my embarkation to this new world, but in her place, Sarah accompanied me. She looked after me on the boat and when we came on land together, she decided to stay with me. Even today, Sarah is my good friend and companion. But we are now going separate ways, as I have recently married and gave birth to a healthy daughter yesterday.

That is why it seems fitting for me to fill another page of this book with my story. I will not forget from whom I am a descendant and my children are also not to forget. I will write down all of my children as long as I live and hope that one day someone else will carry on with this task, so we keep track of our descendants. The cowardly, unnecessary, and brutal murder of my ancestors did not destroy the Cameron clan; it only weakened us. One day there will be just as many Camerons in the world as there were in the past, and then, maybe, the time will come to take our revenge for the injustice. that was inflicted on us.

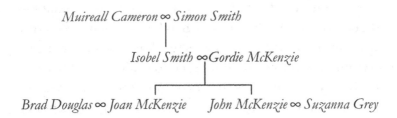

Muireall Cameron ∞ Simon Smith

Isobel Smith ∞ Gordie McKenzie

Brad Douglas ∞ Joan McKenzie   *John McKenzie ∞ Suzanna Grey*

The family tree Muireall had so carefully started here now filled almost the entire book. Page for page, she—and then later someone else—had filled in the Cameron family tree. It was hard to count, there were so many names, but it looked like about ten generations, I thought. Some branches took up whole pages, they'd had so many children; others ended in a single branch. But all in all, I could comfortably say that the Cameron line had definitely not died out. Still, my hands were trembling when I turned to the last page.

The ink was still dark blue, not faded like it was on the first pages. In my grandma's pretty handwriting was written:

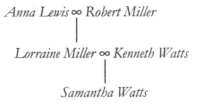

Anna Lewis ∞ Robert Miller

Lorraine Miller ∞ Kenneth Watts

Samantha Watts

So it was true. I was a descendant of the Camerons. But I wondered why it mattered after such a long time. And I asked myself, was it fair to condemn Payton for something he'd done in such a different era?

Over and over, his kiss went through my head. That kiss had been real and full of love; I had felt it. Again, tears rose in my eyes. I was head over heels for that unusual Scot, and everything I had found out seemed to indicate that what he and Roy had told me was the truth. And then there was the necklace from Grandma's attic. I shut the book and chewed my lip.

Payton!

I couldn't dwell in my thoughts because the picture of him kept pushing itself to the front of my mind. I could still feel his hand reaching out for me, could hear his voice singing that beautiful old love song, could see the depth of the pain in his eyes when he got too close to me.

Payton!

Sobbing, I threw myself onto my bed. The day slowly faded, dusk turning to dark, and Payton's smile playing in my dreams.

CHAPTER 23

The motel on the South Dupont Boulevard was pretty run-down. But the location—right on Route 113—was convenient, and Cathal, Nathaira, and Alasdair preferred to avoid crowds. For what they were planning, it was better to have few witnesses. They had arrived in Delaware the day before, and it hadn't taken them long to track down Samantha's address. They planned to use the day to spy on her home. Should they find the opportunity, they wouldn't hesitate to grab the entire family.

They had been waiting for over an hour near the house in their dark-blue rental van when at last, the front door opened. Alasdair nodded. That was the girl who had gotten away from him. A second girl, blonde and slim, came out. The two of them got into a car parked in the driveway and drove off. Alasdair was about to follow, but Nathaira insisted that they wait for the girls to return and, in the meantime, see who else might be home.

She pulled open the van door and stepped out, yanking her long dark hair over one shoulder as she strode to the house. She knocked—once, twice—but no one answered, so she strolled back to the van.

The three of them had almost fallen asleep from boredom when the car finally rolled up into the driveway again. The blonde was carrying an armful of bags, including one that looked like it had come from a fast-food restaurant. They watched as Samantha then got out of the car, heavily laden with more large shopping bags. She nudged the car door shut with her hip and balanced her load. With a loud bang, the front door slammed behind them.

"And now what?" Alasdair asked.

"We'll wait," Cathal answered.

"Wait for what? Let's grab the girl and get away from here," Nathaira said.

"No," Cathal said. "I want to know who that other girl is, the blonde. We don't need any witnesses."

"We could just take the both of them," suggested Alasdair. "Then we wouldn't have to worry about what Blondie might say later. And who knows, maybe she is a Cameron, too."

"But she doesn't look like a Cameron."

"Well, Cathal!" Nathaira's voice was full of contempt. "Do you believe that a family resemblance would be so obvious after so many years?"

"That Samantha certainly shows a strong resemblance."

"That's just a coincidence. You cannot rely on that."

"Still," Cathal said. "We are going to wait!"

Nathaira gave in, crossing her arms in a huff.

About a half hour later, the door opened again. This time, only the blonde came out. She looked around, as if checking to see whether anyone was watching, and then she sat down on the step in front of the house and lit a cigarette. She breathed the smoke deeply into her lungs and blew it out slowly. She kept glancing over her shoulder, but nobody disturbed her. The cigarette had almost burned down to the filter when she jumped up and quickly stamped the cigarette out.

Samantha opened the door and called, "Ashley! Uncle Eddie's on the phone."

"OK! Tell Dad I'm coming."

With that, the two of them disappeared into the house again.

The three secret observers in the van were content. Now they knew that the girls were related, and that meant that they had to grab both of them; no Cameron should get away. They still didn't know how many other Camerons might be romping around Milford. There was no sign of the girls' parents. But they hoped the two girls would have some answers to their questions.

~

"Hey, Sam," Ashley said. "My dad said that he'll probably manage to get here by tomorrow night. At the latest, by the day after tomorrow. I know this might sound insane, but I'd really like to see Ryan again to say good-bye. Maybe I can get a little closure. Is it OK if I skip the Chinese food and go out tonight?"

Huh, I thought. Apparently, our relationship really had improved; otherwise she would have never asked me for permission. And since I was definitely cured of Ryan Fever, I thought she should at least have a chance to smooth things out with him. I had firsthand experience with broken hearts and sudden endings.

"Sure, no problem, go ahead. I called Kim awhile ago, and she said she might come over in a little bit, anyway."

I was worried that Kim might show up with Justin, but I figured that was still better than having to spend the evening alone. Meanwhile, my anger toward Payton had given way to feelings of pure helplessness. What if I were to forgive him, I asked myself. Could I accept the fact that the times had been different back then, that he hadn't really had any choice in the murders? I loved him so much that I wanted to forgive him. But if I did, what would that change? It seemed futile. I was, after all, on a different continent. I wanted to tell him that I loved him, that I didn't give a damn about his curse. I just wanted to be with him.

But, of course, it wasn't that easy. Payton had said that I was changing the curse, and no one had a clue what would come of that. It sounded like his family thought that they would all die; that's why they wanted me gone.

Since I'd been home, I had pushed away that thought—that someone might actually want to do me or my family harm. I knew I should have talked to my parents about it, but I didn't know what to say. Gosh, Mom and Dad, I met this immortal Highlander, and guess what, we're going steady?

Well, anyway, the situation was totally screwed up. School was starting again soon, and I had no idea how I was going to manage that. I could just imagine what would happen when Mr. Schneider asked me about Scotland; instead of answering his questions, I'd probably burst into tears.

"I'm off. Could be late," Ashley said, poking her head into the room. Whoa, I thought, she looked fantastic! I hoped Ryan would leave me in peace after seeing her.

"Good luck," I called after her, but she was already gone.

~

The three Scots across the road jolted to attention when the blonde girl—apparently called Ashley—exited the house and started walking down the street. The night was hot and still, and totally quiet, except for the growling and hissing of two cats. Without another word, the three slipped out of the van and followed the girl.

Cathal's steps were almost silent as he got closer and closer. When Ashley was only one step ahead, he grabbed her in a flash. She put up a struggle, but that came to a halt when Alasdair rushed in to subdue her. She tried to scream, but Cathal pressed his hand strongly against her mouth. Together the men shoved her into the van. Nathaira got in behind Ashley and closed the door. Cathal and Alasdair straightened their clothing, glancing around to make sure no one had witnessed their little interlude. Then they got in the van as well.

The street remained quiet. Only from inside the van could Ashley's terrified cries be heard. The van slowly rolled down the street before turning left, out of sight.

~

Two trembling figures peeled themselves out of the shadows behind the trash cans, mouths open in disbelief.

"Quick," Kim said. "You have to follow the van. I'll go to Sam to get help. Try to stay behind them for as long as you can, and be careful. Don't let them know you are following them!"

Kim gave Justin a push in the right direction. She could hardly believe what they had just seen. She hoped Justin would be able to catch the van and tail it for a while. She didn't think they'd seen his car. She sprinted to Sam's house and rang the doorbell urgently.

∽

I turned down the music when I thought I heard the doorbell. Someone was pressing the button repeatedly.

"All right, all right, I'm coming!" God, I said to myself, why was Kim in such a hurry?

When I opened the door, Kim practically fell on top of me. Her face was white, her voice shaking.

"Quick, call the police! Ashley has been kidnapped."

Before I fully understood what she'd said, she grabbed the phone in the kitchen and started punching in the numbers.

"What? Calm down! What happened?"

I took the phone away from her and pressed it back into the wall mount.

"Wait a second, Kim. Tell me what's going on!"

She pushed me away and grabbed the receiver again. Only when I shook her by the shoulders did she snap out of it enough to fill me in.

"Two men just dragged Ashley into a van. Justin is following them. We have to call for help!"

"What men? Did you see them? What did they look like? What kind of car was it?"

"A van, a dark-blue van. It all happened so quickly I didn't think to get the license plate. The one guy I couldn't see very well, but the other one had blond shoulder-length hair. And he was tall, really tall!"

My knees buckled. I thought I was about to pass out. I clapped my hands to my face and let myself slide down the wall. My thoughts were whirling: Could this be happening? Had they followed me to America? That seemed impossible. But what else could it mean?

"Kim . . . I think that was Alasdair Buchanan."

As soon as I said the name out loud, I knew I was right. And if Alasdair had followed me here, then we were all in great danger. In mortal danger! The pendant flamed hot, burning against my skin.

CHAPTER 24

Fair Isle

The little boat was rocking under Payton's feet, and he jumped onto the jetty. He thanked the fisherman who had brought him to Fair Isle and waved to him as he departed, watching for a moment as the small boat bobbed up and down like a waterbird.

Fair Isle. Here, at last, he should be able to find some answers, to find out more about the curse, and if there was any way to lift it. The waves were pounding high, and the white foam from the sea was washed far up onto the beach. A cold wind blew into his face, but Payton didn't feel a thing.

Since Sam had left him, his world had become dull again, with less and less feeling every passing day. As if the weather were adapting to his mood, the sky was full of dense clouds. The sun was nowhere to be found, and even the time of day seemed to have lost its way, getting stuck somewhere between morning and evening.

Payton walked along the jetty, across the wet sand, up to a stony embankment forming a natural dam. Payton climbed up the steps hewn into the stone and got his first view of his destination.

The island was small and sparsely populated. There was only one village, and the people lived just as their ancestors had for hundreds of years—raising sheep and catching fish. Their little stony huts were placed haphazardly, as if a giant had dropped them from above. Each one faced a different direction. Some roofs looked badly damaged, bowed down almost to the ground. They were mixed in with newer-looking houses, which were painted white.

In the middle of the village, Payton could see the largest building on the island, next to a large square, surrounded by trees. A kind of church, he thought, or maybe a temple of some sort.

A narrow path led from the water to the village, and Payton decided to follow it.

The first buildings he passed seemed deserted, with doors that looked like they hadn't been opened in ages. The large square was empty too. There was no light through the windows of the houses and no smoke rising from the chimneys. He was getting a bit worried that he'd come here for nothing.

Yet the village didn't seem to be completely abandoned, as everything was well kept and tidy. In the front gardens, the last summer flowers were blooming next to precisely laid-out herbal beds, and the paths in the village had recently been swept. Here and there, bean plants had sent their runners creeping up rods; the plants looked healthy, sure to provide a good harvest.

Payton knocked at every single door, but not one was opened.

Disappointed, he sat down on a bench and waited. His gaze landed upon his arm, and he studied the scar that his last trip with Sam had left him with. It was hardly visible any longer, but he stroked it with his finger and wished for that moment when he could still feel pain, when he had still been near Sam.

He had been daydreaming for quite some time when he heard voices from a distance. A short while later, some people appeared under a grove of trees at the edge of the village. The men were pulling a cart piled high with peat. The women carried baskets hanging from their arms, and their children were running around behind them. It must be a big family, or a group of friends, he thought, from the way they were laughing and joking with each other.

A little boy, not more than five years old, grabbed an apple from one of the baskets and quickly hid behind his friends. A woman raised a finger in reprimand, but she didn't look angry. It was clear that she loved the little group of children.

Bit by bit, they all made their way into the square. Payton stood up, and when the villagers got closer, he stepped forward in a friendly manner.

"*Latha math!*" he greeted the people. Curious eyes followed him when he approached the closest man.

"My name is Payton McLean. I have a puzzle in my life, and I'm hoping that you will be able to help me. I'm looking for someone who can answer my questions about a woman called Vanora who lived on this island long ago. Do you know whom I should turn to?"

The man returned Payton's greeting, but shook his head.

"*Tha mi duilich*," he apologized. "We can't help you. But there might be someone who can. Can you tell us more about yourself?"

Payton didn't want to reveal anything, but he could tell the villagers weren't going to give him much access unless they felt they could trust him.

"I am Douglas, by the way," the man said. "It's too late to find someone to talk to now anyway. It's about to get dark."

"But it's important."

"Hmm. How about this. We could use some help unloading the peat. We have a lot of work ahead of us. In exchange, I'll give you a roof over your head for the night. What do you say?"

Douglas turned his back on Payton and stepped toward the other men, who were already lifting the heavy lumps of peat off the cart. Most of the women had already disappeared inside, and the children had gathered around one of the huts, where they were listening attentively to an old woman's story.

Payton didn't need long to think about it. He had to find answers. And if that meant being tested by the villagers, well, he would dig up all the peat on the island if he had to.

He set down his jacket and his bag, and rolled up his sleeves. Then he grabbed the thick, heavy bundles one by one, and lifted them off. Two of the men started hacking the big bundles into smaller hunks. When the cart was empty and the pile of peat had grown high, they began stacking these smaller hunks in front of each hut.

Payton worked along without complaint. After a while, the curious glances from the working men stopped. A white-haired woman approached the men. As she got closer, Payton realized that she couldn't be older than twenty, but her hair was such a light blonde that it seemed to be white. Her tender beauty seemed almost spooky. She brought refreshments—a big hunk of cheese, some apple slices, and bread that was still warm from the oven.

"Tapadh leat," he said in thanks.

"Where are you from?" the young woman asked. She lowered her head so that her hair fell like a protective veil in front of her face.

Payton noticed that the other men were watching him, and he didn't know whether it was a good idea to talk to the girl. He was just about to murmur a short answer when she grabbed his arm.

"I can see a lot of what you aren't saying," she said. "But if you are looking for answers, you must trust me. Ignore the others. Only I can help you! I will wait for you. Come to my hut tomorrow at dawn. Then we will talk."

She turned and disappeared into her hut.

Payton ate his bread and drank some cool water. He worked with the men until darkness fell.

"Payton! Thank you for your help. Come now, we deserve a decent meal and a warm bed."

Douglas clapped Payton on the shoulder and led him to the outskirts of the village. There, in a hut that stood alone, a warm, inviting glow illuminated the windows. Payton had expected to find Douglas's wife waiting there, but the hut was empty.

"You live here alone?" asked Payton, the smell of fried meat drifting into his nose.

"Yes, like most of us here. But the women from the village look after all of us. They cook together and every hut gets its share. Just like with the peat. And I suppose with everything else, too."

After the meal, Payton asked, "Why do you not look for a wife?"

"Well, Payton. Here on Fair Isle, it's a slightly different view of marriage than in other parts. Here, the women decide on the man they want. They are the wise people in our village. But even they can't decide freely. They follow the predictions and prophecies made by our ancestors."

"And the white-haired woman—who is she?"

"Her name is Uisgeliath."

Payton's heart leapt. Uisgeliath was the woman Roy had told him to find. Payton had been afraid to ask for her by name when he'd first arrived on Fair Isle because he thought it might scare the villagers off.

"She protects our past," Douglas said. "And she has an eye that opens up your soul. Nobody can lie to her. That is why it is important that you talk to her tomorrow."

"But why were the men watching me so closely when she was talking to me?"

"Well, they wanted to see if you could withstand her eye."

"And . . . did I?"

"Yes, otherwise you wouldn't be here."

Douglas yawned. "It's getting late. You can sleep over here on my bed. I will sleep in the chamber over there." He started to lie down on a roughly hewn bench.

Payton tried to refuse, but his host declined. In the end, he took the bed, but he remained wide awake. When the moon broke through the layer of clouds, the little hut lit up slightly through its only window. Payton shut his eyes and pictured Sam in front of him. Sam lying next to him on the beach that night. How when she woke up, the moonlight had reflected in her eyes. Payton had felt her love, so despite the pain, he had reached out for her hand. And now, just as then, he wasn't to find any sleep.

~

The next day started with a big surprise. It was still dark, but the little village was already bustling. There had been another new arrival, and it turned out to be Blair. When he had finally convinced the villagers that he was Payton's brother, he was led to Douglas's hut.

"Blair? What are you doing here?" Payton asked when his brother appeared in the doorway.

He made introductions, and all three of them sat down for a quick breakfast. Payton hadn't forgotten his promise to meet Uisgeliath at dawn.

Blair reported that he'd been sent by Sean, and he handed over the letter Sean had given him.

With each line Payton read, his face turned paler until he set the page down on the table and banged his fist.

Curious, Blair picked up the letter and skimmed over the few lines. "What is this? Why would Cathal do this? He gave us his word!"

"Sean is going to try to stop him," Payton said. "He writes that he is going to follow Cathal and his crew to the United States. But he doubts that he will be able to prevent what they have planned."

"Yes, I can read, too. But why didn't Cathal wait for your return, as he promised?"

"Because he isn't the one who makes the decisions, it's Nathaira. I'm sorry, Blair, but it's true. And she wanted Sam to die right from the start!"

Blair stood and laid his hand on his brother's shoulder. They both knew that whatever Nathaira wanted, she got.

"Then we mustn't lose any more time. We will look for your answers and then get in touch with Sean. In the meantime, we have to trust that he'll find a way to keep your Sam safe. Come on!"

They said a hasty thank-you to Douglas and rushed to Uisgeliath's hut. She had obviously been expecting both of them, as there were already three steaming mugs of mulled wine on an old oak table. She gestured to the brothers to sit down.

"Last night I questioned my ghosts, and they agreed to accompany you to see Beathas," she told them. "She is the village's eldest. Nobody knows how old she really is. She has just always been here." She took a sip of wine. "You must know by now that our people have many secrets. We have often been hunted, caught, or threatened. That is why our ancestors found it necessary to create a secret place for our history to be safely kept. Beathas is the warden."

She drained her cup and motioned for the brothers to do the same.

"We should get on our way immediately."

Uisgeliath wrapped a woolen cloak around her shoulders and led them out of the village. She walked silently in front of them, moving so smoothly she almost seemed to float over the rocky ground. Looking neither left nor right, she seemed to find her way easily. When they reached the coast at the north of the island, Uisgeliath ordered them into a small rowboat. It rocked and lurched and almost sank completely under the weight of the three of them.

Although Uisgeliath seemed so delicate and small, she insisted on rowing. With powerful strokes, she navigated the boat into the current a short way from the coast. Then she pulled in the oars and let the current take over for several minutes.

As if pulled by an invisible hand, the boat steered directly toward a dark spot on the rocky coast. They could see a split in the rocks, a crack that looked narrow from outside but that widened inside to a large and very dark cave, and Uisgeliath took up rowing again. They could hear only the swishing of the water and the echo of the oars dipping, dripping, and dipping again.

Uisgeliath lit a lantern. The light reflected eerily from the damp walls of the cave, creating dancing shadows on the rocks. Again and again, the cave branched out, until it became an underground labyrinth. Payton hoped the white-haired woman knew the depths of the island well. He was close to losing his own sense of direction entirely.

Neither Payton nor Blair had any idea how long they had been traveling through the dark passages, but when the water became shallower and ended in an oval basin, they got out of the boat. They no longer needed the lantern, as a bright light shone before them. They stepped across sparkling turquoise stones into a large templelike dome. Separated rays of sunshine reached the ground through tiny holes in the ceiling.

Uisgeliath stopped.

"Here we are. I will wait at the boat. Beathas is expecting you."

And, as if on cue, an ancient lady came toward them. Beathas's skin was white as paper, almost translucent. But despite her obviously advanced age, she was standing up-right and looking them up and down with bright, alert eyes.

"*Latha math*," she said politely. "Good day. I have been expecting you. Please follow me."

Beathas went ahead of them. They crossed through the large room and ducked down through a low archway. A library was certainly not something Payton had expected to find in a sea cave, yet there it was. Illuminated by rows of neatly placed candles were countless rows of books and bound papers. A large table, with chairs around it, filled the center of the room. A book was open on the table.

She invited them to sit down and pushed the book to Payton.

"Here is everything that is left of Vanora. It isn't much, but I think you will find what you are looking for here. I wish you the best of luck."

Payton started to ask the old woman a question, but she shook her head before he could utter another word.

"I can't help you. You must find out the truth yourself."

Then she disappeared through the arched door. The two brothers looked at each other for a moment.

Payton didn't want to waste any time. He bent over the book with focus, trying to make out the old words. The first pages appeared to be Vanora's family tree. Then there was something written by her father recounting the day that his daughter was taken from the island together with the other seven girls. He only glanced at this entry. That wasn't what he needed.

"Somewhere in these papers, there has to be something about the curse," Payton murmured.

Their courage faded with every page until they came to a collection of old letters, all signed by Vanora. The first letters described her arrival at the castle of her kidnapper and of his hope that she would use her powers as a weapon against his neighbors. She wrote that she certainly did not intend to do as he wished, and she swore she'd never show him how powerful she really was.

In the next letters, she seemed discouraged. She had suffered terrible punishment for claiming to have no powers. And she had heard of a plan to lock her in a tower until she did what the chieftain wanted her to do. Then there were no letters for a very long time. Payton guessed that she didn't have the chance to write when she was imprisoned in the tower.

When she next wrote, she had given birth—to a daughter, the letter said—but the father had taken the baby for himself and chased Vanora away. She hated the father. Not only had he stolen her child, but he had forced himself on her. In the end, she had found shelter in a neighboring land and still hoped to see her daughter someday. With that, the last letter ended.

Payton's desperation rose.

"There are only a handful of papers left, and we haven't found out anything!"

Still, they carefully unfolded another piece of paper. And it was exactly what they had been looking for.

Vanora had written down one of her visions. She had seen the day of her death. To avenge a terrible injustice, she would pronounce a curse upon her enemies. But then she herself would die at the hand of her own daughter. The curse would last for many years, even centuries, until the injustice was made up for by a selfless sacrifice of love. And her daughter would be the one to lift the curse.

Payton banged his fist on the table.

"Damn! What does this all mean? This can't be right."

Blair nodded. "Yes, you are right. The witch was wrong! She cursed us, and it lasted as long as she predicted, but her daughter didn't have anything to do with it."

Payton stared at the rows of candles, deep in thought. "It might be useful to know who her daughter was," he mused.

"It wouldn't matter. She's long dead by now and will hardly be able to help us."

"But if Vanora was right, then her daughter should still be alive, shouldn't she?"

"Payton, face the truth. She was wrong. We both know who killed Vanora. It was Nathaira, not Vanora's long-lost daughter."

"I know. But I just can't believe all of this was for nothing!"

"I know how difficult it is for you. Nevertheless, we should try to reach Sean. Then we'll decide how to proceed."

Payton dug his face in his hands. He couldn't just swallow his disappointment and move on. He knew there had to be a logical explanation. He wished she had written down who the child's father was, or even which clan had kept her prisoner for so many years.

The letters had made it clear that she'd found shelter with the Camerons. And she had mentioned finding refuge with one of the neighboring clans. That meant that she had fled from either the McLeans, the McInrees, the Stuarts, or the McDonalds. The only place he could rule out for certain was his own home, if only for the reason that they didn't have a tower. And his father had been a peaceful man, who would never have done such terrible things.

He supposed he would have to talk to Cathal again, to see if he had any ideas. After all, the Stuarts' castle did have a tower dungeon. And they had always had bad relationships with their neighbors. Still, it seemed unlikely, Payton thought. He would have heard something if Cathal's family had ever caught a Fair Witch.

That left the McInrees and the McDonalds. Maybe Sean would be able to help. At the time of the curse, his brother had an eye on almost all the girls in the land. A witch's daughter would surely have caught his attention.

Feeling more confused than ever, Payton stood up. The brothers took their leave from Beathas. As they turned to go, the Wise Woman reached for Payton's hand and whispered, "When you understand the truth, darkness will devour you—but you will be happy."

The old woman's strange words fluttered around in Payton's thoughts on the boat ride back, but he didn't have much time left for thinking. The brothers had hardly regained solid ground when Blair ran off and found a young fisherman to take them back to the mainland. Then after a disconcerting phone call with Sean, they were on their way to Delaware.

CHAPTER 25

Delaware

Just like the Stuarts who had arrived the day before, Sean had to find out Samantha's address before he could make his way there. No sooner had he arrived than he witnessed Cathal and Alasdair kidnapping a young woman who was a complete stranger to him. He had no idea what they could want from her. Totally confused, he followed them to a motel at the outskirts of the town, where he parked directly next to the van.

He was steaming mad as he stepped up to the three of them, just as they were dragging the girl out of the van.

"What is going on here? Are you crazy?"

They were not at all happy to see him.

Nathaira was particularly unhappy. "Are you spying on us? What in the world?"

She swore loudly at Sean and went for his neck, but Cathal's thundering voice stopped them in their tracks.

"Quiet! We can discuss everything inside. We need to get the girl off the street before somebody sees us!" He pushed Ashley roughly, and she stumbled forward.

They led her up the metal staircase on the outside of the motel that accessed the rooms on the fourth floor. Ashley had stopped struggling and looked utterly terrified. They shoved her onto a bed and tied her to a bedpost. Her eyes were wide-open with fear and she was quite pale.

Sean felt the urge to wrap the girl in his arms and comfort her. He also wanted to attack the others, to make them pay for deceiving him and the rest of the clan. But he did neither, knowing that wouldn't be a smart approach. Instead, he demanded answers. "You need to tell me right now what you are doing!"

Cathal, who desperately wanted to avoid a nasty fight, positioned himself between his nagging sister and the unwelcome new arrival. "Steady now. Everyone sit down. First of all, why are you here?"

Sean knew he needed to keep a clear head to represent Payton properly. So, he did as he was told and sat down. Alasdair and Nathaira reluctantly took a seat, too.

"Payton sent me to keep an eye on Samantha," Sean lied. "He wants to stop her from doing anything stupid, or doing us any harm without meaning to."

Cathal seemed to buy that answer, but Nathaira looked skeptical.

"But now, you have some explaining to do," Sean said. "Have you become criminals who kidnap little girls?"

"Rubbish! We have to find out why the curse is changing, so we need Samantha," Alasdair explained.

"Have you actually taken a close look at the girl? That isn't Samantha," Sean said.

"We know that, you idiot," Nathaira said. "But she is related to Samantha and therefore is also one of the Camerons."

Sean turned his attention to the beautiful prisoner. "Is that true? Who are you?"

"I . . . I . . . Please . . . let me go, please . . . I don't know why I'm here!" Ashley cried.

Nathaira's anger boiled over. She slapped Ashley, who was now sobbing, in the face and yelled, "Answer his question or things will only get worse!"

"Stop it," Sean said. "Can't you see she's scared?"

"And since when have you been a saint?"

Sean turned to Ashley. "Who are you?" His tone was kind. He wanted her to see that he wasn't like the others.

"I'm . . . I'm . . . Ashley Bennett. What do you want from me?"

She looked at Sean.

"Nothing will happen to you, I promise," he said, trying to comfort her.

"You'd better not make a promise you can't keep," Nathaira snapped.

"What are you going to do to her?" Sean asked. "Were you planning to kill her, just because she might be descended from the Camerons?"

"We will see," Nathaira said. "First, we need to talk to Samantha. That is the top priority."

"Yes, but it's too late for that today. First thing in the morning, we will deal with her," said Alasdair.

As all the others nodded approvingly, Sean kept his thoughts to himself. He certainly wouldn't give up now. Again, his eyes wandered to the frightened prisoner. It was odd, he thought, given the situation. But when he looked at her, he felt a slight stirring of desire.

"Well then," Cathal said, "Nathaira and I will go to our room, while the two of you look after our guest." The two siblings left for the room next door.

Sean didn't want to share a room with Alasdair, but he wasn't about to leave the poor innocent girl alone with him. Alasdair didn't seem to mind. He poured himself a glass of water and plunked down in front of the TV.

Unsure what to do, Sean stood opposite Ashley. He didn't think it was necessary to keep her tied up, but he knew Alasdair would disagree. That hard warrior wasn't known for being merciful. He sat down next to her carefully, so as not to intimidate her further. Shaking, she turned away from him.

"I'm Sean. You needn't be scared of me."

"But you are with this group here, aren't you?"

"Well, it depends. Actually, I came here to help Samantha, but I presume you will not understand everything just now."

"Sam? What does she have to do with this?"

"Ashley, are you related to Sam?" Sean asked hesitantly.

The fear he felt as he waited for her answer confused him. The whole girl confused him. Her large eyes, her golden hair, and her shapely body were awakening feelings in him, feelings that he hadn't experienced in a very long time.

In his first life, as he frequently called the time before the curse, he had been a skirt-chaser, running after all the girls in the village, stealing more than a kiss from a lot of them. He didn't think he had ever been in love; he was too jumpy for that. But then everything had changed, and he wasn't allowed to be in love.

He had almost completely forgotten that tingling feeling in his belly he used to get around a pretty girl. But he sensed that his feelings for Ashley were more than lust. He felt the urge to protect her, to take her in his arms, and to

---

never let her go. Whatever Cathal and his crew were going to do, he would stop them, he decided. He hoped Blair and Payton would show up soon.

Ashley wiped away a tear, took a deep breath, and started to talk. "I am Sam's cousin, but I still don't see what that has to do with anything?"

"It's simple: you are both Camerons. That means your ancestors are from Scotland and—ach, forget it. Whatever it means," he whispered, "I promise, I'll protect you."

Ashley furrowed her brow and smiled at him timidly.

"Thank you," she whispered back. "Are they going to try to get Sam tomorrow?" It was clear that she was worried about her cousin.

He nodded. But he mouthed, "Not if I can help it." And he gave her a wink.

Slowly Sean could understand why Payton was so desperate. He himself felt more alive next to this pretty young woman than he'd felt for nearly three hundred years.

Looking both relieved and exhausted, Ashley shut her eyes and fell asleep a short time later. Sean lay down next to her, and tried to go to sleep, too, but his newfound feelings kept him up. Carefully, so as not to wake her, he wrapped a strand of her hair around his finger and enjoyed the warm, electric feeling. He had a feeling this was going to be a long night.

～

"Alasdair Buchanan?" Kim wasn't panicked anymore, but she sounded irritated instead.

"Yes, the Scottish man who tried to kill me."

"Are you sure?" She shook her head as if to clear it. "Never mind. It doesn't matter. Ashley's missing. I still think we should call the police."

I chewed on the inside of my cheek. I could hardly think straight: Alasdair had followed me . . . Did Payton know? Was he maybe nearby, too? My heart felt a tiny glimmer of hope.

"We can't call the police. They'd never believe us," I told Kim. "They'd think we were drunk teenagers. 'Yes, officer, immortal Scots that want to kidnap and kill us because of an ancient feud.' I can't imagine them taking that call too seriously. Let's wait to hear from Justin, and then we'll see what to do."

Just at that moment, Justin burst into the house, panting heavily. He needed a moment to catch his breath before he could tell us anything.

"Did you find them?" Kim asked.

"Sort of. I followed them onto Kings Highway. They were going faster than me, and I was trying to make sure they didn't notice me, but I saw them turn south onto Dupont. But by the time I made the turn, I couldn't see them anymore. I'm sorry I lost them." He looked from side to side. "Where are the police?"

"Sam doesn't want to call the cops!"

"What? Ashley has been kidnapped! Who knows what they're going to do to her!"

"Just listen to me!" I tried to get them both to pay close attention to what I had to say. "I know the kidnappers. And I think I know what they want. The thing with Ashley must be a mistake. I think they meant to take me."

"What do you mean? What do they want from you?" Justin looked confused.

"It's a really long story. I can't tell you everything now, but you have to trust me."

"So what do you suggest?" Kim asked, getting right to the point.

"Let's go back to Dupont and look for the van," I said. "There isn't really anything else we can do. But if I'm right, we won't need to find these guys. They will find us."

"That's not very comforting," Kim said.

"Kim is right," Justin said. "We should at least call Ryan."

"Ryan? What does he have to do with this?"

"His dad is a cop—and he collects guns. Maybe he could snag something out of his dad's cabinet and supply us with some actual firepower?"

"Great, now we're stealing guns?" I said. "I really don't think we need to drag him into this."

But Justin was already dialing Ryan's number.

"Look, Sam. If you're not willing to call the police, I at least want to get some help. I don't think I could take those two guys on my own. And unarmed."

Reluctantly, I had to admit he was right. Only too vividly could I remember how serious the fight between Payton and Alasdair had been. And Alasdair had another distinct advantage over Justin: he was immortal.

"Just please tell him to keep his dad out of this. That would be the last thing we need."

Fortunately, Ryan wasn't the type to ask a lot of questions when his friends needed him. And when he heard that it was me who was in danger, he immediately took one of his dad's guns. He must have known he'd be in a world of trouble if his dad ever found out. But I was impressed that he didn't hesitate when we asked for help.

"OK, let's get going," Ryan said, as he rushed into the house. I wasn't sure he grasped how deadly serious this was, but I knew I couldn't face this situation alone.

We piled into my mom's car and drove along Dupont, where Justin had last seen the van. I wasn't sure how we could possibly find the van on this stretch of road. There were just too many places to look—office buildings, the park and ride, motels, stores, not to mention private parking garages, some underground. It would be awfully easy to hide out in a place like this. There was also the possibility that the Scots had already left town. Ashley could be anywhere by then.

We looked everywhere we could think of, checking out every parking lot along that stretch of highway. But it was getting harder to see things in the dark, so when we got to the edge of town, we turned the car around.

While we were searching, I tried to tell Justin and Ryan the whole story. But when I got to the harder concepts, like the curse, immortality, and the fighting clans, I could tell they thought I was nuts. But since Ashley really was missing—and Justin was absolutely sure of that—at least they weren't going to institutionalize me on the spot.

When we got back to my house, Ryan locked the door, closed all the blinds, and explained that it would be safest for all of us to stay together. He suggested the living room. We could keep an eye on the door there and, if all else failed, we'd have another way out, through the back door. Whether his safety strategies were inspired by the movies or all those years of listening to his dad, I didn't know, but it sounded good.

After he checked that all the windows were properly secured, and the door chain was latched, we all tried to relax. Kim was sitting on Justin's lap in an armchair while Justin rubbed her back. Ryan and I sat on opposite ends of the sofa.

"Hey, Sam, do you want a back rub, too?" Ryan asked, grinning.

"Oh, can you not just give up!"

He raised his hands in apology. "I thought danger might turn you on."

I was pretty sure he was joking. At least, I hoped he was joking. So I joked back. "All right, I'll forgive you, but only because you're the one with the gun!"

Ryan laughed, and I smiled at him thankfully.

We all grew quiet. I don't think anyone got much sleep. We spent the night worrying, dozing off once in a while, and shifting around on our seats. Kim and Justin whispered to each other from time to time; Ryan kept checking the windows, and I sank into my memories.

I went over everything in my mind. That poor woman, Isobel, who died trying to save her child. The dark sky, the sudden lightning, I could see it all right in front me, just like in my dream. What had Vanora said to me? Face your destiny. Remember those you are a descendant of. Beware of the fall. The fall. What did she mean by that? Fortunately, in Milford there were far less hills to fall from than in the Scottish Highlands. But the fall could be a metaphor, I realized. And if so, what for?

My restless thoughts wandered on to the Scotsmen. Alasdair was really threatening, and if he wasn't alone, as Kim and Justin had said, then he definitely posed a danger. I considered calling my parents. No, I thought. If Alasdair were intending to finish what he'd started, it was good to know that my parents were nowhere nearby.

I wasn't really worried about Ashley. After all, she wasn't a descendant of the Camerons. She was my cousin on my dad's side; she had nothing to do with the Cameron bloodline. Once they figured that out and got ahold of me instead, the angry Scots were bound to let her go.

I wished with all my might that I could talk to Payton, to ask him what to do and to make sure he was all right. But I had deleted his number awhile back, thinking I could erase him from my life.

I wondered if he knew the danger I was facing, and if he was trying to help. But in the back of my mind I also wondered if he had turned his loyalty back to the clan. After all, he was bound to the clan by oath. Would he dare, after all that had happened, to defy them out of his love for me? I didn't think so. But maybe. He had told me that there was something very special between the two of us.

Ugh! My thoughts were running around in circles. I could pluck petals off a daisy and know as much as I did now . . . He loves me. He loves me not. He wants me dead. Or maybe not.

Ryan's return from one of his security rounds interrupted my dark poetry.

"Hey, don't you want to try to get some sleep?" he asked.

"I don't think I can."

"I know. But you should try." He plopped back down on the couch. "Hey, I was wondering . . . where was Ashley on her way to, when they grabbed her?"

"Actually, she was coming to see you. Her dad is going to come and pick her up tomorrow or the next day. She wanted to say good-bye."

"Oh no! It's my fault, then."

"Don't say that. It's definitely not your fault. But I think she really likes you, and if you weren't always such an idiot, you would have realized that by now."

"Sam, seriously, I have never once met a girl that really likes me for me. They like me because of the way I look or because of the parties they'll get invited to if they're with me."

"Well, maybe that's because those are the only sides of yourself that you let people see. You're actually very similar to Ashley. She hides her soft center behind her sexy clothes and her hard exterior. But I think that since her mom died, all she really wants is someone who will be there for her."

"That's a bunch of sentimental BS," he said. "But thank you."

I yawned. "Maybe you're right—I should get some sleep." At first, I just wanted to stop talking to Ryan, and I pretended to have fallen asleep. But at some point my exhaustion must have gotten the better of me, because I woke with a start when the doorbell rang.

Everyone was immediately on alert, and the two boys stood protectively in front of Kim and me. I took a deep breath. What felt like a day passed, though I'm certain it was only a few seconds.

"Go on . . . Open it up," I said to Ryan.

"And if it's them?"

"They'll get us sooner or later, anyway. Just do it!"

With a quiet click, Ryan released the safety on his dad's gun, and he quietly crept toward the door. Then he tore the door open in exactly the same way it's always done on TV and expertly aimed the gun at the two tall men.

~

I let out a sharp shriek, as the world around me started to spin and my knees caved beneath me. Was Payton at my door, or was it just a dream?

Never had I thought seeing him again would shake me so much, but there I was, with tears in my eyes and words that just wouldn't come out of my throat. All I could do was look at him. I wanted to let my inhibitions go. To touch him and feel his strong arms around me, which would make everything all right. But I did nothing of the kind. I didn't move and didn't utter one word.

So it was up to Kim to clarify what she had guessed by my reaction. "I guess that one of you must be Payton?"

Blair eyed his brother, who also seemed to have turned to stone. He nodded and pointed to Payton. "Good guess," he said. "That's Payton. And I'm his brother Blair."

Payton's whole body was trembling, and his sweet lips were pressed tightly together in a narrow line. He curled his hands into fists, pushed past Ryan and his gun, sank down to his knees next to me, and pulled me into his arms. A muffled sound of pain made its way to my ear, but I wasn't willing to give up our embrace. It was too wonderful to feel Payton's hands on my back and to inhale his familiar scent. I pressed myself tightly to him.

Only slowly did my brain start working again. A full mountain of questions swam to the surface of my foggy mind. And plenty of doubts. How had he found me? Was he working with the others? Was I safe? Or in the worst danger of my life?

Slowly, I raised my eyes. When I saw the immense pain in his face, I was terrified.

I couldn't stop second-guessing everything. Was his expression because he was close to me, or because he'd come to finish me off? The poison of mistrust had mixed itself into my blood and I was fully incapable of freeing myself. I just plain didn't know who I could trust anymore.

I stood up and pushed Payton away, crossing my arms over my chest to keep the warmth of his body with me for a moment longer.

"So what are you doing here?" It took every ounce of energy to keep the emotion out of my voice.

Payton looked surprised. "What? I had to see to it that you were safe."

His voice touched my soul, but I struggled to build a barrier to protect myself. My heart was already in shreds, and I couldn't allow him to hurt me again.

Payton took a tentative step toward me, but I shied away.

Ryan had been watching the whole scene quietly. He cleared his throat and motioned to the door with his weapon. "I guess you should go now. I don't think you're welcome here."

The Scots ignored his remark. They hadn't crossed the Atlantic to be given orders by an American high school boy.

"Sam, oh Sam, *mo luaidh, tha gràdh agam ort.* Please forgive me, *tha mi duilich,*" begged Payton.

He grabbed me by my shoulders and pulled me close. He whispered in Gaelic in my ear, while tears ran down his face. Being so close to me must have given him great pain. And though I didn't know the words he spoke, my heart understood.

Still, I couldn't trust him. Again, I pushed him away from me, and Ryan hurried to my side. He directed Payton and Blair to the door with his gun.

"I will not hesitate to use this if you don't leave immediately!"

Then everything happened very quickly.

Payton hit Ryan hard, and Ryan sank to the ground. Blair picked up Justin by the throat, and Justin struggled to breathe, his feet dangling in the air. Kim shrieked and I just stood there.

"Sam, listen to me," Payton pleaded.

"No! What are you doing? Are you trying to kill all of us? Do you always just strike down people who you are supposedly worried about?"

It was over as quickly as it had begun. Trembling, I knelt next to Ryan on the floor and brushed his blond hair away from his forehead. Blood was trickling out of a cut above his right eye. Blair let go of Justin, placing him back on his feet. Kim ran to him, crying quietly on his shoulder while he sucked in deep breaths and rubbed his sore neck.

I wasn't scared, but I was very, very annoyed. Payton seemed destined to wreck my life. My cousin had been kidnapped; Ryan was knocked out cold with a gun in his hand; Justin nearly got strangled; and still, my treacherous body yearned for Payton's touch. My brain, on the other hand, told me to get as far from him as possible.

"Oh Sam, please forgive me," he said. "I need you so much, please, you must believe me. Please forgive me! I love you." He moved toward me slowly, took my hands in his, and looked deep into my eyes. "You are always in my thoughts, my dreams, and in my heart. I see you in front of me, how you laugh, how you cry, how you reach for my hand. I can't bear to lose you forever, having finally found you. Please believe me, I will never stop loving you."

I knew he must be in incredible pain, but he didn't move away. I could hardly breathe. He was so strong and invincible, and his words were full of passion and desperation.

Then I realized I hadn't given him a chance to explain his side of things. I was the one who'd left him behind in Scotland. I didn't move.

Payton looked disappointed. He shook his head and turned away from me. Right away I found it easier to breathe.

I got a damp cloth from the kitchen and dabbed the blood off Ryan's forehead. I was glad for something to do, to distract myself.

Whispering in Gaelic, Blair and Payton stood with their heads together, occasionally throwing a worried glance in my direction. I quickly forced the thought away that the two of them might be plotting how to kill me. I was starting to hope that they really were here to help.

When Ryan came to a few minutes later, we helped him to a chair. Then we all sat down reluctantly, but at least peacefully, and talked about the situation. Blair and Payton had heard from their brother Sean that Ashley had been abducted, and they had also learned where she was and that she was doing OK, all things considered.

"And from the way he sounded on the telephone, I wouldn't be surprised if our Sean has noticed your cousin's beauty. Perhaps he's getting some feelings back, too," said Blair.

That remark provoked an evil look from Ryan, who was obviously not happy with these invading Scotsmen, who seemed to do whatever they felt like with whomever they pleased.

Thanks to Sean, we now knew where to find Ashley. But we still didn't have any idea how to proceed. Still, we knew that working together was our best chance.

"We can charge the building," suggested Ryan, who still seemed to be itching to use that gun.

"No. Are you crazy?" Kim said. "The best thing would be for us to call the cops."

"Silence!" Blair's clear order interrupted the chaos. "Cathal and Nathaira are after Sam. I also presume that they will realize soon that Ashley is not a Cameron—if they haven't already. That means that she is not a danger to them. If we now offer to bring Sam to them in exchange for Ashley, they should agree to that."

"No!" Ryan objected loudly. "That's absolutely out of the question. Who knows what they would do to Sam. Forget it!"

"It's OK, Ryan," I said. "I actually think Blair is right. They want me, not Ashley. The first thing we should do is get her to safety. Then we'll take it one step at a time and figure out what to do next. And I wouldn't go there alone—Payton and Blair would come with me." The thought of meeting up with Alasdair again had my stomach in knots, but I knew it was the right thing to do.

"Sam, please, you can't go!" begged Kim, whose fear for me was written all over her teary, blotchy red face.

"Kim, it's our only option! If we don't go to them, then they'll come here. This way, we at least have the element of surprise on our side. I also think there's a chance that everything can be cleared up if I can just talk to them."

"You don't have to do this, Sam," said Payton. "You need to understand this is dangerous." He gestured to his brother. "Blair and I can go alone and free Ashley with violence if we have to."

"What for?" Blair said. "Cathal gave us his word that he wouldn't harm Sam. We can just go and clear everything up." The McLean chieftain was clearly less than enthusiastic about the idea of using violence against others in the clan.

"How much is Cathal's word worth? If he'd been intending to stay true to his word, he would have stayed at home in Scotland!"

"Payton, you are wrong! You can trust Cathal!"

"Yes, Cathal maybe, but I don't trust Nathaira, or Alasdair! And I am not going to give Sam over into their hands just like that."

～

"What do you mean, into their hands? We'll be there to protect her."

"Then we should all go there with Sam," Ryan said.

"No, you stay here. We can't look after you, take care of Sam, and protect ourselves."

"I'm the one with the weapon. A weapon from this century, I might add. And I don't trust you two as far as I can spit. So forget it. Either you take us with you, or I'll inform my dad. He happens to be the chief of police."

Oh boy. What a mess! I wished I could slide under the kitchen table and dissolve into the floor. But I knew that I had to face my destiny, if not for myself, then for my ancestors. Just as Vanora had foretold it. And this terrible discussion was only wasting time. I wanted to get everything over with.

To make things worse, Uncle Eddie could turn up any moment to pick Ashley up, and he'd be pretty alarmed if she weren't here to claim. Until then, we had to somehow ease the situation.

"Now listen, everybody." I was yelling now. "We are all going to do exactly what I say. First of all, I am going. Secondly, you are all coming with me."

I banged loudly on the table, so hard the ball of my hand was throbbing and I hoped I hadn't broken any bones. As inconspicuously as possible, I rubbed my hand under the table and waited for opposition. Incredibly, there was none.

The pendant was burning hot on my skin. I wanted to laugh. Like I needed a warning sign of the impending danger!

CHAPTER 26

We took two separate cars to the motel. Payton, who refused to leave my side, was sitting in the front next to me, with Blair in the car, too. Ryan was following us with Kim and Justin. We had agreed that the three of them would wait for Ashley in the parking lot; if it should prove necessary, they would call the police.

The last thing I wanted to think about was any kind of escalation. I couldn't really think, anyway, because being so close to Payton completely threw me off balance. After I rebuffed him at my house, he had hardly said a word. His face was tight, and the warm glow had disappeared from his eyes. It was as if a Scottish wall of mist had pushed itself in front of his feelings. He didn't even seem bothered to be sitting close to me. Either the pain he felt near me had gotten weaker, or he had become accustomed to it. I knew that I was getting used to my pendant; I could hardly feel the burning sensation anymore.

I so wished I could go back to the beginning, when Payton and I had first met. Before all the doubt and distrust. Just the dizzy excitement and rush of new love. When I didn't know he was deceiving me—that he had followed me, spied on me, to find out who I was. I sighed. Looking back, it seemed to me that it was only my feelings for him that had been so strong—not his for me. I closed my eyes and tried to bring back the memory of that magical night at the beach.

We were on the same road as the day before. But we hadn't seen anything unusual then at the motel we were driving up to now.

I asked myself whether Blair had been right. Was Sean feeling attracted to Ashley? They were both good-looking and, as I had experienced firsthand, Sean was a real charmer. Somehow, the idea made me feel happy for Ashley. Maybe this terrible, scary night could have a good side.

But there was still the question of what would happen to Sean—and Payton—if the curse were lifted. Could it really be that they would all just drop dead, or would they only lose their immortality and grow older, like the rest of us? Or could it be that nothing at all would happen? That Payton and his family would carry on living exactly as they had up until now, because neither I nor anyone else was actually capable of influencing the curse? There was, after all, nothing in my grandma's book about the Camerons being destined to lift the curse.

~

Blair turned into the motel's parking lot and stopped the car. When Ryan and the others had pulled up behind us, we all got out. Nobody except me seemed to have any difficulty moving; my legs would hardly obey. I had to force myself to put one foot in front of the other. Ryan tried to comfort me by patting my shoulder, but I was so on edge I jumped as if he'd attacked.

"Sorry, I didn't mean to freak you out."

"It's fine. My nerves are just shot," I said.

"If you don't want to do this, then you just call it off. We can easily call my dad, and he'll deal with everything."

"No, I know it seems crazy—but trust me, this is the only option."

"All right, but shouldn't we all go in together?"

I shook my head. "That would be way too dangerous. Let's stick with the plan. As soon as Ashley is free, you get her away from here and wait for me at home."

He bent down close to me and whispered, "Do you really trust these men?"

Well, I actually still didn't have an answer to that one, but I knew Ryan would never let me go upstairs if he thought I was in doubt, so I answered firmly, "Yes, don't worry. It'll be fine."

Ryan looked me deep in the eyes, and then he nodded and squeezed my hand.

"Ryan," I called as I walked away, "today I almost like you!" I winked.

"Nice. But after seeing you with Payton, I know that's not going to help my case. Your heart obviously belongs to him." He turned to head back to his car.

As Blair, Payton, and I started up the motel's outer staircase, I asked myself what Ryan had meant. Was it clear to everybody that I loved Payton? And if it was so clear, why did everything have to be so complicated?

≈

"Sam, *mo luaidh*, you don't have to do this." It was Payton's turn to try to comfort me.

His soft voice almost succeeded in collapsing the dam holding back my tears. But I wanted to learn my destiny. And if it was here, waiting for me in this shabby motel, well then, so be it.

"Payton, please. If everything that you say is true, then we have to protect Ashley and get her out of here. We'll see about everything else later."

"What can I do to make you trust me again, Sam? I love you and will defend you with my life."

"I don't think I'll ever be able to trust you. It's too late for that." I shook my head sadly. "Let's just focus on what we have to do now."

"Sam, please."

In the meantime, we had reached the fourth floor, and Blair was knocking on one of the doors. I scrambled behind him quickly, seeking protection behind his broad back. Still, I shrieked when the giant Alasdair opened the door.

"Blair. What a surprise . . . First Sean and now all the others, eh?"

Blair wasn't used to explaining himself to anybody, much less Alasdair, and he pushed his way past him into the room. When Alasdair saw me, his grin became wider, and he gave me a sneering mock bow.

"Ah, and our Miss Cameron is here, too!"

Every fiber in my body was screaming for me to get away from there as quickly as possible, but Payton's hand on my shoulder gave me the necessary strength to go in. The room was dark and stuffy.

"Sam! Help me!" Ashley shouted when she saw me. "Please!"

My cousin was sitting upright, but with her hands tied to one of the bedposts. Sean was standing protectively in front of her. At least I knew she wasn't in serious danger just then.

"Don't worry, Ashley," I said. "We'll get out of here."

Every inch of space in the room seemed to be taken up. The size of the immortal Scots really was impressive. Even Nathaira was several inches taller than me. She was the first to speak.

"Blair, who have you brought with you?"

"Hello, darling. Interesting to find you here. You don't seem to think it's necessary to discuss a trip to the United States with your fiancé? You went behind my back."

At these words, Alasdair twitched slightly and lowered his eyes with a guilty look.

"Do you think I will ask you for permission before I leave the house?"

"No, I don't expect that," said Blair, "but it does seem as if you were all intending to leave me in the dark about what you are up to just now."

His eyes darted from Nathaira to his best friend Cathal, who looked remarkably calm.

"Don't get upset. Now we are all here and so is the Cameron girl. I don't see why we shouldn't just clear the situation once and for all." Cathal stepped toward me, studying me from head to toe, as if I were a rare plant. "The similarity in appearance really is astonishing, don't you think?"

Nathaira and Alasdair nodded in agreement, which made me feel even more uncomfortable. I reached for Payton's hand. He twitched in pain at my unexpected touch.

"Sorry," I whispered.

He squeezed my hand and smiled.

"How sweet," snarled Nathaira.

Great, we had attracted her attention. But I knew she wouldn't have let me out of her sight, anyway.

"I fear, Payton, that the love sessions are over for you two now. That girl is harming us. But not for long. We can make sure of that!"

Everyone started speaking all at once. It was all in Gaelic, but they were obviously talking about me. I was relieved to see that Payton and his brothers were still standing by my side. The exchange of words got louder and more aggressive by the minute. Then suddenly, the volume dropped, and we could all hear the sound of Ashley crying.

I gathered all my courage and used the break to my advantage.

"May I please say something, too?" I said. "This all has to do with the Cameron clan, doesn't it? I understand that you want to clear things up with me, but you don't need Ashley here. I'm the one you really want. She has absolutely nothing to do with it."

"Is she not your cousin? Your own blood?" Alasdair asked roughly.

"Yes, but my mom's side is the Cameron one. Ashley's mom is my dad's sister. She's not a Cameron."

To prove it, I pulled Grandma's book out of my jacket pocket and pointed to the last page. There, at the bottom of the family tree, stood my name.

I lifted the book up, moving it from one side of the group to the other so that everyone could see what was written there.

"What is that? Where did you get that?" Cathal asked.

"I found it, purely accidentally, in my grandmother's attic when we were clearing out her belongings after she died. It seems someone named Marta McGabhan started these notes."

"Who is this Marta supposed to be?" Alasdair asked.

Since I had some leverage, it seemed like a good time to make a second attempt to get Ashley out of there.

"I'll tell you later, but first, you need to let Ashley go. As you can plainly see, you don't need her."

Nathaira started to contradict me, but Payton cut her off.

"Exactly," he said. "This all seems to be between me and Sam. It's only when I am near her that I'm in such unbelievable pain—and only when we are close to her that our self-healing abilities are affected. Samantha's cousin has nothing to do with it. We should let her go."

Cathal and Nathaira's eyes met briefly. I held my breath. At last, Cathal went to the bed, cut the ropes, and pulled Ashley to the door.

Turning to Blair, he growled, "I hope she's worth it for you."

"May I remind you, I am the one being betrayed here," Blair said. "The three of you have created this divide and abused my trust." Blair opened the door for Ashley and demanded of Cathal, "And now, let her go!"

Cathal released his steely grip on Ashley's arm, and she ran off crying.

I saw the relief in Sean's face as the door closed behind her. It looked as if a great stone had rolled away from his heart. It was obvious to me that his feelings were almost back to full strength, and I hoped the others didn't notice how much weaker the curse had become.

With all eyes on me again, I felt really sick. My heart was beating like a drum, and my blood was pounding in my ears. I had never felt so scared before in all my life.

"Cathal, I have found something out," Payton started. There was a layer of sweat on his forehead, and the tendons stood out on his arms. He was still holding my hand, standing close by my side, but his face stayed blank.

"About the curse. That witch, Vanora, wrote everything down. Blair and I found her writings on Fair Isle. She had a vision before our attack. She saw almost everything in advance. In her last letter, she wrote that there would be a possibility to lift the curse. We don't have to harm Samantha. There is another way!"

"And what is that supposed to be? I can hardly wait to hear about it," Alasdair said snarkily.

Somewhat abashed, Blair confessed, "We are not really sure. Supposedly, the witch had a daughter who would lift the curse."

Cathal shook his head in disbelief. "A daughter? Who would bed a witch? And anyway, that child would long be dead."

"We don't know that. We ourselves are the best proof that she could very well still be alive. We must not forget that her mother had extraordinary powers," Payton explained.

～

Nathaira had gone white, but her closed expression gave no hint of her racing thoughts.

"*Sguir, mo nighean. Mo gràdh ort.*" That was what the crazy old woman had said the night of the massacre. In all her years, Nathaira had never forgotten that moment. The moment the dying witch claimed that Nathaira was her daughter—and told her that she loved her.

~

"How are we to find this daughter?" Cathal asked.

"According to our information," Payton said, "Vanora was imprisoned by a clan that was a neighbor to the Cameron clan. That is why she fled to the Camerons and then stayed there with them."

I was starting to feel hope that they could actually settle things peacefully. Cathal was listening carefully to what Payton was saying. Even Nathaira had not raised any objections for the last few minutes. She seemed to be deep in thought.

I myself was so captivated by what I was hearing that I hardly thought of the danger I was still in.

The next sentence that Blair said changed everything.

"But maybe the witch was wrong. She claimed that her own daughter would kill her. But as we all know, it was Nathaira who killed her."

Cathal's expression fell in horror. But before he could say another word, Nathaira burst out in hysterical laughter.

"You idiots!" she shouted. Her face had contorted into a sneering mask as she pulled out her dagger and came closer to me, step by step. "Of course the witch was right! I am her daughter!"

Cathal shook his head. "You?"

"Yes! Do you want to hear how I know?" She looked her brother in the eye. "Your mother told me when I was ten years old. She said she hated me. She said I was a monster of wickedness and that my real mother was a dirty devil's bride whom my father had taken whenever he had wanted."

Nathaira's anger was now aimed directly at Cathal, who seemed to hardly believe his ears.

For me, though, the pieces of the puzzle were slowly fitting together. The pendant was burning hotter than ever, and I was not going to ignore it. Slowly and inconspicuously, I tried to move closer to the door. Payton also seemed to sense the danger, and he shielded me a little bit more with his body. But Nathaira was no longer paying any attention to us.

"I knew that your mother had told me the truth," she said. "I could feel Vanora's power inside me, even if I didn't inherit any of her abilities. I was but a child, Cathal. Do you understand that? And she told me that she hated me. The only mother I'd ever known. That's when I knew what I had to do. That's why I poisoned her. Everyone thought she died of consumption."

Cathal turned as pale as the white wall behind him, and his whole body shook.

Blair intervened. He grabbed Nathaira and slapped her with all his might.

"Shut up! What has got into you? Do you know what you are saying?"

Nathaira's cheek turned blazing red where she'd been hit. Her black hair fell into her face; her eyes were full of hatred, and her nostrils flared with every hectic breath. She looked like an animal in a trap. But if I had expected that Blair's intervention would silence the woman, I was wrong.

"You," she now attacked Blair. "You failure!" She shook her hair out of her eyes and pushed him away.

"If it hadn't been for me, you wouldn't have had any other choice than to play husband to one of those Cameron women. Just like your father had planned on."

"That is rubbish!" Blair said. "My father wouldn't ever have wanted an alliance with the Camerons after Kyle's death. That cold-blooded murder had to be avenged and that is exactly what we did."

A triumphant expression set itself on Nathaira's face. She was almost smiling. Slowly, she let her hate-filled eyes wander—first to the giant Alasdair, who looked strangely in-different, and then to her brother Cathal.

"Brother, don't think that I don't love you. For you I gave up Alasdair and would have even married Blair. And the Camerons, well, that was also my gift to you. Without me, that night would never have ended that way."

The atmosphere in the motel room was getting more and more heated. Blair was darting angry looks at Alasdair; Cathal looked like he might collapse. Sean had stepped up to Blair, seeming ready to jump in to prevent his big brother from doing anything rash. He was also keeping an eye on me.

I had already gotten quite a bit closer to the door. But just one step farther and it would be pretty clear that I was intending to run. Payton let go of my hand and took a stance nearer to his brothers. Being so close to me was probably draining too much of his strength. Without him by my side,

I felt more vulnerable. On the other hand, I could react more quickly on my own.

Cathal shook his head, confused. "Nathaira, sister, what does all this mean?"

"Think for yourself! If Kyle hadn't died, the McLeans wouldn't have fought. They would never have taken part in the massacre of the Camerons if they hadn't had a personal reason to join in. I killed Kyle for you!"

She was standing with her back to the wall, holding her long dagger protectively in front of herself.

Everyone was speechless. The air was crackling, that's how strong the emotions were in that room. Hundreds of years' worth of anger, hatred, pain, and triumph—feelings that had not been aroused for centuries—were quickly rising to the surface.

Very slowly, Sean pulled his *sgian dhu* from its sheath. His eyes drilled into the woman he thought he'd known for so long. The charming young man I'd met in Scotland vanished, and in his place now stood a real warrior—a man who had killed before, and who was willing to do so again.

"You rotten bitch! I am going to give you one more chance to explain yourself before I shove the dagger into your heart. Then the world will be rid of one more witch. Remember—you are not invincible now."

He was gripping the knife so hard his fingers were bloodless. He looked ready to thrust. But Nathaira was not impressed. She let out a gravelly laugh.

"Well then, if you want to hear the whole story, here you are. As you all knew, that brat Kyle followed me. He should have listened better to his brother. Blair had explicitly told him not to come, but he did." While she was talking,

Nathaira meandered over to Cathal and softly stroked his arm—but her dagger was still held fast in her hand.

"After the conversation with Fingal, it had become clear to me that the McLeans would just support us, not fight with us. Even then, Blair was not man enough to stand up to his father. That worried me. Cathal's position was not secured. Had we only exchanged words with the Camerons, the attacks would have carried on and he would never have managed to stay in power. That alone would have been enough for me to commit a murder. But with Kyle, I had a very personal motive as well. I hated him! That half child had dared to pick a fight with me. The idiot had called me a dog's daughter."

Payton's breaths were coming in rasps.

"I must admit that I had not planned his death," she said. "In retrospect, it seems it was fate. Blair sent me, of all people, to encourage his brother to turn back. And inside me everything was boiling at his behavior that afternoon. When Kyle recognized me, he stiffened in his saddle. He was hardly able to greet me. What was the worm thinking? Did he think he could punish me with contempt? Whatever it was, I wanted to rid him of his arrogance. So I slid out of my saddle and grabbed his horse's reins. He, of course, wouldn't have that, so he dismounted, too. He tore the leather out of my hands and yelled at me. 'What do you want? Why aren't you with the others?'

"I made fun of him. 'Because they want me to be your nanny. The child is to be put to bed.'

"Kyle wasn't listening to me, he wanted to get back on his horse again. So I grabbed his plaid. With more strength than I would have expected from him, he grabbed my arm.

"'Away with you, otherwise you'll be sorry. Bad enough that a woman should behave like you!'

"I was boiling with anger by then, and his disrespect made me furious. 'You're the one to go away! Blair doesn't need boys when he's going to battle!'

"But Kyle pushed me, and I fell backward to the ground. He turned his back on me and left me lying in the dirt, that fool! There was nothing else I could do. I got back up, pulled out my dagger, and rammed it right between his shoulders. Right at the first sound of surprise, he was coughing up blood. Slowly, he turned around, would probably have fallen if he had not kept a tight hold on the saddle. When I saw his mouth open in disbelief, I had to laugh. His breath was rattling, blood was running out of his mouth onto his shirt. He tried to reach out for me, hoping for help. I looked deep into his eyes, which had already lost their life, and at last I could see it: his arrogance had disappeared. He sank to the ground, gasping helplessly, and his last breaths sounded almost like a whistle. I stepped up to him, pulled my dagger out of his flesh, and cleansed my weapon on his plaid.

"Once I knew he was dead, I went on my way to tell you about the terrible assault." She looked from Payton to Blair, and then to Sean. "I was scared you wouldn't believe me, but my tears were enough to fool you stupid men. That my skirt was almost completely saturated with your brother's blood was something I could easily blame on the fact that the poor boy had died in my arms, after he had told me that a Cameron trap had taken his life. So, you see, the whole story was logical. And I wasn't only rid of that child forever, but I could also be sure that you McLeans would really be on our side in the fight."

Nathaira's words hung in the air for a long time. Nobody said anything. No one breathed. It was like the air itself was holding everyone prisoner.

I took another small step toward the door, touching the doorknob behind my back. I wanted to get out as soon as possible if all hell were about to break loose. And it was pretty clear that was going to happen. Sean looked like a wild animal ready to attack Nathaira at any moment. Only Alasdair seemed to keep his calm reserve.

He came back to the original topic, without paying any attention to the McLeans. "If you are Vanora's daughter, then you must know how the curse can be lifted, right?"

"No," Vanora snapped. "And I have no intention of lifting the curse, anyway. I want everything to stay the way it is."

"So you wish, just like me, for that mountain of feelings that is crushing you to go away again?" he asked. "That everything could be the way it was a few weeks ago?"

Nathaira's eyes suddenly met mine, and the hair at the back of my neck stood on end. The world started to spin around me. Everything seemed to be taking place in slow motion. I couldn't hear what she was saying, but I recognized the glowing hatred in her green eyes. She raised her dagger. As if from a distance, the men's cries made their way to my ears. Gaelic mixed together with Payton's screams.

I hurled myself against the door, turned the doorknob, tripped backward over the doormat, and tumbled onto the stairwell. Payton threw himself in Nathaira's way, but she dug her blade into his upper arm and pushed him aside.

She was so close. My limbs felt like they were made of lead. I wanted to run, but I couldn't. I held my breath, steeling myself for the wound she would inflict. The pendant burned my skin, hotter than ever. Nathaira raised her dagger, the polished metal gleaming—and stabbed.

Payton grabbed the witch by her hair and tore her back. Her blade missed its destination, cutting my hand instead. Payton wrestled her away from me, but before he could overpower her entirely, she distorted her mouth to produce a joyless laugh and shoved me against the railing.

Her strength knocked the wind out of me, the metal cut into my hips, and I lost my balance. Wildly, I flapped my arms, trying to get a grip somewhere, and toppled over the edge.

The fall!

The memory flooded me:

"Vanora? But what do you want from me? What's going on? I'm scared!"

Her hand was resting on my head, as if she were blessing me.

"Face your destiny. Remember those you are a descendant of. Fear not. But beware of the fall."

This was it, then, I thought. The moment of death. The fourth floor of a cheap motel. Time was relative. I took in everything around me. High up in the sky, a plane was leaving a white trail; way down below, police cars were pulling into the driveway of the motel.

A shrill, bloodcurdling warrior's yell pierced my consciousness. It sounded awful, but it made my heart sing. Like a steel claw, Payton's fingers dug into my arm. A hoarse wail left my throat as something inside me tore, and my shoulder made a loud grating sound. The pain made it almost impossible for me to see. But the film of my fate continued to roll. Nobody could press the pause button.

The desperation in Payton's eyes was terrible to behold. His jaw muscles stood out from strain of keeping me in his iron grip. Warm blood swelled out of the cut in my hand, drawing a red pattern on Payton's fingers. I knew there was no way he could hold me much longer. Inch by inch, I sank farther and farther, slipping out of his grasp.

Sean pushed Nathaira to one side, but his knife clattered out of his hand, and he couldn't stop her from coming at us again. Like living snakes, her hair wound itself around her thin body as she dove toward my arm. Twisting violently onto his side, Payton steered his own body into the dagger's path. He jerked in pain as Nathaira drove the blade into his flesh.

∿

Suddenly, black clouds drew up, darkening the day. Lightning bolts struck across the sky, and the wind whirled sand and dust through the air. The police car's light seemed spooky in the sinister twilight. My earlier conversation with Payton thrust itself into my head:

"What can I do to make you trust me again, Sam? I love you and will defend you with my life."

"I don't think I will ever be able to trust you. It's too late for that."

How could I have doubted him?

Vanora's face became visible as a ghostly apparition in the sky. Everyone froze, their eyes on her. Like the penetrating sound of the bagpipes across a loch, each of Vanora's words reached my innermost soul, melted with my blood, and penetrated my heart:

"The power of a curse may never change, but should fate intervene and the destiny be fulfilled, then all powers of nature can combine and free the damned hearts once more. This sacrifice of love and the act of forgiveness are the keys. The devils in your hearts have disappeared and their evil poison no longer is in your blood.

I free your souls. May they now leave their old lives behind them."

With the last flash of lightning, she was gone. Without warning, reality descended again. Time shifted from slow motion back to normal speed. Only a lingering burning smell was proof of what had just happened.

Sean tackled Nathaira, and the two of them fell, grappling on the ground. Payton was still hanging on to my arm, his eyes locked on mine. But I was still slipping, bit by bit.

There was an honesty in his eyes that said he would never leave me, that he would hold me to the end. But I could see that his strength was dwindling. His own blood was puddling at his feet, and sweat covered his forehead. But what shook me the most was what else I could see: Payton was scared.

∼

Payton couldn't believe it when Nathaira attacked him.

Her terrible revelations had been truly shocking. Her treacherous murder of Kyle and her lack of remorse had taken his breath away. He'd felt as weak as a child, hardly able to keep his body under control. Cathal had seemed to feel the same way. He had watched as the hardened warrior sank weakly to the ground and cried in his hands. The words his beloved sister had said seemed to have broken him.

But Payton's attention was abruptly turned back toward Nathaira when she raised her dagger and lunged at Sam. Using all his strength, he had grabbed Nathaira's hair and yanked her back, away from the woman he loved.

What had happened next was literally his worst nightmare come true: Sam fell over the railing outside. At the last moment, he had managed to grab her, and he clung to her as if she were life itself. He would not let a woman fall into the depths, ever again. This repetition of events: the same desperate look in those beautiful Cameron eyes. He would not believe it was his destiny.

He was so caught up in the nightmare, so concentrated on it, that he had almost forgotten Nathaira. But when he saw her move out of the corner of his eye, he knew what he had to do. He would risk his own life, just to see love in Sam's eyes one last time. He turned into Nathaira's swing, prepared for death. And he was flooded with a mighty feeling of happiness.

He knew the curse had been lifted.

Payton had settled his guilt, followed his heart, and sacrificed himself selflessly for Sam. And just as was written in Vanora's prophecy, the witch's own daughter had been the one to make it possible. Yes, with her own selfish behavior,

Nathaira had lifted the curse that her mother had inflicted hundreds of years before.

"When you understand the truth, darkness will devour you—but you will be happy."

Beathas's words of farewell rang in Payton's ears, and for a moment, he didn't feel the blood drenching his clothes, didn't realize that Sam was slipping more and more. He was only glad that he had escaped living for eternity without love.

He already knew what was to come. He had seen enough men die on the battlefield to know what was a fatal wound and what was not. He had lost a huge amount of blood. He could feel the end coming closer with every breath he took. He coughed and tasted blood. Despite the certainty of having done the right thing, he began to feel scared.

∾

With a powerful jerk, Blair grabbed me under my arms, reaching over Payton and pulling me back to solid ground. Together, the three of us sank to the floor. Only now did I notice the tears I was shedding, and the trembling that seized my entire body. My shoulder was sending shock waves of pain through my limbs, but I couldn't take my eyes off Payton.

I didn't realize at the time that Sean was still fighting Nathaira and Alasdair, and that he was on the verge of not being able to bear many more of Alasdair's hard blows. I had no idea that the police were storming up the stairs with their guns drawn. I only half registered the sound of the shot that brought Nathaira down. I didn't know that she had mumbled words in Gaelic as she lay dying, or that Sean, huddled next to her, had hastily made the sign of the cross while a final flash of lightning lit up the sky.

I was aware of none of it. I only had eyes for the man in front of me.

Payton. His love had saved me. How stupid I had been to doubt him. I realized how unfairly I had treated him, but it looked like it was too late. His eyelids fluttered. He coughed and gasped for air. I pressed my hand on his wound, but the bleeding wouldn't stop.

His hand reached out for my face, stroked my cheek, and barely skimmed my lips. Again he drew a pressed breath.

"Please . . ." he barely managed to say.

Tears ran down my face uncontrollably. I told myself this couldn't happen. But the certainty in his eyes destroyed my hopes.

"Please . . . Sam," he repeated, desperately.

I knew what he wanted.

A kiss.

But I didn't want to kiss him, not then. To kiss him and allow him to die. No, I wanted him to stay with me, to kiss me every day from now on, to hold me lovingly in his arms.

"Payton, please stay with me, stay awake. The ambulance will be here any minute!" There was so much I wanted to say. I wanted to order him to get well again, to forbid him to die. I even wished the curse would come back, with all my might, if it would mean healing his injury.

His hand fell limply from my cheek, and he closed his eyes.

"No! Payton!" My loud sobs almost suffocated me. "Please stay here." I leaned my face down and begged. "I love you . . . I need you . . . I can't live without you. Please . . . Don't leave me!"

After every single word I kissed his face—his eyelids, the little scar on his chin, the tip of his nose. I felt a weak puff of air on my skin when I got close to his mouth, and in desperation, I kissed him. Our lips touched and our tears blended.

Then he moved no longer.

"No!" I cried, shaking him until the pain in my shoulder forced me to stop. Then a paramedic pushed me aside, and I leaned against the wall, numb.

"No pulse, no respiration," the man drily noted as they bundled Payton onto a stretcher

Trying to blind out the world, I shut my eyes. I wished I could shut off everything. I didn't want to hear anything else, didn't want to feel any more pain. It was my fault, I thought. None of this would have happened without me.

Finally, Sean knelt next to me and lifted me up, carrying me like a child down the steps. I hardly noticed the strained, worried faces of my friends behind the police line.

~

During the ride to the hospital, I couldn't get one question out of my head:

My one true love—had that been it?

Epilogue

So there I was, on a sterile white hospital bed. My shoulder and my whole right arm were wrapped up in bandages. I was pumped full of pain medication, but it couldn't ease the agony in my heart. My mom had pulled a few strings at the hospital, so I was given a private room. The pale coral paint on the walls was supposed to convey a feeling of comfort and cheer, but the strong smell of disinfectant and the glaring artificial light destroyed any illusions that I was at a spa.

I could hear Kim's voice. I had noticed earlier that she was sitting with Ashley in the hall. A nurse had obviously forbidden them to disturb me, and I was very grateful for that. I just wasn't ready yet. I'd been sitting on the side of the bed for quite a while, but I couldn't decide whether it would be better to lie down to regain my strength, or if I should summon the courage to go out to my friends. A tear fell into my lap.

What kind of medication had they given me, I wondered. Placebos? Nothing seemed to be working. But I knew at some point, the pain would ease. My throat still felt corded up when I thought of our last kiss. Payton's soft lips had been so full of hunger, wanting more. Without the pain that had always forced him to keep away from me, he had savored that kiss. Our lips joining together had touched off an explosion of emotion. He had lost consciousness with a quiet and happy sigh.

"Oh God, Payton."

No, I couldn't summon the strength to see my friends. I threw myself on the bed and buried my face in the pillow to muffle my sobs.

A touch on my shoulder made me jerk in surprise. I involuntarily asked myself what I looked like. My eyes must have been red-rimmed and swollen, my nose raw from constant blowing, and my hair sticky with dried blood. Not to mention I had a monstrous bandage on my shoulder. Still, my visitor smiled at me. This day had also left a mark on him.

"Hi, Sean."

There was no sign of his usual carefree manner. Dark shadows lay under his eyes, and a stubbly beard covered his thin face. His lips were pressed together into a worried line.

"Hi, Sam, are you doing all right?" He patted my hand. "Ashley and I . . . we are worried about you."

"I guess I'm OK. But I really want to know what happened to Payton. No one will tell me. Do you have any news?"

I didn't really want an answer to that question. Didn't want to hear what I already knew. That he hadn't made it.

Sean avoided my eyes, stepped back from the bed, and brushed his hand through his hair.

"Well," he muttered, "I don't quite know how to tell you."

Although I had feared as much, my heart skipped a beat. I jumped out of the bed, howling "No!" as I hit Sean again and again with my healthy hand. My cries and sobs must have penetrated the whole floor.

Finally, Sean held my fist in his hands. He looked a little sheepish as he kissed me on my head. "Sam, listen, I am sorry. I know that you love Payton, but I swear I'll kill him if he asks me again when he can see you. You should get to him as quickly as possible!"

"What?" I pushed Sean away from me and looked into his face. His eyes were radiating happiness, and he was grinning from ear to ear.

"What? Why?" I couldn't think clearly.

"Sam, I am sorry. I shouldn't have teased you, but I haven't been happy for hundreds of years. So please forgive me. I am obviously not of sound mind. Now go to him. Go! He's in the ICU."

Overjoyed, I ran through the corridors, almost knocking over a nurse, as I laughed and cried with relief. I fumbled into a sterile mask and gown before they'd let me go in. The seconds felt like hours. I stepped through the door.

There he was! I would have loved to run to him, squeeze his body next to me, reassure myself that his heart really was beating, but the tangle of cables and monitors held me back.

Slowly, he opened his eyes.

"Sam, *mo luaidh*! I've been waiting almost three hundred years for you, almost let myself be killed for you, and now this? Lying here was almost the worst torture of all because I couldn't bear to be away from you. Come here!"

Payton pulled me down into his strong arms.

"You still owe me an answer," Payton whispered into my hair. "My third question . . ."

I groaned. "Not this again."

He continued. "The third question that I want an honest answer to is: Do you love me the way I love you? Can you not take a breath because your love is taking your breath away? Does your heart skip a beat like mine when we are near each other? And the most important thing: Don't you want to kiss me, really kiss me, at last?"

I wanted to laugh and cry. I couldn't swallow and could hardly speak. "I love you!" was all that I could say. My heart was beating far too quickly, and I knew that we wouldn't allow anything to come between us again. We lost ourselves in our emotions, sinking tenderly into a deep kiss. A kiss full of forgiveness for the past, full of promise for the future, and full of immortal love.

~

Sean was still sitting in Sam's hospital room when Ashley came in and sat beside him. She put her hand on his and smiled. The events of the past few days had brought them close to each other. Sean was entranced with Ashley's beauty, and she in turn seemed smitten with him. They had talked for hours, consoling each other. They'd also given their statements to the police, leading to the arrest of Cathal and Alasdair.

"I think we can take off. Sam and Payton are in good hands here," Ashley said.

"I'll be there in a moment. Go on down and try to get a taxi. I presume we'll have quite a lot of explaining to Sam's parents to do."

"To be honest, I'm not sure I want to let you out of my sight," Ashley said.

Sean got up, pulled Ashley into his arms, and kissed her tenderly.

"Ashley, you don't have to worry, I am not intending to let you get away. But now go, sweetheart. I'll be right with you."

Ashley seemed to float out of the hospital, looking like a girl who had finally found true love. She had no way of knowing what dark thoughts were occupying her boyfriend's mind.

Sean paced up and down the room like a tiger. He tried to gather his thoughts. Could what he know destroy the young happiness the two of them had found?

Maybe he didn't have to tell anyone. He wasn't even sure that he had completely understood. He would keep it to himself for the time being.

Only he would know of Nathaira's final words.

And of her curse.

CHARACTERS

The Stuart Clan:

Cathal Stuart: 29-year-old chieftain of the Stuarts
Nathaira Stuart: Cathal's 27-year-old sister, Blair McLean's
    fiancée
Kenzie Stuart: Cathal and Nathaira's 17-year-old brother,
    who dies in the Cameron massacre
Alasdair Buchanan: Cathal's follower
Grant Stuart: Cathal and Nathaira's father
Kinnon Stuart: Cathal and Nathaira's grandfather, Grant's
    father, Caitlin's brother
Caitlin Stuart Cameron: Lachlann Cameron's wife, Cathal
    and Nathaira's great-aunt

The McLean Clan:

Payton McLean: 19-year-old who falls in love with
    Samantha Watts
Sean McLean: Payton's 25 year-old brother
Blair McLean: Payton's 27-year-old brother, McLean
    chieftain, and Nathaira's fiancé
Kyle McLean: Payton's 16-year-old brother, who dies in the
    Cameron massacre
Fingal McLean: Payton, Blair, Sean, and Kyle's father

The Cameron Clan:

Lachlann Cameron: Caitlin Stuart's husband, Eideard's father
Manus Cameron: Caitlin's second husband, Lachlann's
    brother
Eideard Cameron: Lachlann's son, Tomas's father
Tomas Cameron: Isobel's husband, Muireall's father
Isobel Cameron: Muireall's mother
Muireall Cameron: Sole Cameron survivor of the massacre
Marta McGabhan: Muireall's nanny

The Watts Family:

Samantha Watts: high school student from Delaware who
    falls in love with Payton McLean
Anna Miller, née Lewis: Samantha's grandmother
Lorraine Watts, née Miller: Samantha's mother
Kenneth Watts: Samantha's father
Ashley Bennett: Samantha's cousin from Illinois
Eddie Bennett: Ashley's father

Other characters in the United States:

Ryan Baker: Heartthrob at Samantha's high school
Kim: Samantha's best friend
Justin Summers: Kim's boyfriend, Ryan's best friend
Mr. Schneider: Geography teacher who recommends
    Samantha for exchange program
Lisa: Popular girl

People on Fair Isle:

Vanora: Old woman who inflicts the curse
Brèagha-muir: Wise Woman
Beathas: Another Wise Woman
Douglas: Man who hosts Payton during his visit
Uisgeliath: Young witch

Other characters in Scotland:

Alison and Roy Leary: Samantha's host parents in
    Aviemore
Cathy: Sales assistant in a souvenir shop

GAELIC GLOSSARY

A dhiobhail!
You devil!

Bas mallaichte!
Bloody hell!

Ciamar a tha thu?
How are you?

Cuimhnich air na daoine o'n d' thanig thu.
Remember those you are a descendant of.

Daingead!
Damn!

Ifrinn!
Devil! / Hell!

Latha math!
Greetings to you! / Good day!

Madain math.
Good morning.

Mo charaid.
My friend.

Mo luaidh. / Mo luaidh, tha gràdh agam ort.
My darling. / My darling, I love you.

Nighean na galladh!
   Daughter of a dog!

Pog mo thon!
   Kiss my ass!

Seas!
   Stop!

Sgian dhu
   A small dagger

Sguir!
   Stop it!

Sguir, mo nighean. Mo gràdh ort.
   Stop, my daughter. I love you.

Slàinte mhath!
   Cheers!

Tapadh leat.
   Thank you.

Tha gràdh agad oirre?
   Do you love her?

Tha mi duilich.
   I am sorry.

Teine biorach.
   Sharp fire or will-o'-the-wisp.

ABOUT THE AUTHOR

Photo: Guido Karp for www.p4ld.com

Emily Bold, born in 1980, has already published a number of books including her debut novel *Gefährliche Intrigen*, a best-selling eBook in Germany. She writes historical romance, and her novels are full of love, passion, and adventure. Emily also writes young adult fiction.

The Curse: Touch of Eternity is Emily's first book translated into English. The publication of *The Curse: Touch of Eternity* with Amazon Crossing is a big dream come true for Emily. Don't forget to have a look at her book trailer!

Find out more about The Curse at: http://thecurse.de

Find out more about the author at:

http://emilybold.de

http://facebook.com/emilybold.de

http://twitter.com/emily_bold

http://www.youtube.com/user/EmilyBoldTV